Luke O'Grady

Leaving Home Behind

"I saw the bench that had been almost like a home, or at least a refuge, to me for several hours last night. I had the urge to sit there and get my thoughts together. I tried to do so, but the moment I sat down I was immediately compelled to do something else even more strongly. It was as if while I slept my subconscious had come up with a plan to improve the odds of my survival and decided to act upon the plan before letting me in on it..."

Molloy had to leave home. He felt compelled to get a tattoo he feared may curse him forever. Were *The People For a Better World* really who they said they were? Could he survive on his own? Have a normal life?

Luke O'Grady was born and raised in Ontario. He is a pharmacist, and enjoys reading, writing and cycling.

Leaving Home Behind

Petra Books | petrabooks.ca
Cover sketch: Kumi Matsukawa

Leaving Home Behind

Luke O'Grady

Library and Archives Canada Cataloguing in Publication

O'Grady, Luke, author

Escaping Home / by Luke O'Grady. -- 1st edition.

I. Title.
PS8629.G733N67 2016   C813'.6   C2016-907161-8
C2016-907162-6

c. 80,0000 words
Bookman 10/12 serif
Herculanum sans serif

Petra Books | petrabooks.ca
Design, publishing

This is a work of fiction and all names of people are imaginary.

Frontpiece sketch: Isezakicho street view, Yokohama.
watercolour and pen. by Kumi Matsukawa

Cover photo courtesy Tom Fisk Photography

Sketch: Isezakicho street view, Yokohama.
watercolour and pen, by Kumi Matsukawa

I thank friends, family and fate for giving me the experiences and inspiration to write this novel. I would in particular like to thank my son Nathan, sister Kim and friends Andrew and Chris for their encouragement and for reading the manuscript and giving me suggestions for improvement. I would also thank my editors at Petra Books for their excellent advice, patience, and support.

I dedicate the book to Nathan for his consistent support to me through the good, and difficult times.

— Luke O'Grady

"For a while I just sat there looking around. It was peaceful...playful city lights blotted out nearly all the stars. This reminded me I was a long way from home where hundreds of stars could be seen...only an hour away by train, but an eternity away in many other ways."

Table of Contents

Part 1

Where I Am Now
and Where I Was Then

1

A Day In The Life

Each morning between six and six-thirty an unidentified agent of *The People for a Better World* puts my list of daily tasks through the mail slot at the bottom of the stairs. There is usually a map included to offer quick and easy tips to get to the locations where the tasks take place. I have considered hiding outside, waiting, and spying on them as they deliver the list, but I cannot see what that would accomplish and I expect *The People* would frown upon it.

They would certainly frown upon what I am about to do, copy a list of my daily tasks and show it to you, the reader. The list is to be destroyed upon completion. To release details of our actions apparently puts us at risk from our competitors. I use the word our because although I am struggling with the concept I am presently a member of *The People for a Better World.*

Today's Tasks

08:20---Pick one healthy looking tulip, preferably, but not necessarily red, from the garden at 134 Front Street. Walk at a normal pace to 157 Front Street and set the tulip on the front porch near the door. If there is someone nearby to observe you at the time, walk once around the block and try once more to place the flower unseen. If you are still unable to complete the task undetected on the second try, simply leave the task unfinished and throw the flower into a trash container several blocks from Front Street.

09:35---You will find a cinder block near the Norman Street entrance to the pedestrian path beside the O-Train railway track. Carry the cinder block along the path to the pedestrian bridge leading over the tracks to Young Street. Set the cinder block down in the longer grass at the corner where the path meets the bridge. Walk immediately home when you are finished this task and do what you like inside until your next task.

11:45-12:45---Simply be within the large boundary of Brewer Park. Do not attract undue attention to yourself, but otherwise do as you wish for this time in the park. Strolling peacefully around the park, relaxing on one of the benches, or shooting a basketball on one of the courts are good examples of what you might do.

13:45---Enter the Microplay video game store on Bank Street and investigate the variety of video games for rent on the wall display for about twenty minutes. Spend the majority of that time looking at the Ratchet and Clank series for the Playstation and the Gears of War series for the Xbox. After about twenty minutes approach one of the counter clerks and ask if the new Gears of War game is available yet. If staff asks if they can help you before the twenty minutes are up reply with the same question. The answer will be no. Request to be phoned when it arrives so that you can purchase it. When asked give the name Gordon Thom (pronounced Tom). Give the following phone number...

When the previous task is finished, take the bus to the Rideau Mall to be there in time for your next task. Your destination at the Rideau Mall is The Bay. You will likely have time to grab a bite to eat on the way.

15:00---Enter and browse through The Bay department store for up to half an hour. Find a reasonably priced, practical item that will be useful for you at home and can be carried easily. Do not spend more than ten minutes finding your item. After obtaining the item pretend to continue to shop for the remainder of the half hour. Your real objective during this time is to be on the lookout for an obviously balding man well over six feet tall. If you see him, nonchalantly intercept him and ask him the time. After his reply thank him and ask him jokingly if he has seen anything a grumpy old man might like for his birthday. Depending on his reply, continue and end the conversation in whatever way seems appropriate and friendly. Purchase your item with your employee credit card and walk home.

16:00-17:00---Data Entry. Data entry is a relatively mindless task that nonetheless requires concentration. It is dull work, but precise enough in nature that I will not do a proper job if I let my mind wander. It can be meditative if you are in the perfect mood for it, but otherwise it is pretty tedious. It also seems as meaningless and random as the more interactive daily tasks I have described. It is certainly difficult to imagine how my acts, data entry or otherwise, somehow make the world a better place.

Here is a quick description of data entry. I bring up the client's file using the client identification number then double-check that I have entered the proper client identification number before data entry. Except for this identification number there is no other information on the computer screen except for the numbers and symbols I enter into two small fields beside the ID number.

Here is a small sample of today's data entry.

```
4529317@      *       42
3173261       $$      167
691           *       12
2242          +=      27
71412         "+      6
858919        *       !4713
84163214      ??      113
925413        &%      313
```

Over ninety percent of the time the second column is two symbols and the last column is one to three digits. The odd time it is outside of this norm I used to get a ridiculous thrill that I might be part of something special when I typed it into its space. I had to remind myself that it was still random gibberish to me no matter what symbols or numbers the area contained. I do not get this little tingle of excitement anymore. I have improved that much at least.

This is an example of a typical day of tasks for an entry-level member of *The People for a Better World*. Some days I may have a higher number of less time-consuming tasks. On occasion I may spend the entire day completing a single lengthy task or even the whole day doing data entry. The day-to-day details of my tasks may vary a lot, but in essence they are the same.

This rigmarole is enough to make me question my sanity at times; taking a bus five kilometres to put a hockey card under the windshield of a Buick station wagon, walking around a particular block at a particular time whistling a particular tune ready to give a particular reply if a person fitting a particular description asks a particular question. This nonsense makes up a very significant portion of my life.

As I have described, my daily list of tasks sometimes requires me to purchase something with an employee credit card specifically for that purpose. I also have a debit card linked to an account which I use for living expenses and to receive my pay from *The People for a Better World*. I have a separate account at a separate bank that I use for my personal savings. My intention is to keep my account separate and secret from *The People*, but it is easy to get paranoid sometimes and wonder if anything is secret from *The People*.

I should point out that my compensation from *The People* seems to be fair. My basic living costs are well covered, and depending upon my performance I may receive bonuses. I gave my information to *The People* so they could take care of my rent and utilities. I use the organization's credit card for basic living expenses such as food. The bonuses for performance are the obscure part of the equation, but I get them quite regularly. It is the bonuses which help me build my separate savings.

My involvement with *The People for a Better World* is far from the beginning of my diary. However, since it is this situation that finally prompted me to get serious about editing and organizing my diary into a coherent work, I decided to start out with this chapter.

What is the true nature of these things I do? To what purpose and for whom? I am one of many who perform similar duties in the name of *The People*. Why do we have to be completely in the dark about the reasons for these strange tasks? I expect most of us were in the same lonely and desperate state when we joined *The People*, happy to belong to a common group serving a purportedly noble purpose. But what evidence is there that we work toward a better world?

Occasionally, when someone is bold enough to ask, our supervisors tell us our lack of knowledge make it easier for *The People* to keep a low profile and avoid the notice of our antagonists and our competitors in making the world a better place. Does that even make sense? Are our competitors called *The People* For a Nastier World?

I cannot stop asking myself these questions. It occurs to me that it makes more sense that secrecy might be the root of all evil.

At this point the goal of this diary is to organize my life story, keep it honest, and identify a path out of this mess. I suppose I am trying to write myself free.

2

Back to the Beginning: Brockville

I grew up in Brockville, a town with a population of about twenty thousand people. Brockville is a working class town where most of the money is old money and the bad parts of town are more dishevelled and grubby rather than truly bad. I guess the rest is in the middle or at least slightly less dishevelled. We lived in the dishevelled, grubby part of town.

Somehow or other the population seems to always hover at around twenty thousand. Most of Brockville's children who finish high school seem to move on and only come back to visit, but I guess the rest stayed and expanded into little families to even things out. And occasionally a new factory would spring up providing a cluster of new, decent paying jobs which also helped to keep the population stable.

I wondered sometimes if they just could not be bothered to change the sign and reduce the number on the highway sign that read:

```
Brockville Home of the Thousand Islands
           Population: 20,000
```

Then again, to be fair, Brockville did not seem to be getting any smaller. If anything, the city limits seem to gradually expand and the number of fast food restaurants has more than doubled over the last decade.

The family had already fallen apart when I decided to leave. It was only Dad and I before I left. Right up until the end I generally went to school, but at the time I do not think Dad knew, cared, or even thought about whether I went to school or not. He certainly never asked about it. The most common thing he said to me in those days was, "I guess it's just the men now, eh, boy?"

Before I leave Brockville I will introduce you to my family.

3

Dad

"Get up, kids! Come on, Mother!"

It was so early on Sunday morning I guessed even the sun might still be drowsy. It had to be Sunday because Dad was up earlier than everyone else and was shouting for all of us to get up. It was a tradition that occurred roughly twice per year at random intervals. I wondered what Dad had done that had him feeling guilty enough that we all had to go to church. He could never go make amends with the Lord by himself. We all had to go.

My Dad was the youngest of eight children born to strict Catholic parents. I am not sure why there was such a gap between Dad and his next youngest sibling, five years. One sister and one brother still lived in Brockville, but the rest have moved away. I have met both the remaining siblings and I pass them now and then on the street. We say hi, but we do not get together anymore. Not even at Christmas. I do not think I have met any of the brothers or sisters who moved away. If I did meet them I was very young at the time. Dad's Mom and Dad, my grandparents, are not alive anymore.

As for Mom's parents, I have only heard her speak of her mother. As far as I know she is still alive, but lives far away in Nova Scotia. Mom talks to her on the phone once in a while. I have even talked to her on the phone a couple of times at Christmas. She is nice enough I guess, but she does not say much to keep a conversation going. Mom seems to do most of the talking as far as I can tell, but I have not overheard a phone call between them over the phone in quite a while. Mom has not mentioned her. Mom said I met her Mom, my grandma, when I was very young. Dad says that about his Mom too, but I do not remember either of them. Dad's dad died before I was born.

Anyway, it seems the strict Catholic upbringing never completely left my father, but neither did it take root and become a part of his day-to-day life. It just flared up once in a while like a virus. Around two Sundays per year I presume guilt overwhelmed him and we would have to attend the earliest Sunday mass available. We could never simply *not* go. We had to scramble around to make sure we dug up at least a couple of coins for the collection plate and look as halfway respectable as we could. The event came infrequently enough and Dad was intense enough about it that nobody ever bothered to try and talk him out of the ordeal. We just went with it. I also do not think anybody had the nerve to try and argue we did not need salvation.

"I'll make breakfast," Dad yelled.

That generally meant toast and coffee for my parents and toast and milk for me. Sometimes we also had fried potatoes or tomato slices with salt and pepper. In retrospect, I admit I feel vague internal warmth when I remember those strange, rushed breakfasts. At least we were doing something together, heading in the same direction. Unfortunately, upon closer examination, this togetherness was just another symptom of our disease.

In keeping with Dad's inconsistent religious obsession I was sent to a Catholic public school then afterward a non-denominational, public high school. I think I inherited his inconclusive faith. I too have never been able to altogether abandon nor embrace the concept of God.

A second memory of my father can also be a small introduction to Mom since she is present as well.

Sporadically, like his church moods, Dad would suddenly feel the need to teach me a useful skill. The teacher, the student, or both were flawed because it never ended up with me learning much of anything. The following example stands out best in my mind because it was the first time my parents clearly showed their disrespect for one another in front of me.

On this occasion Dad decided to teach me how to fix cars. I stood on a milk crate in the driveway beside him staring into the open hood of a dark green car we had recently acquired. He leaned in over the engine with a tool then reached down and moved his hands around in there. I heard clinks of metal on metal.

"Get over here." he said, "You're not going to learn anything if you're not looking at what I'm doing."

I leaned in a little further, closer to his hands. I could see his hands move, but not what was going on underneath his hands. My head felt like a carved Halloween pumpkin; empty, mute, and filled with only an imaginary awareness. I dreaded the inevitable moment when he would ask me a question about the insides of the car to see if I was paying attention. He said words like transmission, idle, carburetor, running smooth, tube, and line. If any of these words meant anything to me it was not in connection with automobiles. Many years later I still do not know shit about cars.

Following the script, it was not long before Dad started to become frustrated with the slow pace of my learning and the fact that the car still did not work. Not long after he started to get annoyed Mom appeared and confronted him.

"Why are you doing this?" she shouted, her arms perpendicular to her sides. "For one thing, he's too young to learn about cars. He should be playing with other kids, reading his books, using his imagination, having fun."

My Dad shook his head.

"So typical."

He looked to the sky for strength before continuing.

"Maybe you can also tell me who's going to pay him to read and imagine so he can earn a living when he grows up. Christ, all he does is read anyway."

Mom laughed in a mean way and slapped herself on the forehead.

"The nerve! Imagine you teaching someone how to earn a living. Christ have mercy."

"That's it, swear in front of the kid."

"If he's old enough to earn a living he's old enough to hear swearing."

"Are you done?"

"No, I'm not. I want you to answer one more question that has me a little confused. What makes you think you can teach anyone how to fix cars? Whenever we scrape up enough money for some piece of trash it breaks down within a month and not once have you even come close to fixing it. It's just an excuse for you to be not doing the other things you should be doing. In the end I'll end up pretty much having to shove a stick of dynamite up your ass just to get you to have it towed away to get the mess out of sight. Bye the way, we drove this heap for four and a half days. So far it's been broken down in the driveway for seven days. Are you starting to see the pattern I'm seeing?"

"I may not be a licensed mechanic, but I'm mechanically minded. It might take me a while, but if you'd give me a chance I can figure out these things. Besides, we got this car basically for free."

Mom threw her hands out in front of her chest.

"Give it up. Give me one shred of evidence in all the time we've been together that you're mechanically minded. Just one. You can't because you're not and there isn't one."

"I've had just about enough of this."

Dad threw a wrench wrapped in an oily rag into the open hood of the car with a clank. He stomped down the driveway then along the sidewalk away from the house.

I hated the fighting, but I was glad the car-fixing lesson was over. It was more efficient. I learned the same amount of nothing in less time. I sat on the milk crate near the car and waited for Mom to go inside so she could calm down, but she came over to me instead.

"Come on inside, Molloy. I'll make you some soup. Sorry to fight like that in front of you. I just get so damn frustrated. Sorry for the swearing too."

I walked with her to the front door, but just before we went in she stopped and looked at me.

She said, "It's an awfully nice day. Maybe you should stay outside and play a while instead. Sometimes I think you spend too much time up in your room reading. Why don't you play outside until you get hungry, then come in and I'll feed you. I'll have soup ready."

It was an unusually pleasant day. It was clear and blue with fairly green, healthy lawns all around when normally several brown patches were the norm. I don't remember what I did exactly, but I stayed outside until I was really hungry.

4

Mom

Mom entered my room very late one night while I was asleep. She snuck in quietly and turned on the small bed-side lamp I used to read in bed. I had had the lamp as long as I could remember. The lampshade had a decal of Piglet on it. Eeyore was on the base. I was much too old for the lamp, but I had gotten past that fact. Now I thought of it as I did everything else that was part of my very own room. It was my own, private and special.

Around Piglet the lampshade used to be almost white, but now it was almost yellow with age and the accumulation of human interactions.

With the lamp coming on it awakened me, and Mom spoke. I could barely see her at first in the dark behind the bright light, but gradually my eyes adjusted. She whispered something.

"Hi, honey. Can I talk to you? I know it's late. I'm sorry."

"Mom? What time is it?"

"Sorry, it's late. It's not time to get up."

I had to squint at her through my fingers until my eyes got adjusted to the light.

"What is it, Mom?"

She put her fingers to hers lips and quietly shushed me.

"Can you keep a terrible secret, Molloy?"

Despite me grogginess, the words terrible secret whispered by my mother in the middle of the night made the air feel electric and icy. Everything went kind of still and silent except for Mom. I just looked at her, waiting.

"Okay," I said.

She took a deep breath and closed her eyes. She spoke very quietly.

"I'm sure you've noticed this family of ours has problems, right?"

I was not absolutely sure at the time, but I had wondered if it was the same for other families, especially with the fighting recently, so I nodded. If Mom thought so it was probably true. She should know.

She smiled a kind of angry, one-sided grin.

"Not hard to tell, I guess, not even for a little kid."

She stared straight into my eyes for what seemed like an eternity. Tears started to gather in hers, but they did not fall. They just sat there, stuck and pooled in her lower lids. Her voice was even quieter the next time she spoke.

"This is the hardest thing I have ever done."

She hugged me while she sniffled quietly in my ear. I could feel her tears on my neck. It felt warm and nice in a way, even though I wished she was not sad. Even though I knew something bad was happening. I could feel it deep down and quiet somewhere inside me. After a while Mom pulled back from me and took another deep breath. She still had tears in her eyes, but she had pulled herself together. She looked determined. She still spoke softly, but more firmly now. Again, she looked me directly in the eyes.

"Being in this family isn't good for any of us, Molloy. It wasn't good for Kim either and that's why she left."

Kim is my sister. I did not think about her that much anymore. I missed her in a way, but I felt as if I barely knew her. She was quite a bit older than me and always seemed to have a lot on her mind. She was never mean to me, but I felt as if I was the least of her concerns. I had not seen her in a long time.

"Where is Kim?" I asked.

Mom shook her head and made a brief crying face. She rubbed her hand over her eyes and forehead for a couple of seconds until she was back in control of herself.

"Kimmy isn't too far away. She doesn't come by because there's nothing for her here and she's got to deal with her own life. And she's definitely not Kimmy anymore. She's Kim. She's old enough now and has enough to worry about now that she's an adult whether she's ready or not."

Suddenly Mom spaced out like she was not even in the same room with me. She looked through me as if she was talking to someone else.

"Kim's not a grown-up though," she said. "How can I even pretend that? She's got a grown-up's problems, but she's not a grown-up. She wasn't ready to leave, but she had to leave. Being in this family isn't good for any of us and that's why she left."

Mom was very quiet for a few seconds, still looking far away. Then she made a face like she was screaming, but she only whispered.

"Jesus fucking Christ I am a terrible mother."

Then she really did start to cry a little bit.

"You're not a bad ma'. I like you."

Dad says women say love and men say like or appreciate.

It did not take long before Mom stopped crying and looked determined again.

"No," she said. "I have to be honest here, Molloy. I am a terrible mother. That's the reason I am here talking to you in secret in the middle of the night. I can't stay here and live like this for the rest of my life. Someday you'll wake up and I'll be gone, and you may not see me again for a long time. Like your sister, Kim, I'm going to run away and start out fresh. It will work out better for me. I'm smarter, more experienced. I've got to do something. I don't know exactly what I'm going to do or when I'll go, but I didn't want to do it without telling you first."

"Okay," I said.

I thought I might be dying or something for a second. Maybe I went into a kind of emotional shock if there is such a thing. Mom was going to run away and leave Dad and I. But she was upset. Maybe Dad and I could make her feel better and she would change her mind. What was I supposed to say or do?

Mom looked bewildered at my reply. She shook her head slightly as if to say she did not understand me. She probably expected me to cry. I felt like I wanted to, but could not. I felt semi-paralyzed. She took my hand.

"Promise me you will keep this a secret between us?"

I nodded.

"I promise."

She hugged me.

"Thank you, Molloy."

She started to cry her hardest yet now, but still quietly. It sounded loud, but I know it was because her mouth was right next to my ear. Her voice came through in breathy sobs.

"I don't deserve you. I don't even deserve the right to tell you I love you."

I did not know what she meant by that, but I did not say anything. She continued.

"I'm sorry, baby. It's late and I shouldn't have woken you, but I had to tell you."

"It's okay."

She managed to smile.

"Say a prayer for me before you go back to sleep?"

I nodded.

"Thanks, baby. Someday, somehow, I know you're going to shake this shit off and be the best of any of us."

She stood then bent down and kissed my forehead.

"Goodnight, sweetheart."

"Night, Mom."

She rubbed my hair near where she kissed and left the room.

I sat for a long time with the bed table light on staring out the window. It was a small bedroom. The single bed took up half the floor space. But it really was my very own room. Hardly anyone else ever came in. I was trying to think of a prayer for Mom. I did one, but I do not remember what exactly.

Outside I could see the beams from car headlamps going by once in a while. Also, there was a single star bright enough to be visible despite the little light on in the room. It was as if it had the entire sky to itself. Being a star might be a nice happy simple life even though I know stars are not alive. It could twinkle in the sky, a pinhole of brightness in the black silence of outer space. It might be lonely, but you could grant the wish of the first person that saw you each night. If they were a special person with a special wish, you could even help make the world a better place.

Eventually, I fell asleep with the light on. When I woke up it was too late for me to get to school anywhere close to on time. The last thing keeping Mom at home must have been telling me she was going, because that was the last time I saw her.

5

Missing Sister

My sister, Kim, left home well before Mom ran away. How long before I am not exactly certain. We never played or hung around very much even as little kids. She was about five years older than me and the age difference combined with the gender difference made the gap between us large enough that we rarely attempted to bridge it. It is strange and perhaps a little pathetic that I cannot pin down more accurately when Kim left home, but I can only say with confidence that it was more than a year ago and less than three years ago. The past few years have been something of a blur.

When Kim was around she fought a lot with my parents, especially when it got closer to when she left. Maybe subconsciously I stayed away from her then to avoid collateral damage from the fighting. Also, she certainly did not seek me out. I would not have been much assistance to her.

You should know that dredging up and dusting off these old memories is tiring work. It might have been impossible had I not kept a diary. My original diary was meandering and repetitive, but a useful enough conduit to tease hazy, trod upon memories more clearly to life. During orientation, *The People for a Better World* crews encouraged stepping away from the past, shedding the old skin that stunted our growth, and starting out new. I bought into the idea enough in the beginning that I might have lost contact with my past had I not had my own notes to guide me.

Back to my sister, I think I may have seen her a single time after she left home. It was not long after Mom took off. From the second I saw the woman half a block away on the other side of the street some instinct assured me it was Kim, but in truth I cannot be certain.

It was an overcast and unusually chilly day in April filled with tiny pinpoint swarms of raindrops. I had not expected the cold and I had not dressed well. I was heading downtown with a few quarters in my pocket to play some pinball. I was one of the few guys who had not switched over to video games. They kept a couple of decent machines around for us old school types.

Dad had given me the quarters in exchange for agreeing to pick him up a racing form from Ritchie's on the way home. Richie's was an old general store that had off-track betting in the backroom.

As happened a lot in the time following Mom's departure I thought about what she said to me before she left. She said eventually I was going to leave home like she did. Lately, I had been coming around to thinking she was right. I was suddenly feeling like I was finished up here in Brockville. I only had a month or two until I finished high school, but even that was starting to feel pointless. There had not been any talk about me going to university or college and I was sure we could not afford it anyway. I was doing pretty well on my tests and assignments, but what did it matter? Was I going to work in a factory and live with Dad?

Whatever superficial friends or acquaintances I had at school I felt I could do without. I wondered what learning a little more math and science was going to do for me. As far as English and reading comprehension, even the teacher said I was already past the high school level.

Dad did not seem concerned about whether I went to school or not. He actually seemed a little friendlier toward me since Mom left. Maybe he was just minding his own business more and leaving me alone.

These were concerns that floated around in my head as I paused for a moment in my journey to consider the most efficient route to get the racing form then go to the arcade. I did not want to be underdressed in the cold for any longer than necessary. A child's shriek from up ahead on the other side the street interrupted my navigational computations.

Half a block away I saw a chubby young woman pulling a red plastic wagon whose cargo was a little boy around two years old. The boy was screaming unintelligibly, perhaps because he, like myself, was not dressed properly to protect him from the weather. Even from a distance he looked unkempt, his face was smudged with something and his hair was sticking out. There was something about the woman, the boy's mother I presumed, that even viewed from the back commanded my attention.

She was ignoring the yells of the boy, but I could tell from her posture she was frustrated and embarrassed. Normally, I would have ignored this sort of spectacle. Young children often have tantrums. However, the pair completely drew the focus of my attention. I was convinced I knew this woman. I felt sure it was my sister, Kim.

I stopped walking and raised my hand to about shoulder height as if to give a feeble wave even though neither of them were looking in my direction. This action only allowed them to move farther away so I could see them less clearly. I could still hear the boy shrieking clear enough. He was good at it. I tried to call out, but the air stuck in my chest. What if it was not my sister? What if it was? What would I say?

Before I could come to any decision about whether to call out or not the woman snapped. She spun around to face to child and lowered her face to within inches of his and shrieked back at him.

"If you don't shut your mouth I'm going to slap you in the stupid face."

The tantrum only got worse. The woman did not make good on her threat to slap the boy. She simply turned away and never faced him again. She pulled the wagon looking straight ahead, and argued with the wordless cries and tears of the boy I presumed was her son.

"Just wait 'til we get home."

"You'll be very sorry you're doing this to me."

"No dessert for a week."

"No going to the park this afternoon, that's for sure."

"As soon as we get home you're going straight to your room until you apologize to me and promise to be a good boy from now on."

For the life of me all I could do was to stand shivering in the drizzle and watch them, wondering if they could be my sister and nephew.

To this day I have no proof these people were related to me, but somehow the experience was the final mental shove that convinced me it was time to leave Brockville. It was still a couple of weeks before I left, but from that moment on I knew I was going. I just had to put the last pieces together. I would run like my mother, run as if to stay would curse me for the rest of my life.

6

Tattoo Vision

I should tell you about the tattoo I am going to get before I leave home.

The notion to get a tattoo haunted me for years before I decided to do it. I forgot about the idea from time to time, but it never left me for long. It lodged in my mind like an unfinished task in my destiny.

The tattoo came to me as something I can only describe as a vision which struck me as I walked through a park on my way home from school when I was eleven years old. It was quiet and raining gently. It came from nowhere and it took my breath away. I had to sit on a park bench for several minutes until the feeling passed. I could sit there in the drizzle and look at the tattoo upon my back and see it clearly as if I were looking at a different individual. However, in the vision I knew I was looking at my tattooed self in the future.

Except for the vision I could still see normally. I could see the park around me. I could even worry that someone would come by and see me in this strange state. Yet the vision was clear. It was my tattoo and I knew I had gotten it because God had abandoned me. It frightened me. It frightens me still the odd time when I can relive the sensation particularly well.

I sat on the park bench until the sensation stilled enough that I could shove it to the background. I noticed I was breathing more quickly than usual. I was a little sweaty. I wondered what had happened, what it meant.

This is what the tattoo looked like more or less:

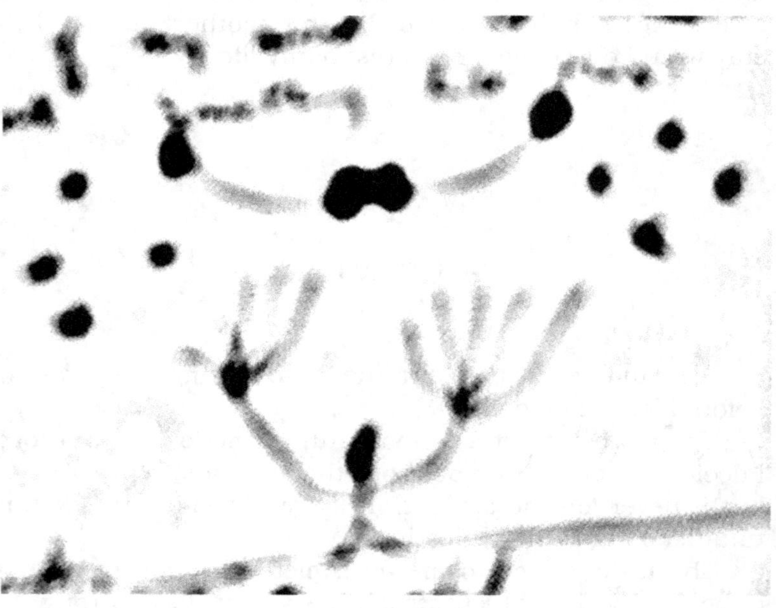

Essentially, the concept is this: the pleading, down on his luck human faced with the reluctant All-powerful, the weak and desperate pleading with the deaf, mute, and cryptic Almighty. The idea never rose up in me as powerfully as it did that first time, but a weaker vision bloomed in my mind often enough. The tattoo was a permanent curse toward God upon my flesh.

Perhaps the inconsistencies in my upbringing regarding God played a part in my mind's behaviour. I went to a

Catholic public school, but otherwise only heard tell of God through curses or Dad's random, maniacal, religious exacerbations. I only ever went to church through school.

Like any child exposed to God's potential greatness, I prayed occasionally in desperation for aid and to heal my family. Prayers went only as far as my breath could carry them in front of my face. My family continued to take on more water, to shift and sink.

After the vision, praying seemed ridiculous. It was so clear and real I felt as if I had already committed the sin of getting the tattoo — signed the contract. There was no turning back. God and I had officially abandoned one another. If I was going to act and feel as if I had gotten the tattoo then I might as well go ahead and get it.

The strangest thing about all this was I could not even say for sure whether I even believed in God. I guess that means I did not truly believe, but in my own mind it was not that clear. I was not sure if God did not exist or just did not care about our family. Just in case it was the latter, I wanted to get the tattoo that told Him to go fuck Himself.

7

Tattoo Me

The ongoing strain of my family's disintegration fuelled my decision to leave Brockville. The seed of this idea had been forming for nearly a year and now was coming more clearly into view. I had pretty much decided upon Ottawa as my destination. I hoped it was not so far away that I felt completely out of my element, yet it was a large enough city it should be easy enough for a young nobody to dissolve within. I had also pretty much decided to take the train. I had definitely decided to get my tattoo before I left. The only tattoo parlour in town was downtown, a little off King Street, Brockville's main street. The sign out front advertised the place opened at noon. I arrived there only shortly after the church bell tower finished sounding its twelfth dong.

The shop looked to be divided into halves by a long counter that split the room. The center portion of the counter could be lifted on hinges to allow access between the two halves. The half of the room where I entered was scattered and dusty. It looked like a storage room for various things the owner did not need at the moment but was unsure whether he should throw them away. There were partly unpacked boxes, odds and ends of small furniture, and a couple of stacks of framed photographs or artwork of some sort.

The other half the room behind the counter looked strikingly clear and tidy by comparison. There were lots of designs for tattoos on the wall back there, as well as a couple of basic wooden chairs, a tall stool, and a large, more comfortable looking, padded chair where I presumed the person getting the tattoo sat. At the back of the room there was a large unusual piece of furniture I guessed might be a designing desk with lots of small, makeshift shelves and paper stuffed pigeonholes above it.

The tattoo artist all but ignored me as I walked tentatively toward the counter dividing the room. He was on the other side of the counter moving around somewhat aimlessly as far as I could tell. He glanced at me once as I approached, but continued whatever he was doing without a pause. He was a smallish skinny man with a moustache perhaps long and thick enough to make up for his slight stature. The store was not particularly bright, but even inside he wore sunglasses with small round lenses.

He graced me with his attention when I cleared my throat and spoke up.

"Hi. I was hoping to get a tattoo. I have something particular in mind. Do you think you could help me out?"

He nodded gently and frequently at every word I spoke, but he did not say anything until I was finished. Then he shot me down immediately.

"You're way too young, dude."

I pulled out a wad of cash to show him I was serious.

"Believe me, kid, I could use the money, but I'd be shut down and prob'ly run out of town. I've had these problems before and I can't have them again. I'm on thin ice as it is."

"How can I get a tattoo then? It's for something very important."

He peered out over the top of the dark lenses of his sunglasses at me for several seconds. Then he shrugged and wrote something on a yellow post-it note and handed it over the counter to me.

"Ask for Angel," he said. "And don't mention who sent you. In fact, don't mention to anyone that you ever came here."

I took the scrap of paper and looked at it. It was an address. I showed him a thumb up. I could play ball.

"Why would I come to a place like this? I'm way too young to get a tattoo."

"You got it, kid."

The tattoo artist turned his back to me and resumed his puttering. I waited ten or fifteen seconds, but he never glanced back toward me again. I left.

Since I was on a mission and in the proper frame of mind to get this tattoo done, I decided to walk to the address written on the yellow paper square right away. I thought I knew pretty much every street in Brockville, but this address did not ring any bells. I dropped in at the nearest gas station to ask directions. It also had an auto repair shop so I figured they must know how to get pretty much anywhere for towing broken down cars or whatever. The gas station attendant knew exactly where the address was without even looking at a map.

It turned out to be practically in the country on the very western edge of town on Highway 2. It was a long hike, but I was pumped to make this tattoo a reality. I started walking. Fortunately, it was not a complicated route. It would be almost impossible to get lost. Highway 2 went right through Brockville's downtown where it became Brockville's main street, King Street, then changed back to Highway 2 once it got past the town. The vast majority of my trip was a straight line. I walked more than two miles before I came to the address on the post-it note. I figured it must be one of the last houses still considered to be within the city limits.

The house was large and far back from the road. It looked like a solid house with repairs being done when needed. However, the repairs were the kind of work that did not try to hide the fact that things had needed fixing. Several repairs stood out around the place and the relative age of each of the repairs was evident even to a novice like myself. The repairs were often unpainted or not completely symmetric in some way. There were some motorcycles, two old cars, and a huge truck spread out over a wide gravel parking area beside the house. I could hear unfamiliar rock music blasting away inside.

I could see a side door and a front door. I chose the front door because it had a doorbell I thought might be easier to hear above the music. It took a long time for anyone to answer. Just as I reached to try the bell again the door swung inward. A very tall, thin guy with long, straight hair, a long, straight beard, and a giant can of beer gazed at me.

"What's up?" he said.

I was starting to wonder what the hell I was doing here, but I was here and I had come a long way on a mission.

"I'm looking for a lady called Angel. I heard she might be able to give me a tattoo."

The guy burst out laughing. When he had gotten himself a bit under control he managed to spit out a sentence fragment between snickers.

"You did, did you?"

"Yeah. Seems like you don't think it's a good idea. I'm kind of desperate so I thought I would give it a try."

My skinny friend still had to pull himself together between giggles so he could talk, but whatever the joke, it gradually wore off so he could keep himself together and talk.

"Sorry, I'm kinda drunk and kinda stoned. Why don't you ask her yourself? Come on in."

The door opened up into a very large room that must have taken up most of the ground floor. There was a big fireplace, a few tables, a couple of couches, and a multitude of chairs of all different descriptions scattered about the place. There were a few large, wooden ceiling fans whirling up above and a large staircase along the far wall leading to the upper level.

My host went to the bottom of the stairs and screamed upward.

"Angel, you have a gentleman visitor."

After a few seconds the music cut off only to be replaced by the sounds of laughing, shouting, and the sound of large men moving around overhead. I heard a door open on the second level and then steps coming closer from above.

A bunch of guys filed down the stairs to the ground floor. It hit me. My face got hot and I mentally kicked myself. There were no females. Angel was a guy...likely a large, tough guy by the looks of things. Once the men got a few feet away from me they stopped coming forward. They formed a semi-circle on one side of me. One man, Angel, I presumed, came all the way up to me. He was well over six feet tall and looked to be three hundred pounds of muscle covered with a thick layer of fat and hair. He looked tough, but he exuded a slightly milder manner than his friends. He only seemed slightly threatening when he stepped in front of me to size me up. If anything he seemed disinterested, maybe slightly annoyed.

"You looking for me?"

"You Angel?"

"Yup."

"I want to pay you to give me a tattoo."

He did not say anything for a while. He just stared at me up, down, and into my eyes with flat expressionless gaze. I did my best to appear non-threatening, yet non-petrified. I'm sure I played the non-threatening part perfectly. I avoided looking Angel in the eye except for occasional glances to let him know I was still attending our interaction. I tried to smile a couple of times, but they felt more like grimaces so I stopped trying.

Eventually, Angel said, "Go back to what you were doing fellas. I'm going to need some time alone with my gentleman caller."

There was a bunch of loud hoots at the comment, but before long the guys started shifting around and for the most part started heading back to the second floor.

Angel said, "Come into the kitchen."

He turned and led the way into an unusually large kitchen. I wondered if this place with its huge front room, massive kitchen, and long, wide staircase had once been a small hotel, a lodge, or large, themed restaurant of some kind.

Angel closed the kitchen door behind us. The room looked surprisingly sanitary. It did not look overwhelmingly tidy or organized, but things were noticeably clean with no dirty dishes in sight. There were two very large refrigerators along the outer wall.

Angel got me to sit across from him at the end of a long wooden table big enough for large groups like the one upstairs.

"Listen to me," he said. "I'm not gonna bother with any bullshit about who sent you here and you're too young to get a tattoo because you already know you're too young and you don't even know the name of the guy who told you about me, right?"

I nodded, "Yeah."

"Okay. Look at me when I'm talking to you, please."

"Okay, sorry."

"Never mind. I'm pretty much done with tattooing, okay? I liked the work for a while and I suppose it treated me well enough helping pay the bills over the years, but it's not taking me anywhere I want to go these days. You get my drift?"

"Yeah, I think I know what you mean. Your life's changing direction. It's where I'm at now too. Staying in this town doesn't seem to be getting me anywhere I want to go so I'm leaving. Getting this tattoo is important to me before I leave. For whatever reason I feel like it's something I've got to get done."

Angel kept looking at me with that flat look, but his face changed a little bit behind the stare somehow. I could see he was not a wild, young man anymore. Or if he was he realized it could not last. He was trying to find a way to change the ending to his life's story.

Angel's softer look did not last long. His eyes hardened and, if anything, he looked a little angry. The quick change startled me, but the anger did not seem directed at me.

"Let me guess, kid. Family's all fucked up? Dad grinding you down?"

"You could say that. Family's blown apart. It's just me and Dad now. He doesn't even bother grinding me much anymore. It's like the life is being sucked out of him and I've got to get going before it happens to me. I'm getting a tattoo before I go."

"Listen, kid, I hear you and I feel for you, but I don't want to hear about it, okay? I know it sucks, but I couldn't help you even if I wanted to. You know you've got to figure it out for yourself. That's why you're going away."

"Yep."

The big man took a deep breath and finally looked away from me. He rested his forehead on his fist in silence like the modern, North American, biker version of The Thinker.

"Okay," he said. "What's your name?"

"Molloy."

"What you got in mind for a tattoo?"

I had my design in my pocket. I took it out, unfolded it, and flattened it out facing him on the table. He stared at it for a while without touching it. I felt a little embarrassed for some reason. Because my tattoo was private, I guess, and the idea had been private for a long time. Just because it was important to me did not mean another reasonable person would not find it childish. The whole idea did initially come to me as a child.

"Hmmm," Angel said. "Interesting. Tell me a bit about it. Make sure we're on the same page. Why did you make this?"

It was hard to talk about it.

"It's about me and God mostly, I guess."

He looked at it again for a bit, then nodded.

"I follow," he said.

Then Angel laughed. It pissed me off, but of course I did not say anything.

He kept looking back and forth between my design and me, chuckling to himself. His eyes were bright, almost manic.

"You know," he said, "it's actually kind of fucking crazy. Would you get freaked out if I took off my shirt and showed you something?"

His tone was friendly, not mocking. My defences eased off.

"Sure," I said, "go ahead."

With a significant amount of effort Angel managed to peel the sweaty sail of his gray t-shirt over his head to expose an expanse of his pale, hairy, tattooed flab. The number of tattoos he displayed was briefly startling as none had been visible while his wore his shirt. He turned his back to me and with his right hand reached over and pointed down over his left shoulder.

"Do you see it? Sort of like an eyeball thingy? I know it's a shit tattoo, but I still want to show it to you. I had pretty much forgotten about it until you showed me your design. I haven't thought about it for years. I was just a year or two older than you when I got it, but tattoos were newer back then and kids seemed younger somehow. Now it seems as if just about everyone who's not retired has a tattoo."

He stood still and pointed in the general direction of the eyeball thingy. It was just under his left shoulder on his back. Angel was large enough around that he might never get to see this tattoo again unless someone took a photograph for him.

"Do you see it? What do you think? Do you see what I'm getting at?"

His tattoo looked something like this:

I was not absolutely sure I got it, but I might have if some of the assumptions I made were correct. I assumed from his reaction that the theme for his tattoo was similar to the theme I ascribed to my own tattoo design. This in turn assumed Angel correctly identified the theme I had in mind for my tattoo. This seemed reasonable since I gave him a decent hint regarding the idea behind my design. In any case, I did not care to discuss with Angel whether my assumptions were correct or not.

I said, "Yeah, I can see the idea you're trying to get across for sure."

Thankfully, he did not ask me to explain. He pulled his t-shirt back on then sat across the table from me again and got back to business.

"Just so I can envision it, where are you planning on getting this tattoo?"

"On my back."

"Okay," he said.

Then Angel closed his eyes and sat silently for more than a minute. At the same time he opened his eyes he snapped his fingers.

"I think I got it. I'm going to give you your tattoo, but not today. I was just starting to party and I want to get back to it before everyone gets too wasted for me to catch up. Can you come back in two days around the same time you came today?"

I was shocked the negotiations were suddenly finished. I had expected a lot more static if not a flat out refusal to make the tattoo.

"Sure," I said.

"Can I keep the picture you made of it? I want to study it and think about it a bit. Maybe I can tweak it a little and give you some ideas you like. I won't do anything without running it by you first."

I took it back out of my pocket and handed it to him.

"No problem. I've got a few more at home. I've doodled it more than a hundred times I bet."

Angel took the picture and winked at me.

"You stirred up some ghosts for me," he said. "Reminded me not all the shit I got repressed back there is bad. I got some good memories too."

He held out his big hand toward me and we shook.

"Don't worry," he said. "I'll make you a reasonable price. This tattoo could be my last and I'll try to make it a good one for ya."

"Thanks, Angel, I appreciate it."

"No sweat. I'll see you in a couple of days."

Angel turned, walked to one of fridges and took out three big cans of Molson Canadian. He saluted me and rushed out of the kitchen.

"Bye, kid," he yelled.

"Bye."

I let myself out and walked home.

8

Money

To run away requires some money. I have enough, but not enough to make it easy. I had a paper route for a couple of years when I was younger. I worked in a bookshop for a couple of months one summer before the store went out of business. I have my name in down at the youth center for odd jobs that come up now an again, mostly painting or manual labour.

I keep an education fund where I put money in the unlikely hope I end up going to school past high school. I pretty much gave up on it quite a while ago, but I kept the premise and the education account alive in the hopes of getting bits of university cash for birthdays and Christmas instead of the usual useless crap. There is not a ton of money in it, but usually I have resisted the urge to dig into it. I do not have any expensive hobbies.

Altogether I have a little more than a thousand dollars in the education fund and a bit of cash hidden in little spots around my room. I figure it is enough to give it a decent try to make a run for it.

I intend to waste some of it on my tattoo before I go.

9

Inked

I went back to the property where Angel lived at precisely the appointed time. Things looked pretty much the same there on the surface, but the atmosphere was different. Only the big truck and two motorcycles occupied the gravel parking area beside the house. I heard no music coming from inside.

I rang the doorbell. Angel answered wearing a large, sleeved, beige apron made of canvas with a row of pockets along the front. The garment was covered with ink stains of every imaginable colour.

"Hey, Angel."

I must have look mesmerized by his outfit.

"Don't worry about the get-up, kid. It's just something I had made that I find convenient to wear when I do ink work. I've had it a long time. You feel ready? Committed?"

"I'm ready."

"Good. So am I. You're name's Molloy, right? I don't wanna keep calling you kid."

"You got it. It's Molloy."

"Alright, Molloy, c'mon. I'm set up in the kitchen."

We ended up sitting across from each other again at the big kitchen table. Angel pulled some papers out from one of his apron pockets and tossed them semi-crumpled onto the table in front of me.

"Here's a few ideas I had on that tattoo. See if any of them work for ya'."

He turned slightly to the side then and looked away as if studying something over in a corner of the kitchen. Then he got up and walked a few steps in the direction he had been looking, but he did not seem to be really doing anything. I wondered if he might be concerned I would not appreciate his ideas the same way I had worried when I first showed him my original design. As it turned out he had nothing to worry about. I liked all of his designs better than my own. He had made quite a variety and it was clear he did see where I was coming from.

I chose the one that was essentially just an improved styling of my original design. I wanted it to be as close as possible to my own creation.

He said, "Okay. I thought you might pick that one. Good choice. I probably would've picked that one if I were you too. You said you want this thing on your back. Whereabouts? On your back how?"

"I've been thinking about that...I don't want it too big. Not over my whole back or anything. What do you think?"

"I was thinking the same as you, not too big. I think it might work best with something like a six-inch tall, eight-inch long rectangle in the middle of your back just below the shoulder blades. It's not too over the top, it's a bit different than what you usually see, and it can be like a little window to what's inside. What do you think?"

"Sounds good. I like it. Do it."

"Okay, good. I think it will have a pretty cool style and it will be easy enough to cover up whenever you don't feel like showing it off for some reason. That's why you can hardly see any of my tattoos unless my shirt's off."

Angel seemed to have put more thought into all this than I ever had. His ideas were certainly better than anything I had been able to dream up. It was a little embarrassing. I had been mulling over this tattoo on and off for years. Angel had patched up the holes in my plan in less than a thousandth of that time. But I was more grateful than anything. I tried to give him some credit.

"I really like your idea where to put the tattoo. Thanks."

"Don't sweat it. That's why you came to me. I have experience in these sorts of things."

Angel laughed and then continued.

"I know you really came to me because you had nowhere else to go, but it worked out. That sucky tattoo I showed you was one of my first ones. It turned out shitty 'cause I went to a hack who just did what I asked as quick as he could."

"Well thanks for not being like that guy."

Angel showed me a thumb up.

He said, "Are we done with the chit-chat? Are you ready?"

"Yep."

"You sure?"

"Yep."

"Last time...positive about this?"

"Do it."

"Take your shirt off, sit backward on the chair and lean your chest on top of the back of the chair. It'll hurt some so you can squeeze and pull on the spokes at the back of the chair to let some stress out if you need to. I can't make it not hurt at all, but if it's too much tell me and I'll see what I can do. We can always take a break if we need to."

I did as I was told and never asked Angel to pause in his work. I thought about things even more thrilling, nerve-wracking, and possibly more dangerous than getting a tattoo; running away. Big changes were about to enter my life. My train ride from Brockville to my new life in Ottawa would occur in only a few days, mere moments away in the big scheme of things.

10

Train

I got on the train the evening after I got my tattoo. Once I got my tattoo the last piece of my plan was in place. There was no point in staying. I did not show anyone or tell anyone about my tattoo. I packed a large duffle bag with whatever stuff I thought I would need and snuck away.

I contemplated saying goodbye to Dad, but somehow it did not seem appropriate. In all my contemplating about leaving home, I ran away. All the plans I made were made with running away in mind. The process made me sympathize with Mom a little more, though in truth she ran away from me as well as from Dad even if she did say goodbye.

I had never traveled on a train. I liked it. It was dusk when the locomotive pulled us out of Brockville. I had nobody in the seat beside me. The train was half empty. I turned off the overhead lights in my section to minimize any inner reflection that might hamper my view of the settling day.

The train made a number of stops, planned and unplanned, along the way, but it did not matter to me. I felt I had done my part and gotten on my way. I could utterly relax for a little while. Until I arrived in Ottawa I decided I had a free pass from worry, fret, or fear even if the worst was yet to come. The train ride could take the rest of my life for all I cared.

I wondered about the lives of the people in the country homes and little towns we passed between Brockville and Ottawa. I tried not to think much about what lay ahead. That was all I had been thinking about for several days, and I could not think of anything I had not already considered several times over. Whatever was going to happen would happen and I would deal with it as best I could.

I observed the sun sink and fade as the train progressed along its halting path northeast to the country's capital. The trip was about an hour and a half. My tattoo itched, tingled, and stung beneath my shirt the whole way.

It felt good rolling, watching, and often barely thinking as I moved from one life to another. If anything it seemed too soon when the train made its final braking coast into the Ottawa train station a little behind schedule.

Part 2

Ottawa

11

Arrival

As soon as I stepped off the train into the station I emerged from my trance. The more practical sections of my brain warmed up and started to work. I sat down in a row of chairs next to a discarded newspaper. My most immediate concern was finding a cheap place to stay for at least one night, next was food, then a job. I grabbed the abandoned newspaper on the chair beside me. I glanced briefly through the classified rental and 'help wanted' sections, only to get a general feel for what was out there. I needed to get my bearings and find a spot to get organized before the newspaper would be much use. I put the classified section in my duffle bag and left the rest on the chair.

The Ottawa train station was nothing like the big-city train stations I had read about. They were often described as old fashioned with large arches, pillars, and cathedral ceilings. The Ottawa station was more a clean, functional, and sparse design. There was only one store which appeared to be a convenience store/deli hybrid of some sort and it was closed. I had expected a little more variety and splendour, but I probably should have been thankful for the reduced temptation to spend the money I would likely need to start a life here. It was easier to just pick up my duffle bag and leave the station.

Outside it was again a bit of a letdown. It did not appear I was in a big city. Other than the train station there was less lights and less going on than there would be in downtown Brockville. The people who got off the train with me were moving so fast toward taxis or the parking lot that they were gone before I could even form a question to ask them in my mind. Back in the station a janitor informed me the station was on a small island of relatively quiet land away from the rest of the city. He did not know of any cheap places to stay for a night, but his best guess for a starting point was the corner of Bank and Gladstone. He directed me to the appropriate bus. Having nothing else to go on I took his advice.

Bank and Gladstone was more like what I had been expecting. The Esso gas station on the corner with a Tim Horton's inside took up most of a block and was more active than all of downtown Brockville put together at this time of night. I sat down on a bench near the bus stop to organize my thoughts. The full realization I was truly on my own suddenly sprang to life within me. Out of necessity I think I had suppressed such thoughts for the getaway, knowing if they were set loose I might lose my nerve. The world changed, became much larger and more unknown in that moment. Whatever became of me now there was only myself left to blame.

I had about a hundred dollars in cash spread around my hockey bag and upon my person. I had another eight hundred or so in my Scotiabank account. I hoped it was enough to get settled, but I knew I did not have a lot of slack. I brought most of my clothes, a few books, pens and blank notebooks to continue my diary, and a set of basic bathroom stuff. There were also piles of semi-organized notebooks and loose pages of writing that eventually got whittled down to the diary you now hold in your hands. With a trace of shame I also admit to taking bread and cheese out of Dad's refrigerator before I left, about a day's worth if I rationed it out.

The sun was down for the night, but it felt warmer in more northern Ottawa at night than it had earlier when the sun was still up in Brockville. It was about time things warmed up. It was almost April. I put my jacket in my bag, comfortable in only a sweater and jeans.

I spent well over an hour roaming the city trying to get a feel for things. The hustle and bustle died down noticeably away from the gas station, but there was still a significant flow of cars and people. The bag was a lesser burden when I looped the handles over my shoulders and wore it as a giant backpack even if it did make me feel like a bit of a freak. I stayed mainly on Bank Street since it seemed by far the busiest street nearby. I felt small, a little overwhelmed, and lost in an unknown place that was bigger in every way than what I was accustomed. I felt fear for sure, but there was something good mixed in with it too. I was more alert, present, and alive than I could ever remember. I was nervous, but I never seriously considered turning back.

During my travels I noted a few places that might come in handy if I lived somewhere nearby. I saw a place to get breakfast for $4.25. Also, there was an all you can eat Chinese food lunch buffet for $8.99. I noted a couple of pharmacies, grocery stores, a laundromat, and a library. I saw two 'help wanted' signs. They were posted at the laundromat and a Subway restaurant.

Ottawa seemed to have a decent amount of green space and parks for a big city. There were even some close to busy Bank Street. I made it far enough along Bank to see the Rideau Canal that I heard had the world's longest skating rink. It was cool watching the canal flow under the bridge in the dark right through the middle of the city. There were already several ducks and geese floating near the bridge. Spring had definitely arrived.

I turned back after I got to the canal. Bank Street seemed to go on forever. Even looking down a long hill before I turned back I could not see the end of it. Except for the bars and restaurants even the stores that were still open gave off the vibe they were about to close. I had not seen anything promising in terms of potential accommodations; none of the cheap hotels or youth hostels I had naively imagined. I had had good luck asking for directions to Angel's at the gas station in Brockville. It occurred to me it might be a good idea to try my luck back at the busy Esso.

By the time I arrived back at my starting point, the Esso gas station, I decided to keep going and try my luck in the other direction at least for a few blocks. The train station employee had presumably chosen Bank Street for a reason when I told him I needed a cheap place to stay for the night. Maybe with a bit of poor luck I had chosen the wrong direction to walk initially. The heavy bag was starting to wear me down, but I could still feel some power in my legs.

After three or four blocks I still had not seen any accommodations, but just a couple of blocks perpendicular from Bank Street, on Somerset Avenue, I saw a garish display of neon lights. It drew me. Whatever it was looked like it was still open. I walked down Somerset on the opposite side of the neon lights to get a better look as I approached. It was a slightly seedy, slightly hippy looking, twenty-four-hour diner. In several different colours and a funky style, the neon spelled out Groovier's. I smirked at the name. It also displayed the third help-wanted sign I had seen that night in less than two hours. At least the signs gave me hope of finding some type of employment. I put my bag down on the sidewalk and stood looking at the diner for several minutes. The scene was weird, mesmerizing. The fact that half of one of the neon o's spelling Groovier's was burned out somehow made it even more fitting.

I decided to go in and order something. Rationally, it was as likely a place as anywhere the staff might know an inexpensive place to stay. Irrationally, I was truly mesmerized and drawn toward Groovier's by the funky neon sign. Going in felt like the right thing to do at the time.

12

Groovier's

Groovier's turned out to be a much different place than I expected. It was less seedy, less hippy, busier and more organized than I imagined. When I say busy I mean it in a relaxed way. At least the customers were relaxed. The staff did not appear stressed, but they were always on the move. I did not have a watch, but I estimated it was around eight-thirty at night.

They let me lean my big duffle bag against the wall in a space between two coat racks and seated me at a small table near the front window. I had not been in many restaurants. I felt a little nervous and out of place, but at this point just sitting down on my ass in the light and heat indoors felt luxurious. Eventually I relaxed and tried to let go of the feeling I was on the run and therefore a suspicious character. The staff and other patrons did not seem to notice anything out of the ordinary about me.

The waiter was at my table fairly quickly, pleasant and efficient. He smiled and set a menu in front of me.

"I'm Dan. I'll be your waiter tonight. I'll be back in a few minutes to take your order. Don't be afraid to wave me down if you need something sooner. Anything to drink before I take off?"

"Coffee and water, please."

"Of course. Coming up."

Since Dad and I had been alone he had been letting me have coffee sometimes. I liked the zing it gave me and I was getting used to the taste. I needed a little energy boost.

I watched out the window. The people walking the streets were thinning out now. Down a ways, on the opposite side of the street, a large park took up the entire city block. The idea of saving money by sleeping overnight in the park scuttled through my mind. It might be warm enough if I dressed properly.

The thought of a chilly night in the park made me even more grateful for Groovier's temporary shelter. For some reason my shoulders, back, and legs ached more now that I had taken the load off them.

The waiter arrived with my beverages. I think he noticed I had not opened the menu yet.

"Here you go. I'll give you another few minutes and I'll be back."

"Great, thanks."

"My pleasure."

He was gone.

I was pretty hungry. I had done a lot of exercise without much food. I also think the nervous energy concentrating on my surroundings and soaking in the new atmosphere of Ottawa burned away calories behind the scenes. For now though the sight, smell, and anticipation of food swept all of my thrills about Ottawa through the door to wait outside.

For food I decided on what I hoped would be filling and cheap...a large plate of fries with ketchup, vinegar, salt, and pepper.

"Coming right up," said Dan.

I let my mind relax and go empty after I placed my order. My mind was as weary as my body. Trying to remain alert enough to notice anything that might help me get a toe hold here in Ottawa was more draining than I thought. I tried to put it from my mind that I would soon have to head back out into the night.

Groovier's décor and vibe was very different from anything I had come across in Brockville. I saw a fair amount of hippy-type décor, but with time, wear, and the modernization of the rest of the building the sixties pieces had slipped into the background. I wondered if I would even have noticed them under different circumstances. The lights looked like they might have been fluorescent, but they held a steady level of brightness over the whole restaurant without any flicker or buzz. I could not help but notice many of the patrons were somewhat dish-evelled, but they seemed calm and content. The business end of Groovier's, the staff, emanated alert, busy, pleasant efficiency. They were helpful, but not cloying. As well, the establishment looked very clean.

When Dan brought me fries I pumped him for information.

"I'm new in town. Know any place I can stay a night for cheap?"

"How cheap?"

"As cheap as possible...as long as it's fairly safe. I just need some uninterrupted sleep for a night."

"Hmm."

He pointed.

"There's a place that rents rooms cheap a couple of blocks down on the same side of Somerset. To be honest though, by the look of the place, I think they're more into renting rooms by the hour if you catch my drift. I can't really vouch for them being safe either."

I thought I knew what he meant.

"Anything else?"

"There used to be a men's shelter up a bit further on Bank Street, but it's probably full. Those places always are. I'm not sure if it's safe either. I'm not even sure if it's still there. I haven't seen the usual bunch huddled out in front smoking in quite a while."

Dan stopped and thought a bit.

"I can't really think of any other possibilities around here. Sorry."

"Okay. Thanks anyway."

He smiled.

"Yeah, sorry. Good luck."

Then he went about his business.

The fries were great. For a while each one I ate made me hungrier, but I forced myself not to eat like a starved animal. I was a little dehydrated too, but Dan filled up my water glass a couple of times while I tried to mimic a normal human eating a snack.

From my position I had a decent view of a corner section of the park through Groovier's front window. I kept wondering over and over how practical it would be to spend the night there. Even if I did not get an ideal night's sleep, saving the money on indoor accommodations was worth something. Then again, a poor night's sleep might leave me in bad shape for starting to get my new life organized tomorrow.

I was running out of options. If saving a night's rent was the best thing I could salvage from the night it was better than nothing. I would at least go over to check out the park and see what sort of vibe I got there.

13

The Park

The park was split into four sections by two diagonal pedestrian paths that went through it corner to corner. About every twenty meters white plastic globes upon black metal posts emitted soft light along the paths. Also lining the paths were wooden benches nearly long enough for me to lay flat without bending my legs. Large healthy looking trees stretched themselves into the generous space provided between them, ensuring their roots and leaves had ample access to water, nutrients, and light. In the early spring their leaves were tiny and new, but there they were, preparing to greet the coming of a brighter, hotter sun. Noticing the leaf buds made me feel a little warmer and hopeful.

I chose a bench I hoped was close enough to the street to discourage potential criminals. At the same time I tried to choose a spot far enough from the street to avoid a policeman's casual scan for vagrants like me.

For a while I just sat there looking around. It was peaceful. The artificial stationary light of the city together with the light in motion from car headlamps made faint shadows shift and play along the ground even at night. These playful city lights blotted out nearly all the stars. This reminded me I was a long way from home where hundreds of stars could be seen — only an hour away by train, but an eternity away in many other ways.

My body was weary, but my mind felt nowhere near ready for sleep. I did not have a clue what to do next. Even if I managed to get a decent night's sleep on the park bench it would only mean I did not have a clue what to do tomorrow morning instead of tonight. Still, I had to get safely through the night before I even had a chance at anything else. Whatever hours of peaceful rest I could manage were a bonus for my state of mind in the morning.

The park was never empty. In fact, it gradually donned on me as I sat thinking, only half aware of my surroundings, that if anything the park was slowly gaining more occupants. I noticed an earlier couple beside the children's swing set now had four in the group. A large tree I felt certain was alone many minutes ago now had two chums standing together near its trunk. More than once I noticed a person or two crossing Somerset between the park and The Beer Store a few doors down from Groovier's. Coming back they usually had cans or six-packs in their hands.

Everyone was split up into small groups. They were generally quiet, but once in a while I heard a clear word, phrase, or laugh catch the air just right. The only other sounds were the background swish of wind through the half-bare branches and the occasional rumble of motor vehicles passing by.

I had imagined my night in the park completely alone with no more than an occasional pedestrian passing through. My biggest concern was a policeman telling me to move along. What were all these people doing here in the middle of the night? Drifters like me? None seemed to be settling in for the night. Some sort of late night amateur music festival or poetry reading? I hoped not. Drugs? Maybe. I could see the winking lights of people smoking and once in a while I thought I smelled something funny. I knew some were at least drinking beer. I just wanted to be left alone to sleep a little.

That did not happen. Instead, a skinny guy, maybe a bit older than me, stopped by to visit me at my bench. His hair was very straight, shoulder length, and parted equally down each side of his face. He had a tiny moustache and a poorly crafted tattoo placed high on the center of his breastbone. He wore his shirt unbuttoned in a manner that ensured the tattoo was visible. It was just letters that looked drawn by a child with a royal blue marker — Tragicly Hip. I assumed it was a misspelled reference to the famous Canadian rock band that had been near top of the charts for several years a while back. I even knew a few of their songs.

He stood in front of me for a while not saying anything, smiling, sizing up the situation in a non-threatening way. He shifted from foot to foot a couple of times before finally saying something.

"Hey, man."

I tried to sound tough and jaded, but not too tough, not confrontational.

"Hey. What's up?"

"New in town?"

"Pretty new. Why?"

"Cool. What's in the bag? Hockey stuff? You play?"

"Naw, just my stuff. Only thing big enough to fit my clothes and other crap in one bag."

"Why are you carrying it around?"

I wondered why he asked and what I should say. I was suspicious of his motives, but it seemed the truth was as good as anything under the circumstances. At least the truth in general if not in detail.

"I just left home today. I'm just sitting here trying to figure the best way to pass the night cheap until morning. This park safe to stay in?"

My visitor seemed to relax a little after my explanation.

"Been there," he said.

His face even looked sympathetic for a brief moment in the poor light, but if there was a flicker of emotion, it vanished as quickly as it arrived.

"Your pa' messing with you?" he asked.

Just like Angel, this cast-off seemed to guess my life's story just by looking at me.

I stared at him, studied him. Was this guy me a year or two from now: a weird, skinny, hungry guy lurking in a park, approaching and starting up conversations with strangers in the middle of the night? I felt like I was standing on the edge of a deep pit with a murky, shadowy bottom. He was still waiting for an answer. I kind of snapped at him.

"I don't know. I guess. Everyone. Everything. I had to go or maybe rot or die there or something."

My visitor did not seem perturbed by me raising my voice.

"Heavy, man. That's tough shit. Good luck to you, man."

I softened my tone.

"Thanks," I said. "I'm Molloy."

"Todd."

We did some sort of weird handshake that Todd started and I tried to follow. After that we were both quiet for quite a while before he asked me for help.

"Say, man, I hate to ask, but you think you got anything you could spare outta that bag? It gets tough sometimes."

I found the request annoying. I suspected this request was the whole reason for his wandering over and the rest was the set up. But I suppose he seemed relatively harmless and maybe as nice as one could expect under the circumstances. And he did look half-starved and a little under the weather. That part seemed genuine.

"Not much, but maybe something small. I think so. Let's just leave it for now until there are not so many people around watching. I don't want to start a lineup for handouts. If you put the word out that I'm a nice guy who doesn't have much and shouldn't be messed with I'll show some appreciation. You can also spread the word I'm looking for a cheap place to stay for a night. We'll see how it goes and talk again later."

"Cool," he said. "It's a deal. I'll put the word around."

Todd took off immediately.

Since the encounter with Todd went smooth enough I felt a little less edgy. I tried to imagine my spot on the bench as a bubble of relative calm within whatever else was going on in the park. I took a few deep breaths and looked around making sure not to stare anywhere in particular for long.

I thought I picked out Todd's silhouette once in a while visiting various small groups scattered around the park. I hoped he was doing what I asked him to do, convincing people I was not worth pestering unless they knew where I could stay cheaply.

It actually did seem as if Todd worked some sort of magic. Whereas before I got the feeling people were looking over at me fairly often, now I almost felt like I was being ignored. The peace helped me relax and relaxing made me realize I was dead tired. I was tired enough to wonder if I might even be able to fall asleep with all these people nearby. I could not help trying to figure out what they were doing here. I figured it must be past ten o'clock by now.

It appeared the separate groups began to mingle more as time went by. In terms of passing cars and pedestrians it grew quieter as it grew later and darker. The park population was in an ongoing state of gradual flux. I watched. A member of one group would break away and visit another group for a spell. Sometimes it appeared as if some sort of barter and exchange was occurring. There had been fairly frequent visits to The Beer Store across the street, but the lights were now out. The light was dim and I watched from a distance, but it seemed some people left the park altogether. I think some of those who left came back and new people occasionally dropped by to check things out.

I do not know what Todd said to the park dwellers, but it worked. I was pretty much ignored. It was as if there was a fifteen-meter impenetrable barrier around my bench. I no longer felt threatened. I almost felt safe enough to sleep, but I was too freaked out by these nearly silent people gathered in the park so late. The question would not leave me. What were they doing here?

As exhaustion ate away at my bewilderment I started to relax. I was really tired. Why would these people care if I slept while they did their thing? Aside from the bit of cash, I guessed my measly hoard would hardly be worth the trouble of stealing. Also, it seemed as if Todd may have got the word out I was not any better off then they were. Maybe they would just leave me alone. I put my bag on the bench so it was tilted up on one of the armrests and I rested against it sort of like a lounge chair. It probably was not that comfortable, but I was tired enough that it felt fine. Before long I was having those half-awake thoughts and visions that meant sleep was just around the corner.

Then a gravelly voice croaked nearby and ripped apart the cloud I was riding to dreamland.

"What you got?"

My glands blasted me with a shot of adrenaline. I jerked upright and around toward the voice. My own voice was startled and a little nasty.

"Fuck. You shouldn't sneak up on people when they're trying to sleep."

My visitor conveyed peace by keeping his hands up where I could see them in a surrender position. He moved around to the path where I could see him better.

"Sorry, man, I didn't know you were trying to sleep."

He was skinny and slightly shabby in a way similar to Todd, but he was taller and older. He was a couple inches taller than me. He looked a little crazed even at first glance.

"Don't worry about it," I said. "I'm not having much luck sleeping here anyway. It's busier than I expected. I'm just waiting and resting until morning. If I'm lucky maybe I'll doze a little. What are all these people doing here anyway?"

He nodded.

"Yep," he said. "We're all looking for a little piece of the demon."

My skinny new friend's jeans were too large for him. His dirty sweatshirt was too small. The top of his ass-crack showed at the best of times and half of his ass showed more then I would have preferred. He wore no underwear. He never stopped looking around, adjusting his loose pants, and just randomly moving in general. He sometimes turned right around and put his back to me while we were talking. This action usually seemed to help his pants slide over his hips to flash me his twig-like hairy butt. I suppose I should be thankful he somehow managed to avoid showing me his cock. He had a bushy beard and large, bulging eyes that made the rest of his face and his body appear even skinnier. He looked insane.

Todd had been working his way around telling my story. This guy knew it.

"Not enough cash for a hostel, eh?"

"Not even close. Why? Are there hostels around here?"

He cackled and shrugged.

"I don't rightly know. I think there used to be, but I wouldn't have a clue these days."

I nodded and shrugged back at him. I did not need this interaction right now. After a pause he asked the question I presumed was the reason he came over.

"Anything to spare in that big bag?"

I looked at him as if he should know better than to ask.

"I wouldn't be here if I had spare would I?"

The freak startled me again by collapsing onto his knees, grimacing and shaking in what I initially took for pain or a seizure. Then he started to make a whining, stuttering sound I eventually recognized as laughter. He had to put one of his arms down on the ground to form a tripod to keep him from falling flat on the grass weak with uncontrollable giggles.

He choked out between spasms of laughter, "That's the funniest thing I ever heard."

Apparently, he did not just look insane.

When he calmed down he hauled himself to his feet and shuffled away. Even then he had to stop once in a while, clutch his stomach, and tremble with laughter.

The unfortunate part about beardy-bug-eye's outburst was it turned a lot of attention my way from the little enclaves sprinkled around the park. It did not last too long though, dissipating completely by the time he dissolved back into the shadows. It took me a bit longer to settle down from the experience.

At this point I was almost regretting not springing for a decent hotel room. Then again, why turn back now? I readjusted my hockey bag again so I could recline on the bench. It was like I was on a miniature hospital bed with no sheets and too short for me to fully extend my legs.

I was tired enough I did not need ideal conditions to sleep. Every time I closed my eyes it felt as if the breeze was gently rocking the Earth and whispering me a lullaby. I definitely dozed, but it was a fitful slumber, the kind when even lightly asleep my dream was to wonder if I would ever get to sleep, dreaming I was awake. I figured any rest I could manage could only make me feel less tired when the sun came up and I had to move on.

It must have been one of those times I was asleep that I felt a hand gently shake my shoulder. I flinched awake and felt my heart jump in my chest. What the hell? Todd? Now what?

I must have shouted the words I thought were only flashing through my mind as I awoke because Todd flinched and looked a little hurt.

"Sorry to wake you, man. It's just that I'm going to be heading out now and I did spread the word you were all right and didn't have no valuables like we said. I even asked around a bit to see if I could find you a place to stay. Not much luck on that part though."

I was groggy enough having a hard time following what he was saying. Maybe I slept more than I thought. He seemed to recognize the blank look on my face and tried to clarify the situation.

"You said you might have something for me if I did all that stuff."

My mind cleared up some. I figured out what Todd was talking about. My muscles were sore.

"Right, Todd. Sorry. I'm pretty out of it."

It was true I had hardly been bothered at all and we did sort of make a deal and I did say I might have something for him. It seemed like bad karma to start out in Ottawa by being a prick. Whatever. I reached into my bag and pulled out the first thing on top, a pair of jeans. I was aware enough to remember I spread my cash around in the bag. I made sure I had not hidden any cash in one of the jean pockets. I had another pair of jeans.

"I wasn't lying when I said I didn't have much, but you can have these for your trouble. Thanks for helping me out."

Todd looked happy enough with the jeans even though they would not fit him well. He was at least as tall as me, but he was skinnier. It might work out if he had a belt or rope or something.

He said, "Thanks, bro."

"Thank you too. Hope they fit."

"I'll make 'em fit."

"All right. Any idea of the time?"

"I'd guess about two in the morning."

"Okay, thanks."

Todd held the jeans up to the light beside the path to get a better look at them. He was smiling and it made me feel good he was pleased with them. I was afraid he expected money.

"Thanks," he said again. "Maybe I'll see you around sometime."

I did not have to reply. As he spoke, Todd turned and ran from the park apparently feeling richer with his new pair of used jeans.

The park population was really thinning out now. I was now sure I could at least grab a few hours of uninterrupted sleep if I was left alone. I lay down on the bench again with my big bag underneath me and closed my eyes. My head buzzed with the desire to be unconscious. Only a few tenuous threads connecting me to the physical world needed to dissolve and I would be gone.

Like a buzz saw words ripped me back into the real world.

"I heard you could maybe use a place to stay tonight."

I jolted up. Now what?

"Huh!? What?"

"Sorry, chief, I didn't mean to scare you. I heard you could use a place for the night."

More evidence that Todd had done what I asked of him. I got up halfway on my elbows. The man continued before I could put my thoughts together.

"I can probably help you if you need a place to crash for the night. Cheap too. If you don't need, you don't need. Just asking. I was told you needed a place."

When my eyes cleared of sleep I could see he was a fairly old guy. Not like eighty, but probably a good fifty. I had kind of figured everyone gathered in the park were younger. However, he was definitely skinny and grubby looking like the other people I'd seen.

"How cheap?"

"Five bucks," he said.

That got my attention. Definitely in my price range. Still, I only had to wait a few hours until morning. But would I be exhausted for my first day in Ottawa with such little sleep?

The guy seemed to take my hesitation as a sign of a lost sale and haggled with me.

"Hey, man, I don't have all night to stand around and chit-chat. It's late. Three bucks. Yes or no?"

Whoa. Really cheap. Why? My mind raced around looking for answers.

"Can I sleep until noon if I want?"

"Sure, pal. Don't touch any food or use any supplies in the house, but you can sleep 'til noon...then out."

What the fuck, I thought. Sold. I did not even have to hunt around in my bag for such as small amount of cash. I had three bucks, a toonie and a loonie, in my pocket. I would be better off with a few extra hours of deeper sleep than I could get outside on a park bench. I dropped the coins in his hand and he immediately started off, motioning me to follow.

"C'mon, it's not far."

It was only three or four blocks.

14

Room for the Night

The house was a lot bigger than I expected, it was huge. It looked decent enough in the dark. As the man led me into the building I realized the house was actually split up into six apartments. There were six letterboxes on the outside. I followed him up to a door on the second floor.

The place was noticeably shabbier within than it had been from the outside view. The steps were bare wood with worn rubber strips covering the center section of each stair. The railing and some of the stairs were wobbly in places. Cigarette burns and butts were common decorations along the climb. A fine powder of grime was noticeable on the edges of the steps and on any windowsills we passed. I did not care. All I wanted was some hours of uninterrupted sleep to help me get through the next day with enough focus to make some progress toward getting my new life up and running.

My host fumbled with a big ring of keys in front of the apartment door. Why did he need so many keys? It was obvious from the first moment the door cracked open that the place was a disaster. The negative impression of the room immediately cut through my exhaustion like a slap in the face. Trash was all over the place; papers, plastic bags, half eaten food, cans, bottles, utensils, curtains that had apparently been torn from the bare windows, a rusty set of barbells, a tiny ghetto blaster, a couple of needles on a small, scuffed coffee table, and a miniature television turned on but broadcasting only silent static. There were also the ends of a couple of mattresses on the floor poking through the piles of old blankets on top of them. Clusters of dust lurked beneath any piece of furniture that had a bare space beneath itself.

Along the wall next to the door we entered, a girl wearing only shorts and a bra was asleep on top of a pile of clothes. She looked to be in an uncomfortable position, but she did not stir when we entered. I guessed there were others asleep under the unkempt blankets heaped upon the mattresses on the floor. In the dim light it was difficult to be sure of anything among the chaotic piles of rubbish. Overhead, a light fixture with three small bulbs in it (one of those was burnt out) lit the room unevenly.

An eerie chill crept through me as I looked around. Was it legal to live like this? For a few seconds I had a difficult time suppressing my laughter, but I managed to hold it in. I felt like I was on one of those prank television shows. I presumed the man who brought me here was the one in charge of this catastrophe. He stepped gingerly through the apartment poking his hands into various piles of clutter with great focus. It was as if he forgot I was there.

"Where do I sleep?"

I was wondering if I should just cut my losses and get out. He did not even look at me, but he answered.

"Wherever you want," he said, "except not in my room."

He then made a pleased grunt of discovery, reached into a pile of trash, and transferred something I could not clearly see into his pocket. He looked over and gave me a thumb up.

"Speaking of my room," he said, "I'm going to bed right now. Gotta' get some shuteye."

He smiled, held his arms outstretched, and turned slowly to encompass the entire area of the apartment.

"Make yourself at home. Just don't take anything and be gone by the time I get home from my early morning appointment tomorrow. Around noon will be fine."

My host then gave me a half wave/half salute farewell, went into his room, and shut the door. I looked around for a non-toxic place to lie down for a few hours. It was extremely shitty accommodations, but for three bucks I guess I was getting my money's worth. If I did not get hurt and I did not have my things stolen I was getting a fair deal.

I could not bring myself to dig out a spot for myself beneath the rubbish in the living room. For one thing I felt sure there were people under there somewhere, and I did not want to tangle with anyone desperate enough to be staying in a place like this. As well, I could imagine many unpleasant, hidden objects down below that I would rather avoid rummaging through. I was so tired I probably could have slept anywhere, but I would sleep more soundly with a better idea of the nature of the filth that surrounded me. I chose the bathtub.

The tub was filthy, of course, splotched with hard grayish-brown grime that was difficult to remove even when I scraped it with a quarter. I was pretty sure it had been a long time since someone had used it to clean themselves. I did not dwell on the dirt. If I could not scrape it off with a quarter it was not going to come off on my clothes or skin. I crawled in and pulled my duffle bag in on top of me upside down, the zipper against my chest, to ward off potential thieves.

I felt pretty foolish scrunched up in a dirty bathtub with a big, heavy bag on top of me for a blanket. I even snickered a couple of times as I reflected on the absurdity of life on my own so far. It was more scary than funny, but in my current state all I could do was laugh.

Eventually I quit worrying. Fuck it. As much as I was able I shut my mind down; my exhaustion helped. The best I could do at this point was to hold on and see what the morning brought. I pulled the mildewed plastic curtain shut for as much privacy as I could manage. I don't remember having another thought. I went to sleep.

At some point somebody came in to use the toilet. It woke me up, but I did not stir or make a sound. There was the sound of peeing, maybe washing hands, and then drinking out of the sink faucet. I still felt the desire for sleep like a soft but urgent pressing on my mind from within. I really wanted to doze more, but something kept prickling at me to get up. My muscles were stiff and my neck was kinked from sleeping in the tub and all the walking with my big bag on my shoulders. Once I was alone in the bathroom again I peeked around the shower curtain. I could tell by the light slanting through the twisted, rung-missing window blinds that the sun had started to rise.

Another discomfort, my chest ached from the heavy burden of the bag on top of it while I slept. I pushed it off of me out of the tub then climbed out after it. I just had to pick up my bag and quietly walk out the door. I kept as silent as possible as I manoeuvered the big bag through the bathroom doorway.

In the weak morning light passing through some uncovered windows and a few hours sleep under my belt the apartment's living room looked even worse than I remembered from only hours before. The walls were an orangey brown likely evolved over years of indoor smoking. The smell supported my hypothesis. Perhaps fortunately, the night before I somehow failed to notice what looked like a six-inch hunk of feces in the corner. Or maybe it was relatively fresh and had not been there before. These could not be legal living arrangements.

The girl sleeping on the pile of clothes last night must have been the same one who used the bathroom before I got up. She was slowly moving around the living room in a daze not bothered by the fact she was shuffling barefoot in a toxic waste dump. She was wearing the same outfit, short red shorts and a bra. In the better light I noticed her face was bruised. When she finally noticed me she looked delighted to see me.

"Oh, hi, God, I wasn't even sure if there was anyone else here. That's great. Do you have any money?"

"No," I said.

I thrust my arms through the bags handles once again to morph it to a giant backpack. It was even less enjoyable this time due to aches and stiffness. As I closed the door behind me I heard her yell.

"Cigarettes?"

I walked quickly, wanting to distance myself from the surreal dive I somehow ended up in last night. Ottawa was not what I expected so far and I would be hard pressed to argue it was better than Brockville. I felt tainted from spending the night in such a filthy confusion of a place, but as I walked, the breeze softly caressed my hair and skin and I gradually realized I at least felt surprisingly refreshed from whatever sleep I had salvaged at the park and apartment. I had also spent much less money than I intended my first night in Ottawa. These realizations lifted my spirits off the bottom. By the time I looked up from my thoughts I was back where I began the previous night, at the park.

By the temperature and the brightness of the day I could tell it was later than I expected from the dim light inside the apartment. A passerby informed me it was nine-thirty in the morning. It turned out I had slept a decent amount.

I saw the bench that had been almost like a home, or at least a refuge, to me for several hours last night. I had the urge to sit there and get my thoughts together. I tried to do so, but the moment I sat down I was immediately compelled to do something else even more strongly. It was as if while I slept my subconscious had come up with a plan to improve the odds of my survival and decided to act upon the plan before letting me in on it. My body shot up off the bench and started off while my conscious mind worked on putting the pieces together. I went straight through the park over to the twenty-four-hour diner, Groovier's. I took the 'help wanted' sign from the window and held it up to the first staff person I saw.

I asked, "Who can I talk to about this?"

I am sure I looked a little crazed with my giant duffle bag backpack and a little rough around the edges from poor morning hygiene and sleeping in purgatory, but I was persistent enough that someone went back into the depths of the restaurant to bring the owner out to see me. His name was Mr. Iaello. He did not look pleased. He asked me to follow him into his office away from the customers.

He told me several times I was not the right sort of person for his diner. He explained things often got very busy and he needed someone with experience. He told me most shifts were hellish, the pay was mediocre at best, and that the customers demanded efficiency and respect at all times whether they deserved it or not.

I told Mr. Iaello things about myself I was not sure were true, but I had little control over myself. From the moment this notion of working at Groovier's hit me on the bench in the park I felt as if I was watching myself from a spot nearby and playing along with the show. I watched myself tell Mr. Iaello I was a fast learner, a hard worker, and had no problem whatsoever starting and staying at the very bottom for as long as it took to prove myself. I also watched myself tell Mr. Iaello at least one thing I knew to be definitely true, that I really, really, really needed this job.

Mr. Iaello looked as if he was preparing to signal someone to physically remove me from the restaurant. He looked past me through his office door that had not been shut during our conversation. A couple of staff members were standing by outside the door to keep an eye on things. He looked back at me, then away again, then back at me. It probably happened over less than ten seconds, but it felt like everything was in slow motion. Then the lines in the owner's face, the light in his eyes, and the tension in his posture altered slightly. Something in him yielded.

"Fine, you're a new hire. You get the worst jobs and the worst shifts to start. You won't get many hours at first, but we'll see how it goes. Come in tomorrow at ten in the morning after the breakfast rush and we'll get you set up and go over some things."

I went kind of nuts and thanked him over and over again without allowing him the chance to respond. I grabbed his hand before he had opportunity to extend it toward me, and shook it over and over. I continued to shake his hand and thank him as he tried to turn away from me to head back to the restaurant and customers.

As I left the building, without looking back, I shouted.

"You won't regret it."

15

Search For a Home

It is hard to describe the energy boost landing my job at Groovier's gave me. Within minutes I locked onto the next most important thing I had to do, find some place to live. I put every ounce of my effort and attention toward that task. In the end, the saying I worked hard enough to make my own luck came true that day. Ironically, I think it was Dad who taught me that maxim.

I got a newspaper, the Ottawa Citizen, and took it to a nearby restaurant to study over breakfast. I was hungry and breakfast was the cheapest meal of the day so I did not skimp. I ordered a full breakfast with an extra order of toast and home fries. I would not eat again until I had a place to live.

I will not submit the reader to a detailed description of my tedious day of apartment hunting. It is enough to say it started with classified ads over breakfast, then calls from a payphone and walks to appointments, and ended in desperation, roaming the streets in search of rental signs within walking distance of Groovier's. It was near dark and my positive energy had finally started to run low when I found success.

From the nearest payphone I phoned the number posted in the front door's window. The lady who answered sounded like she might be from Russia.

"Yes the apartment is still available. Would you like to come and see it?"

"As soon as possible. I'm close to the apartment right now."

"Now?"

"If it works for you I can see it now."

"Well, alright. I live nearby. Meet me in front in fifteen or twenty minutes?"

"Sure, I'll be there."

I was there first and I sat on the front steps for five minutes or so before the landlady turned up. She was elderly, at least seventy I think. Her gray hair was pulled back in a bun and she was plainly, yet nicely dressed. I smiled and tried to put forward my best attributes. I really needed this place at least for a couple of nights. I caught myself silently praying before remembering the blasphemy, my tattoo.

"Hi, I'm Molloy. Thank you for coming so quickly."

She laughed.

"My name is Hilda. It was easy for me. I only live up the street. This is where I grew up, but I live in a smaller house now."

I tried to make it sound real when I laughed in return.

"Lucky for me," I said.

Hilda's tone turned a little more serious.

"I should have mentioned on the phone that the apartment is not a real apartment."

"What do you mean?"

"You would get the top floor which is a bedroom and kitchen joined by a small hallway that connects to the stairway down to the second floor. You would share a full bathroom with the second floor tenant. He is quiet, works during the day and goes away quite often on weekends."

That did not sound like too big a deal.

"That's not too bad for me. I don't spend a lot of time in the bathroom."

"Good. Sorry I did not mention it on the phone. I got sidetracked when you said you wanted to see it so soon."

It seems unnecessary to give the full details of the apartment showing. It was a simple and more than adequate place for me to live. It even had basic furniture. As soon as she told me the price I new I would have a difficult time finding a better solution to my needs.

"It is four-hundred and ninety dollars per month and I need first and last months rent."

I could not realistically give her first and last months rent and survive until my first paycheck, but I needed this place.

"I love this place. I just moved to Ottawa yesterday and I got a job today. My entire savings is first and last. Can I give you first now? Then I'll pay up the last month's rent during the first month once I start getting some pay."

Hilda looked at me, uncertain.

"I don't think so. I have run into trouble making unusual deals in the past."

"I'm not even sure if I have that much money all put together. And I have to at least buy food until my first pay."

"Where is your job?"

"Groovier's, the restaurant pretty close to here."

"Groovier's?"

"Yeah, the one that's open all night, twenty-four hours."

"Who hired you?"

"The owner. Uh, mister, uh...Mr. Iaello."

"I know Mr. Iaello. He is a serious man, but he is also a very trustworthy, dependable man."

"You know him? I'll go with you right now and we can tell him to keep half my pay until I'm caught up first and last. I'll sign whatever I need to make it legal."

"I don't think we have to go that far."

"How about I go and get first month from the bank right now plus an extra hundred. I can live on the rest until I start getting paid."

The landlady's demeanour had changed. She seemed much less hesitant.

"Okay, we have a deal. No need to get the money tonight. Just give it to me the day you move in."

I froze. It had never even occurred to me there was any question of my move in date.

"I want to move in tonight."

"Tonight?"

Hilda's hesitancy was back.

"I don't have any place to stay. I've been looking all day and this place is perfect for me. I'll go to a bank machine right now and get the money."

Now she just looked shocked. She stared at me silently.

"What about your things?"

"I just have that big bag near the front porch."

"That's it?"

I nodded.

"Can I go get the money?"

Hilda shrugged.

"Why not? How did you know there was no one living here?"

It never even occurred to me.

"I never thought of that. Is there?"

"No. Usually there is when I put a place up for rent, but not this time. The previous tenant left on short notice."

"I'll be as fast as I can. Where's the closest bank machine?"

16

Apartment

All I had to supply for the apartment was my bag full of junk. Eventually, I did have to supply a phone and a cheap used computer to have basic contact with the world outside. The bedroom had a bed complete with linens and blankets, a bedside table with a lamp, and a desk with four drawers. I suspect the accommodations were furnished with a student in mind. The bedroom was bigger than the one I had at home. The kitchen had a fridge, a stove, a microwave, and metal table surrounded by three wooden chairs. The kitchen drawers and cupboards were stocked with basic utensils, cookware, cups, and plates. The kitchen was also bigger than the one at home.

All the windows could be opened easily leaving just the screen between the outside and I. Often I would leave them all open and let the fresh breeze blow through the place. The translucent pink-orange curtains moved easily to the beat of the wind.

All I had to do was arrange to have a phone put in.

I loved it.

Exhausted, I was only there an hour or two the first night before I fell asleep, but in those couple hours it was hard for me to imagine I would not succeed in Ottawa. I was my own man, self-sufficient, and ready to build a life. I was not naïve enough to believe my struggle was finished. I knew it had just begun. But for a couple of hours I allowed myself to believe I was making it. I had a job and a place to sleep when only a day ago vagrancy and death seemed more realistic possibilities.

It was as if from the moment I woke up I was filled with a mission and a drive that would not let me fail. My tattoo itched for the first time since the train ride to Ottawa. It got me thinking. Once might argue I had been "blessed" during the day, my good fortune more than anyone could have reasonably hoped. Then again, one might argue the night before was more horrific than I would have reasonably feared. Then again, no harm had come to me and I had spent very little of my money despite my poor planning. Then again things had been going to hellish shit for a long time in Brockville before I decided to split for Ottawa.

Thankfully, somewhere between those muddled thoughts I feel asleep.

17

Family

This point seems to be an opportune time to reflect upon my lost life and family in Brockville. I have reflected upon these things many times, of course, but I am trying to keep this diary orderly and contained. My reflections have been no more or less than any reasonable person would expect, a confused jumble of conflicting emotions; longing, anger, emptiness, sorrow, and guilt, all surrounded by a secret pointless wish that things had turned out differently than they did.

I have portrayed my parents honestly, but poorly and perhaps with too much bias due to the time frame. To be fair, the points where my parents are highlighted in my diary are low points for them, for us as a family. In retrospect it seems we only noticed and admitted something was wrong when it was far too late to fix anything. In truth, I have no idea how it started or how we got there.

Because the better times are more distant and less life altering, I do not remember them as clearly as the worst times, but there are bits and echoes that make me wonder sometimes what it would have taken to keep us on a finer path. Could no more than better luck have made a big enough difference?

Thinking this way makes me remember my tattoo. I forget it sometimes back there, hidden from view...my condemnation of life, circumstances, and any powers that may be.

Allow me to try and put things a different way. I hold definite hope my life and I will turn out well, that I will find a way to navigate the countless obstacles that are and will be in my path. And if I do turn out well? Who gets the credit? Just me? I might be a measure of my genes or my environment or some complicated recipe of both, but my parents were involved in both factors forming the whole.

Perhaps my parents' lives started to unravel and it never let up long enough for them to catch their breath and fight back, let alone find the time and energy to be the type of parents they would have liked. Again, I do not pretend to know, but I do know and remember a few small things I should relate.

Somewhere along the line I developed the courage to go off on my own to a new city and start a new life without much aid. I found the will to put together the skills and knowledge necessary to survive and make a go of it. Until I left home I had always been fed and given shelter. I was rarely spanked and never physically abused. Both my parents smoked, but after several attempts both managed to quit long before I got to high school. In early public school I had difficulty concentrating on class tasks and frequently got in trouble. My parents managed to find and reimburse a tutor for a couple of months who helped me learn how to focus. I believe the tutoring provided me with a measurable, lasting benefit.

When I was very young Dad brought me a large collection of Children's Illustrated Classics from a garage sale. I read them all several times. I suspect these literary comics were likely the seeds for my love of reading and the desire to write something of my own.

During my life Mom once in a while appeared in my room after I had been reading, writing, or daydreaming in there for hours. She often had a cookie or hot chocolate and she would sit and hang out with me for several minutes. She would ask me how I was doing, what I was up to, and chat for a while until she was not sure what else to say. She was trying to connect like a good Mom.

Lastly, Dad is the only one who did not run away. He is the one who is left alone at home. Does that mean he was the core of the problem or that he was the only one willing to stick it out with the remainder of the family for better or for worse?

Again, I am not trying to offer answers. I only thought it was appropriate to write a short entry to let the reader know I think about these things. Also to remind the reader and myself that there is likely always much more to these types of things than meets the eye.

18

First Real Job

I had been working at Groovier's for a few months before I worked up the courage to ask Mr. Iaello about the unusual name of his establishment. The owner said he realized the restaurant's name was somewhat ridiculous, but he kept it the way it was because his clients were used to it, and to remind himself to be humble and to treat everyone with a measure of respect. He had chosen the name Groovier's when he was much younger.

He said, "Having the sign above my restaurant is a constant reminder that everyone makes mistakes, some people just learn from them better than others."

It may be not surprising that Mr. Iaello was something of a father figure to me. I realized it a little at the time, but more so now that we are apart. He may have even felt like something of a father to me. However, when it came time to separate we simply let it happen with a minimum of fuss and emotion. We were both too old for Mr. Iaello to start being my father. I had to find another way.

To date, my experience at Groovier's has been one of the best experiences of my life. I did start out with the crappiest jobs and worst overnight shifts, but it gave my life a focus, gave me some money, and kept me from feeling like easy prey in the city. I was lucky to get a job where I was treated fairly. I was thankful. I was happy for a while.

Many days were very much the same at Groovier's. The first two or three weeks I did all the worst jobs and during the worst shifts, just like Mr. Iaello said I would. I worked from ten at night until six in the morning, lugging garbage, sweeping, dishes, table clean-up, cleaning up the smoking area out back, and washroom duty. After my initiation I was allowed a bigger variety of jobs and shifts. The other staff took their usual turns with the less desirable jobs and shifts. As the new guy, I did more than my share for a while, but things evened out fairly quickly.

It wasn't too long before I could do everything since there were only so many jobs to switch around between and none of them were overly difficult. Serving was the most challenging; lots of carrying and walking, lots of things to remember, and juggling all the customers' different personalities was a handful. Job rotation was nice because it kept any job from getting too mundane. Tip sharing worked pretty well. The staff must have been fairly honest because at the end of the day when the money was split up, I only noticed a reasonably modest increase in my tips when I worked serving meals and collecting money compared to when I cleaned toilets. In addition to tips, I was paid the minimum wage. The benefits consisted of one large free meal per shift.

It seems petty, but fair to describe the clientele as a mangy sort. It would be fair to describe the staff, myself included, that way as well. I fit the stereotype perfectly; from the broken-home of a low-income family, few practical skills, low-income myself, a runaway, my thoughts of the future limited for the most part to a few days from now. I occasionally thought I recognized people from the park on my first night in Ottawa, but it was difficult to be sure. It seemed likely people from the park happened into Groovier's now and then, after all, I am sure a lot of them also fit nicely into the stereotype I described. I recognized this fact, how close I was to the edge of a bare bones existence, as something which I should never let slip my mind.

I am almost positive the skinny, bearded guy with the bulging eyes from the park who thought it was so funny when I replied to him, 'if I could spare anything I wouldn't be here' came into Groovier's one day. In the light of the restaurant he looked far worse than in the gloom of the park. His clothes were dirty and threadbare and when you got close enough to him, he smelled bad. I had the feeling if I knew his age I would be shocked that he was not twenty years older than he was. He wouldn't say anything and he looked quite irritable when anybody tried to speak to him. He dropped a pile of change on the table and motioned for me to take it away and bring him whatever it would buy him. Like a child in a candy store. What can I buy for this? The change pile contained less than two dollars. Mr. Iaello instructed me to take him to a table at the back of the restaurant and give him eggs, bacon, some hashbrowns, coffee with milk and sugar, and a large glass of orange juice. Mr. Iaello seemed to know him.

The bearded fellow ate and drank fairly quickly then just sat there. Mr Iaello went over and said, "So Dave, you don't talk anymore? Is that it?" Dave looked at him and I thought he might say something, but no words would come. His eyes concentrated as his mouth opened and closed slowly with the effort of trying to put something into words, but silence prevailed. Soon after Dave rose, walked out the door, then down the street without looking back. I learned later that he used to be a regular customer with a flat nearby. Mr. Iaello had been expecting his sudden disappearance for years, but every once in a while, maybe two or three times a year, Dave would appear, closer to death and less like a person, but still alive and human. Mr. Iaello told he had been a flamboyant, promising artist with a kind, helpful personality until drugs gradually pinned him to the ground.

I believe Dave was tolerated at Groovier's out of compassion for a fallen man. Also, like the name of the place itself, Dave was a reminder how everyone makes mistakes, how easy it is to lose it all, how the drop is not as far down as we would like to believe.

Part 3

Friend?

19

Todd

I cannot be absolutely positive Dave was the guy I met in the park my first night in Ottawa, but I am sure I bumped into another park guy at Groovier's. It was winter in Ottawa. One Saturday morning it was my turn to tidy up the smoking area out back of the restaurant.

Smokers do not like to think about it, but they are messy people. It is unpleasant for them to recognize their saliva-smeared, fibrous butt with a burnt, ashy, stinking end as garbage so they simply do not think of it that way. After all, what self-respecting Earthling would frequently toss and grind garbage into the ground without as much as a second thought? So they do not give it a second thought. For them it is part of a habitual, inevitable chain of events like breathing or the heart pumping blood throughout the body, an unconscious necessity of life.

I was digging out these discarded remnants from their self-melted burrows in the snow's crust and collecting them in a can for future disposal. Afterward I would kick the spot to scatter the snow to disperse the grubby gray and black-flecked burn mark. I was alone tidying the outdoor patio area when I heard someone open the back door from the inside.

I thought I recognized Todd immediately as he came outside. He had the same innocent, friendly, easy-going, slightly vacant looking face. His hair was straight, medium brown, a bit messy, and parted in the middle so it only hung over the corners of his eyes. He was quite thin, a little taller than me, and likely a little older as well.

He did not bother to sit down at the few tables and chairs I had cleared of snow. He preferred to stand and lean against a corner of the backend of the restaurant. He did not speak to me or even do more than glance briefly at my hunched form digging butts from the snow. He concentrated on getting his cigarette arranged in his mouth and lit. I felt a strong urge to speak with him to see if he really was who I thought. My first night in the park was so strange and isolated from the rest of my life in Ottawa it sometimes felt as if I only dreamed or imagined it. This fellow could be concrete proof it happened.

The more I stole glances at him as I worked, the more I became sure it was the guy I gave my jeans to in the park. I must have been in the right mood at the right time because I just went for it. I am not normally good with names, but his name popped right into my head as I spoke.

"Hey, aren't you Todd?"

He did a little jump, startled, and then squinted at me.

"Yeah, man, how'd you know? Do I know you?"

"Not really, but sort of. I'm Molloy. We met in the park a couple of months ago. Remember? I had a big duffle bag. I gave you some jeans at the end of the night for helping me out."

He looked around thoughtfully over a couple of long slow drags on his cigarette. Then he looked at me and started to nod, once again in a slow and thoughtful manner.

"Yeah, now I remember...kind of...it's still a bit hazy though. I might have been pretty blazed that night. Who knows?"

He laughed at himself.

"You seemed pretty normal to me."

"Yeah? Like I said, who knows?"

Suddenly a quick spark of memory flashed in his eyes.

"Hey, now I remember you. For sure. Yeah, I still got those jeans. I wear 'em all the time."

"Good. Jeans should last a long time if you treat them okay."

Todd laughed again.

"Yeah."

He looked at me, smoking a little faster and more intensely now, still looking thoughtful.

"So, you work here?'

"Yep."

"And you just came to Ottawa, right?"

"Yeah, that night I met you was my first night here."

"How'd you scam this job so quick?'

I shrugged.

"I was desperate. I just applied. I begged. Lucky, I guess."

"No shit. Sweet deal. I guess you the man, bro."

Todd seemed laid back, friendly, and engaging, but he also appeared somewhat robotic at times, as if his responses had been programmed into him and triggered by what I said. His last short burst of gibberish is a good example, but I got the feeling if I did not make some sort of a response the conversation would be over. He might even forget I was there.

So I said, "Thanks."

He looked at me and nodded. Then he looked down near his feet at the general area of the snow upon which he had created a random pattern of flick ash. He continued to smoke with a very thoughtful air. Eventually, he snapped his gaze back toward me.

"Listen, man, sorry, I can't remember your name."

"Molloy."

"Yeah, right, Molloy. Sorry, I'm shit with names."

"No worries. I'm usually pretty shit with them too."

"Cool. Anyway, if you want to hang or something I can drop by sometime. You working here again tomorrow?"

"Yep. Same time."

"When you off?"

"Four."

"Want me to come by around then and we can do something?"

I was a little surprised by the quick, painless offer of potential friendship, but gladdened as well even if I could not imagine what we might have in common.

"Sure, drop by."

"Okay, great. If I'm not here right at four don't bother waiting around for me. I can be a bit of a dumbass with remembering appointments and shit like that so don't waste time waiting around for me if I don't show."

Better useless and honest than clever and manipulating, I supposed. I still liked the idea of someone wanting to hang with me after such a short meeting, like I had charisma or something.

"Alright. Thanks for the warning. Maybe I'll see you tomorrow then."

Todd snorted a short laugh.

"I should be able to get my shit together by four in the afternoon. If not, I'm a bigger loser than I thought."

Then Todd nodded at me a final time and left.

"Keep it real," he said before the door closed.

20

More Todd

Todd continued to drop by Groovier's occasionally, somewhat randomly, and if he managed to stop by at quitting time we usually hung out together for a while. The meetings were much like the previous one I described, Todd was not particularly inspiring company. We generally walked and talked; sometimes sitting over a snack somewhere inside if the weather was very poor. I estimate we hung out around once every two weeks and the visits lasted thirty minutes to an hour.

Whenever we walked through the park Todd would mention his night visits there or someplace similar. The exact location did not seem to alter the stories significantly. At first I was content to listen to the repetitive stories hoping they might shed some light on my mysterious initiation to Ottawa, but that never happened. Apparently the whole story is simply that the park is where an assembly of small groups and individuals congregate to hang out and take drugs or try to bum some drugs from each other and interact a little. If Todd's style of communication is representative of the whole group the conversation likely did not amount to much.

Todd only got a little animated when he talked about the park. He only got excited when he knew he was actually going to have some money to take with him to the park. This only happened once while I had known him.

I asked him, "If the real fun is when you actually have money to buy drugs, why bother going all the time when you don't have any to spend? Isn't it frustrating and waste of time?"

Todd shook his head.

"I don't expect you to get it. I do have mates to hang with there you know. I do sometimes get lucky and score a little even when I don't have cash. I do get info there."

"I wasn't trying to offend you. I'm just trying to figure it out. I don't get it, like you said. What sort of info do you mean?"

"You hear what's going down for one thing. Where the action might be, parties after, who scored big, you know?"

"Oh, that kind of info."

"And other stuff. What buddies been up to and that kind of shit...I don't know. What do you care anyway? Sometimes I might get word about a job. That sound better to ya?"

Todd sounded pissed off. Maybe he had a right to be. Our friendship felt kind of stagnant and I was not feeling too impressed with him. It probably came through in my tone.

"If I sound stupid with my questions and comments about the park it's probably because I am stupid about the park. Even the night I was there I didn't have a clue what was going on."

Todd liked that way of putting things a lot better. He even laughed and patted me on the back.

"You're definitely not stupid. You're smarter than me in most ways. Let's just not worry about it and hang out."

So we hung out. This consisted of strolling around together and speaking now and then. We were unable to stop moving outdoors due to Todd's poor winter gear. He liked to remind me his nuts and hands were about to freeze and fall off.

Eventually, I could not stand the sight of Todd's light-jacketed body, bare hands, and shivering jawbone any longer. The view of his running shoes slipping and skidding across the ice wore thin as well. I took him to a Salvation Army store and bought him a decent set of second hand mitts, boots, and a better coat for about fifteen dollars. I imagine the gear cost a lot less than a good night in the park cost Todd.

I admit I probably should have asked Todd to visit the warmth and comfort of my apartment sooner than I did, but I did not really trust him at this point. There was the drug thing, but just as important was the fact I was unable to connect with him or find much common ground.

To be fair I saw no clear motive for Todd to seek me out as an occasional walking partner after my work shifts. He did not seem particularly interested in getting to know me, but he also never seemed overly interested in gaining anything material from me. I initiated the gift of winter clothes after winter was mostly over and Todd only reluctantly accepted. I occasionally bought him a snack or a coffee, but Todd never initiated the purchase.

I tried several times to inject a little variety and fun into our time together. If I could call anyone in Ottawa my friend it was Todd. If we could only start actually doing something we might have fun.

"We should go skating on the Rideau Canal before winter's over. I've never done that before."

Todd did not reply. I knew Todd probably did not have skates, but neither did I. I heard you could rent them at the canal. I made up something so my offer would not sound like charity.

"I hear they're having an end of season sale. Pay for one rental set and you get a second one free. I'm planning on going anyway. Why don't you come and keep me company?"

Todd did not seem to even consider the idea.

"Nah, it's not my kind of thing."

Another time I suggested, "We should do something other than just walk around and repeat the same words to each other. What should we do? Road hockey? A movie? What do you think?"

Todd sighed in an exasperated way.

"I'm not really into those things."

His voice sounded bored at my childish suggestions. It pissed me off.

"What things are you into then? Anything other than the park, other than drugs? If so, please tell me because I haven't been able to notice anything else."

Todd looked at me as if I had slapped him in the face or spit on him. He was speechless for a few seconds that felt like a full minute. I felt like a shit even before he shouted back at me in a hurt, offended voice.

"You're right. I'm a loser who has nothing to offer you or anyone else. I never pretended to be anything else. Sorry to waste your fucking time."

It was my turn to be speechless for a few seconds and when those seconds were up, Todd was already gone.

21

Favour

Todd stopped dropping by Groovier's after our little spat. I thought he was being a bit of a suck, but it nagged at my conscience that I had hurt his feelings for no good reason. He had never asked me for anything but occasional company and it could be argued that I called him a loser. For days after our disagreement I wondered how I could help him without being condescending or insulting and making the situation worse.

He needed money, but even more it seemed he needed some direction in his life, something to shift his focus rather than just killing time until the park opened at night. My idea came to me in complete form as soon as I remembered Todd asking how I had managed to get such a sweet job so quickly after arriving in Ottawa. Could a job help give some balance to Todd's days and set him on a more constructive path? Could Groovier's work for Todd the same way it worked for me? I was aware of the risks involved, but it was the only plan I could come up with that might offer lasting benefit.

I went into work early one day and asked Mr. Iaello if I could talk with him alone. Todd had stopped by Groovier's enough that Mr. Iaello was somewhat familiar with him as an acquaintance of mine.

"Do you think it might be possible for Todd to get a part time job here? Minimal hours to start, of course, to make sure he's capable and everything."

The boss looked sceptical and I did not blame him. I was taking a risk and I was not at all sure of the outcome. If we got lucky I planned to apply myself even more at Groovier's and personally help Todd to adjust and perform well.

Mr. Iaello did not answer right away, only questioned.

"Todd? Your friend who comes here?"

It was the first time I had seen him a little uncomfortable. I hoped this might happen and I felt slightly guilty using Mr. Iaello's own words against him.

"I am hoping a job will bring him back to Earth; give him an anchor, something to focus on...anything."

Mr. Iaello nodded his head slowly, watching me. I felt as if his eyes penetrated to peer within me. My tattoo tingled on my back for some reason.

"Molloy, let me take a look at the schedule for the next couple of weeks and think about it. I will let you know."

"Thank you, sir. That's all I can ask."

I could hardly believe this ordeal I had agonized over and over again in my mind for days was over in just a few minutes. It was out of my hands at least. I had done my best for Todd even though I was not sure it was in everyone's best interest. I would happily accept whatever the boss decided. It was his business and his call. I put the issue out of my mind and got busy with starting my shift.

With the weight of my duty lifted and the sense I may have done a good deed I felt less fatigued and friendlier than usual during my shift. I made brief chitchat with some of the regulars and gave everyone my best Groovier's service. The night whipped past.

By the end of my shift I had heard nothing from Mr. Iaello regarding Todd yet, but I was not particularly concerned. I had done what I could do. I was tired, but in a decent mood as I packed up to go home when Mr. Iaello called to me from the short hallway that led to his office.

"May I talk to you for a minute quickly before you go, Molloy?"

I figured he might have come to a decision regarding Todd. Everything was happening faster than I imagined it.

"Sure."

I followed him into his office.

Mr. Iaello's office was cramped and the few items in it were small. There was a small desk, a miniature bookshelf, a one cubic foot filing cabinet, and two plain wooden chairs facing his desk. Even the ceiling looked somehow lower than the rest of the restaurant. After I sat down we faced one another. The boss wasted no time getting to the point.

"I am going to give Todd a chance. He will start with a small number of the worst shifts like everyone else and we will see how it goes. I expect he will need support. May I put you on the same shifts as Todd so you can watch over him and mentor him at first?"

"Of course, Mr. Iaello. I'll take responsibility for him. I'll try to help keep him from going under. Thank you."

The boss shrugged and smiled warily.

"I hope we can do more than that for him, but that will be a good start."

I reached out and shook Mr. Iaello's hand.

"I really appreciate it, sir. At least we're giving him a chance at turning things around."

"Have him come and see me sometime in the next day or two so I can talk to him and give him his first schedule."

"Will do, boss. See you tomorrow."

I was in a buoyant, fantastic mood walking home... until I hit the park. The park made me think of Todd. I wondered if he would be coming to the park tonight. I wanted to tell him the good news. I stopped dead in my tracks. I was such an asshole. I had conceived and set in motion the whole plan without even speaking with the main actor in my plan. Todd did not know a thing about my whole scheme even though he was supposed to start his new job in a few days.

I felt like punching myself in the stomach, but I did not have time to mess around with nonsense like that. I had to find Todd and let him in on the news. I did not even know where he lived.

How could I be so stupid?

I continued home to think and plan my next move.

22

Find Todd

It turned out there was not much to think about. I knew of only one place other than Groovier's at quitting time where I might run into Todd and possibly salvage my plan; the park. Hoping to bump into him before he got distracted, I arrived at the park just as dusk began to settle. If there was going to be a gathering at the park this night I was the first arrival. Instinctively, I went for the bench where I spent a good part of my first night in Ottawa. I had a surreal attachment to it and usually noticed it going to and from work each day. It occurred to me to describe it as a personal sacred spot, but can a person who has inscribed a curse against God into his skin claim anything as sacred?

I withdrew from my meandering, philosophical funk and concentrated on the task at hand. If it got much darker it would be difficult to pick Todd out from a distance. I would have to make the rounds to the little spread out groups on foot looking for him. I preferred to avoid that discomfort. I did not trust in my ability to communicate well with the druggies in the park at night.

Suddenly, there he was...the distance and fading light allowed me to see only his silhouette, but I recognized him instantly. Seeing him during all those walks after work must have imprinted his posture in my mind. He was alone as he crossed the street toward the park a block and a half away. I moved to intercept him before he got caught up in anything. I called out long before I got close to him.

"Todd!"

He stopped on the sidewalk across the street from the park and looked at me. His body language sulking, he looked away; but he stayed where he was and allowed me to catch up to him. I found his reaction childish and annoying, but I had to suck it up and try to smooth things out with him. I had foolishly risked both our reputations by involving him in something without consulting him. That was my fault only. I could only hope Todd thought it was as good an idea as I did.

I jogged up close to him, but Todd still did not look at me. I did not have a lot of time to piss around. I dropped the situation into his lap so he could look at it and decide for himself what to do. What I should have done in the first place.

"Hey, Todd. Sorry I was rude the last time we were together. I was feeling frustrated and took it out on you, I guess. Sorry."

Todd still did not look at me, but his posture softened slightly. He shrugged.

"Whatever," he said.

"Anyway, I thought of something to try and make things better and make it up to you. Can I run the idea by you?"

He shrugged again, but this time he looked over at me.

"If you gotta' tell me, tell me."

"Okay. Just say yes or no. How would you feel if you got lucky like me and found a decent job for some spending money?"

"Yeah, so?"

"I asked Mr. Iaello if you could start part time at Groovier's. Just small hours to start, but if you do well you could probably end up with a lot more hours if you want. That's how it started for me and it worked out. I talked to the boss and he says he'll give you a shot. All you have to do is tell me whether you want it, or whether you want me to tell him no."

Todd looked stunned. Not pleased or displeased, just stunned. He did not say anything.

I said, "So what do you think? I probably should have talked to you about it before I talked to Mr. Iaello, but the idea just sort of came to me and I got excited and ran with it. Everything's totally up to you, of course."

The stunned look on Todd's face stayed there, but eventually he said something.

"I don't know what to say...it's out of nowhere...big news for the second time today. Big day all around."

"Big day? Did something else happen today?"

"A couple of things actually. It's kind of freaky really. My Mom got a part time job as a waitress last night and last night was her first night. I didn't find out until this morning when she told me. She got decent tips and she gave me eight bucks of it."

He put his hands in his pockets and withdrew four toonies that he held in his open palm to show me.

"That is good news. And a little freaky like you said. Basically the same type of job at the same time for both of you."

Todd nodded. He was looking less bewildered and perhaps even a little pleased at the turn of events.

"Working with you at Groovier's, eh?"

"Yeah, the idea just came to me and it seemed like a good one so I started working on it right away. I did what I could. The rest is up to you."

Todd definitely looked pleased now. He whistled and rolled his eyes as if the fate of the world rested upon his decision. He punched me softly in the chest, as a friendly gesture, before he spoke.

"I think I'm going to give it a go, but do you mind if I walk around the block by myself to think about it and let it sink in? I'm kind of shocked at the news. In a good way, but still shocked."

"Sure, go ahead. I'll just go back to my bench and wait for you."

I pointed over at my sacred bench.

"Come over and see me when you decide what you want to do."

"Way over there? Why? After I go around the block I'll be right here. Why don't you sit on this bench right here?"

Todd had a good point. I was acting superstitious or something...my bench.

I laughed.

"Good idea. I don't know why I said that bench. I guess that's the one I'm used to. I'll be here."

"I won't be long," he said.

I sat down on the nearest bench and watched Todd's back recede down the sidewalk. I was a little nervous. Part of me wanted Todd to give the job a shot since I had already put the plan in motion, but even though it sounded likely he was going to give it a go at Groovier's I was still unsure how well it would turn out. I could feel the doubt in Mr. Iaello when we spoke about it. I had the same doubts.

I reminded myself it was out of my hands now except for giving Todd a hand to learn the ropes. I made myself relax and notice the weather. It was the warmest evening in quite some time. The first tease of spring was definitely in the air. It made me think of leaf buds and melting snowbanks.

When Todd reappeared he looked happier than I had ever seen him.

"I'm going to go for it," he said. "Thanks for arranging it for me, brother. I owe you. I'm really fuckin' nervous about it already...happy, but nervous. Is it hard working there?"

"It takes a bit of practice to get into a comfortable routine, but I'm sure you can do it if you put your mind to it, and don't let yourself get easily discouraged. I'll help you."

Todd held his clenched fist out for me to bump with mine.

"Right on, man. Thanks. You feel like having a little party to celebrate? Nothing major, but we deserve something."

I was not sure it was a bright idea, but considering we had just patched things up I thought it might be a bad move to reject the idea outright.

"I guess a little celebration is in order. Not too late though. I have to work tomorrow. What do you have in mind?"

"Well, I got eight bucks. If you throw in the same we could split a six-pack and a couple of joints. Just relax and shoot the shit for a couple of hours...maybe listen to some tunes. If we start now we could have a pretty early night."

I only hesitated for a few moments. It seemed like something that could be kept under reasonable control with a bit of foresight. My mind worked quickly.

"I think I could handle that," I said. "I've only had a couple puffs of dope before so I'm not going to do much. I'm not sure how I'm going to react so I'd rather it was just you and me at my place. We have to keep the noise down. There's other people in the house. Only thing is I don't have anything for tunes at my place; not even a radio."

Todd did not seem to care.

"I'm cool with that," he said.

"Okay. Don't forget I have to work tomorrow so I can't be up too late. I know I already said that, but I just want to be clear. If I'm in bed by ten we still have about three hours. That work for you? You shouldn't be up too late either since you have to go in to talk to your new boss tomorrow or the next day at the latest. That's when you can arrange your first schedule."

"Sure, we'll get started right away then we'll have plenty of time for a nice chill session together."

"Okay, let's do it. Last thing I want to repeat is that you have to go into Groovier's today or tomorrow during the day to set everything up with Mr. Iaello, okay? He asked me to tell you and I told him you would be there if you want the job. It will get everything off to a good start if you show up as planned."

"Don't worry. I'll go tomorrow first thing after I get up and get my shit together. It will make my Mom happy too."

I threw up my hands and smiled.

"I guess it's settled then. Now how do we go about collecting our party goods?"

"Leave it to me. Give me your eight bucks and just wait for me on the bench. It will be fastest that way."

I was relieved, wanting to be as little involved as possible in retrieving the booze and drugs. I gave him a ten-dollar bill and sat down. I watched Todd disappear into the gloom of the park's center. I got tingles of déja vu sitting on a bench trying to peer into the dimness and shadows of the park.

I was not sure about this little party I had agreed to with Todd. It was an inappropriate way to celebrate Todd getting a job and hopefully becoming more responsible. I also was not sure about trying to party in my apartment with a shared bathroom. Hopefully things would not get too out of hand with a six-pack and a couple of joints. I did not plan on letting myself get too disoriented. I was more worried about what Todd might do even though it was me who would be more out of his element.

I tried to relax and take deep breaths of the spring-tinged, winter air. My new life started in this park. Maybe Todd could also find a new beginning here.

Far quicker than I expected Todd appeared with six Corona hanging from his right hand. I never even saw him cross the street from the park to the Beer Store. He patted his coat pocket with the other hand.

"We're all set," he said.

"That was fast."

Todd laughed.

"I guess everyone has their special talents."

I laughed too, then stood up and led him to my place.

23

Todd's New Career

The job-celebration party was harmless enough. I felt pretty spaced out even though I did a good job of pacing myself and allowing Todd to partake in the majority of the inebriants. Even high we had a difficult time keeping up a lively conversation, but occasional fits of giggling and illusionary moments of profundity kept us entertained until my self-imposed ten o'clock bedtime.

Todd was true to his word. He did not put up a fuss about stopping the party. I cannot be certain what he did after he left my place, but he did go in to see Mr. Iaello the next day. The interview must have gone well enough. He was put on the schedule for a few shifts to try things out.

For his first shift Mr. Iaello put Todd and I together on a graveyard shift from ten at night on Tuesday until six in the morning on Wednesday, about as quiet as it ever gets at Groovier's. Even then it is far from a graveyard.

Todd's first day at work was about what I imagined in my best-case scenario. I tried to keep a balance between giving him pointers when it looked like he was getting flustered and letting him learn from his own mistakes. I made sure I was never too busy to answer questions.

From the very start of his shift Todd was essentially a new man. He came to work noticeably tidier than usual. He listened to instructions. He asked reasonable questions when he was not sure what to do. He usually did not repeat his mistake if we explained why a different method of doing things was preferred. He wanted to do a good job and he cared if he did a good job. I think that is what it boiled down to on that first midnight shift. I thought I even detected an undercurrent of pride within him as the night wore on and he kept at it, learning what to do and getting through the shift without any major problems. Todd's hands actually trembled when, near dawn, he held them out to receive his share of the tips after our shift was finished.

I said, "This is always the best part of the shift."

Todd started at the money in his hand.

"A decent amount too. Bonus."

Todd looked a full inch taller. Mr. Iaello came by and slapped him gently on the back. He tried to give Todd a little confidence boost and added a little plug for me. Things like that were what made him a great boss.

"Good first day, Todd. Molloy was right about you. Keep it up and you'll be a pro in no time."

Todd and I talked for a little while out in front of Groovier's before we headed home. A sprinkle of fresh snow had fallen during our shift.

I told him, "You did well. How do you feel?"

"Tired, but good. I don't stand up that long during a whole week sometimes."

I laughed, remembering the stiffness I felt during my first days on the job.

"It's even worse during the busier shifts because your walking, hurrying, and carrying more stuff, but you'd be surprised how fast your body gets used to it and in shape for the work."

Todd pulled a wad of bills and change out of his pocket and looked at it.

"Fuck, man, my first real job with real pay."

I held my fist up for him to bump with his like he did sometimes with me.

"Feels good doesn't it. You did great."

"Thanks, bro."

I wanted to give Todd some advice, but I wanted to make sure it did not initiate any potential confrontation and spoil the good cheer.

"Now that you're a working man can I tell you something that I do that gives me some confidence?"

"Sure."

"You should reward yourself for good work, but also put an amount of each day's pay into the bank. It adds up quick and it feels great having some savings behind you in case you ever need it. It's like having a back up plan and it makes you feel more in control of your life."

It looked as if Todd liked the sound of that concept.

"Sounds solid. Think you could help me set up a bank account?"

He did not need my help. If he took some money into a bank they would be glad to set him up. However, since my plan was to help him get some traction in his life I figured it would be best to stick close by him at least until he got some momentum.

"Sure, I'll go with you whenever you want. You'll be amazed how easy it is. Just let me know when and we'll do it."

Todd gave me a hint he saw where I was going with all these plans.

He said, "If this is what work is like it should help me keep control of myself. I'm too tired to even want to go to the park."

"Glad to hear it. That will make it even easier to save up some cash. Wouldn't it be nice to have the problem of trying to decide what's the best thing to do with the money you have building up?"

"Hard to imagine. Does sound sweet though."

"Okay, I guess it's bedtime. Good work."

"Take it easy."

24

Todd's Retirement

Todd had his second shift at Groovier's four days after his first shift. He had not dropped by since then and I was looking forward to seeing him again. As before, I was scheduled with him on the graveyard shift to help him out if help was needed. If Todd had seemed like a new man during that first shift he seemed like an altogether differ-

ent new man during his second shift. He was easily flustered by any little mistake he made and was much less
eager to listen when the correct method was explained.
He took several smoke breaks whereas during his first
shift he took only one. He did his job, did what was asked, but in a joyless, begrudging manner.

His demeanor made everyone want to stay away from
him, including me, but a couple of times I did my duty
and forced my way through his attitude barrier to try to
connect with him.

"What's up, buddy? You seem pretty upset compared
to last time you were here."

He used the sullen tactic of not even looking at me
when he replied.

"Not now, please. Just let me get through my shift in
peace."

In the end I gave up and did as he asked. Then
abruptly, a little past halfway through the shift, Todd's
behaviour improved. He was still quiet and kept to
himself, but he was a much more sympathetic character.
He was no longer short and snappy with customers and
staff. He spoke more politely and was more approachable
regarding being trained for the job. To say he had softer
edges sums up his change best.

I had a hard time keeping my eyes off Todd. His errat-
ic behaviour was disturbing, but fascinating as well.

At the end of the shift Todd went up to Mr. Iaello
immediately afterward and apologized for his behaviour. I
was close enough to hear.

"Sorry for how I was acting tonight. I've got some stuff
going on that's kind of wearing me down. I'll be better
next time and from now on. You don't have to pay me for
this shift if you want."

Before I got a chance to talk to him, before Mr. Iaello
even had a chance to respond to his apology, before even
glancing at his coworkers who were in the process of
divvying up the tips, Todd walked quickly to the change
room, exchanged his work gear for his home gear, and left
through the back door.

We set Todd's share of the tips aside for him, but as it turned out we need not have bothered. To the best of my knowledge, none of us ever heard a peep from Todd or about Todd again.

25

After Todd

Todd's disappearance affected me in a strange, calm way where I was not sure I was feeling anything. I wrote a lot in my diary for a while. In the end, most of that writing went in the garbage instead of the diary. It was mostly shit, but I guess it helped calm my nerves. When Todd vanished I did not have enough information to make a hypothesis about what had happened to him let alone a conclusion. I could only make semi-educated speculations, very similar to wild speculations. Only the least rational of those fantasies had happy endings for Todd. My outward routine stayed essentially the same, minus Todd. Mr. Iaello and I talked about it a bit, but with so few facts there was not a lot to say.

I focused my energy on things I could know and do something about. I applied myself to an even greater degree in my work at Groovier's and believe I may well have become the most valuable worker there aside from the boss. I could handle pretty much any position and I was usually willing to work an extra shift on short notice if anything came up. I saved a respectable sum of money due to my extra work and budgeting. I put away at least seventy-five dollars a week, often considerably more.

I took up running and soon began to enjoy it and miss it if I skipped too many days. I even bought proper gear and ran outside through the winter. Since this activity is the most significant difference in my life after Todd disappeared, perhaps I replaced him with running. My fitness and energy have significantly improved.

Lastly, I read and wrote a lot. As mentioned, the latter produced more quantity than quality.

I do not have a lot to show for it, but I think I spent the end of the winter, the spring, and the start of the summer quietly reflecting upon what had happened and what I was doing here. I did not think intensely or for long periods so it took a while, long enough that I wormed a path back and forth along the shallow groove of my life until it became shallow, smooth, and comfortable. The small number of things I concentrated upon went well with the possible exception of the diary. This small number of paragraphs does not seem particularly worthy of more than a season's work, but it is all that remains.

Eventually, the groove I wore my life into got too comfortable, became a rut, and I started to look for ways to build up enough momentum to break free from it. I started to go for longer walks and jogs to explore parts of the city I had not seen. Having seen very little of Ottawa I had lots of space to roam. I used my runs to explore areas that deserved to be explored more patiently later on with a long walk.

Things happened on these excursions, as they will even when one does not seek them, but in retrospect, I wonder if some of the odd encounters I was involved in were, in fact, merely coincidence. I believe it is possible that a few of these walks resulted in my first contact with *The People for a Better World.*

Part 4

The People

26

Chance Encounters

Coffee Shop

My first such encounter was at a coffee shop, a Second Cup, on Bank Street.

I was alone reading a newspaper at a small table overlooking the ebb and flow of the street. A man I estimate to be between fifty and sixty years old approached and spoke to me. He was well groomed, dressed in a light gray suit, and his brown and silver speckled hair and beard were trimmed in such a manner that his receding hairline suited him.

"Pardon me," he said, "you have the best table in the house for a beautiful day like today. Do you mind if I sit down at your table?"

"Sure, go ahead," I replied.

Although I found it more relaxing to read the paper by myself I was not about to refuse him without good reason. For about ten minutes he seemed content to quietly look out the window and sip his coffee as if I was not there. I pretty much forgot about him.

He spoke to me when I took a break from my reading and glanced around, catching his eye.

"Nice to get away from your life on a gorgeous day like today isn't it?"

He indicated my newspaper with a flick of his gaze down toward it, then continued.

"However, I don't find reading the paper too relaxing these days. For some reason they concentrate their attention on the bad news, the sensational news, don't you find?"

My guest smiled broadly at me as he spoke as if trying to assure me he was not trying to be confrontational.

"You have a point there," I agreed. "You want me to give you a section anyway? I'm almost done with it."

"Sure. Do you have a movie and book review section there? That can't be too depressing."

I passed him the entertainment section and we basically kept to ourselves until I left the coffee shop about ten minutes later. This inconspicuous interaction is only interesting because I had another chance encounter with the very same man about a month after our first meeting.

Arboretum

The arboretum is a large, wonderfully landscaped oasis at the Northwest end of the Rideau Canal. The trees there often have small metal tags identifying their species name. Once you get to know your way around you can walk for an hour without seeing much evidence that you are close to the city's core. There are creeks, bridges, locks, forested areas, and even small wildlife. I like to sit up on the top of the highest hill to enjoy the view. People often bring their dogs, allowing them to spend their energy as if they were out in the countryside. They sprint, chase, and mock battle one another with profound zest and joy the moment their leashes are unhooked. I wonder then if the dogs feel an ancient tingle of some subconscious, genetic memory reminding them of a time when their kind was a different sort of animal, undomesticated and free.

It was at the top of this hill where I bumped into the fellow from the coffee shop a second time. He was alone and appeared to be out for a stroll heading toward me. I recognized him immediately because although neither time we met normally called for such formal attire, he was again in a light gray suit similar to the one he wore at the Second Cup. He recognized me quickly as well.

"The lad from the coffee shop a while ago...what a pleasant surprise. How do you do, sir?"

"Not bad," I said, "how are you?"

He laughed.

"Hard to be bad on a day like today now isn't it? It was also lovely weather the other time we bumped into each other if I remember correctly. A pretty good sign wouldn't you say?"

As he spoke he walked toward me and looked into my eyes. There was nothing threatening, ill natured, or uneasy upon his face. If anything, the opposite were true, his presence seemed to exude peace and contentedness. For some reason, he still sort of put me off, probably because he came a bit too close to me before he stopped. He apparently noticed my discomfort and backed off a little to a more appropriate speaking distance. His calm, slightly mirthful demeanour did not change.

"I see we are headed in opposite directions so I will not delay you long, however, I will say one final thing that may sound strange. If you ever chance upon a red tiger, consider it carefully before walking away. I myself stopped to check it out and I have never regretted it."

He held my gaze for a moment longer, nodded, and passed by. For the rest of my walk I found it difficult to stop thinking about the odd encounter, trying to make sense of it. I also tried to remember our interaction at the coffee shop to try and identify some connection between our two unlikely meetings, but I could not see any. Red tiger? Maybe he was simply old and had a harmless touch of dementia.

In retrospect, I cannot help but wonder perhaps if this man may have been an agent for *The People for a Better World*; however, it is only fair to state for the record that despite many future dealings with the group I do not recall ever seeing this gentleman again.

More Coffee

This coffee encounter was at a Starbucks rather than a Second Cup.

Generally, I slightly prefer the coffee and atmosphere of Second Cup, but where I go mainly boils down to convenience. Atmosphere-wise, Second Cup is often less crowded, therefore more relaxing.

Starbucks got the contract to open coffee shops inside all of the giant Chapters bookstores where I like to poke around. I visit Starbucks if I am in Chapters to enjoy my two addictions at the same time: books and caffeine. I usually borrow books from the library, but I will buy a book if it is one I want for my collection. More often than not if I buy a book it is one I have already read.

I was in the Chapter's Starbucks across from the Rideau Center when I bumped into a woman who also mentioned something about a red tiger. She approached me at the milk and sugar stand. She was kind of sexy in a hectic, frazzled way. She was slim with shoulder length reddish-brown hair and green-brown eyes. Her dress was also a greenish-brown but different than her eyes.

She was about thirty I would guess, and undecided whether she wanted to be preppy or artsy.

I was taking longer than usual to get my coffee ready. I usually took my coffee black, but I was considering whether to add something to it for a change.

The woman came up and said, "What's the hold up, buddy? Do you need a hand?"

She did a good job conveying she was only pretending to be obnoxious. I played along.

"Just hold on. This is a big decision."

I moved over to make room for her, snapping a lid onto my coffee without bothering to add anything. She squeezed in and added skim milk and artificial sweetener to her brew.

Holding up the Splenda packet she said, "A lady's got to start watching her calories when she starts getting older."

She was not old, of course, but I figured I was supposed to say it anyway.

"You're not old," I said.

She smiled conspiratorially at me and winked.

"You're right, but I'm at least getting to the age where I have to keep an eye on what calories I'm stuffing into my body. Every little bit adds up."

"True," I said, "we all have to be careful."

I was not even twenty and I did try to keep some control over my empty calories so I could relate to what she was saying.

I wandered over to the magazine racks to browse while my black coffee cooled down. I only have the few interests

I have already mentioned, but the huge sections of big, shiny magazines available on pretty much any subject amazed me. Investing. Video games. Hockey. Body Piercing. Needlepoint. Fashion. Cage Fighting. Tattoos. Guitar Playing. Writing. Real Estate.

One might think I would have been interested in the writing and tattoo categories, but I was not. I was nearly afraid to read about the proper process of writing, afraid to find out that I was not doing it properly, that the process I had created for myself was a sham. The long, tangled path of my diary was wound so deeply into my secret inner life I feared what would happen to me if I lost hope in my story.

As for my tattoo, I needed to have it done, but it almost feels as if I am finished with it now. It rarely itches anymore and it often gives me a gentle start when I notice it upon my back in the mirror or suddenly remember I have it. The tattoo is a part of me, but it seems getting the tattoo was the difficult, important part; wearing the tattoo is just a record of the act.

Video game magazines on the other hand have a certain mysterious pull on me. I had played very little myself, but even looking at the colourful screenshots of the monsters and powerful weapons gave me a buzz. I remember watching lots of kids in the schoolyard mesmerized by their handheld systems as they mashed the little buttons and stared at the screen, hooked in as if the world around them did not even exist. It looked exciting. Now that I have money saved up I have been tempted to try it out, but so far I have resisted. The video game culture had been fairly strong at school. I had been left out of it then and I had the sense it was now too late to join the party.

On this particular afternoon I did not even get to the magazine racks before the lady from the milk and sugar counter tapped me on the shoulder from behind.

"I know you black coffee drinkers are often the quiet, loner types, but would you like to sit and chat with me for a few minutes? I prefer chatting than sitting alone."

"Sure," I said, "I was just going to look around while my coffee cooled."

"Okay, there's a little free table off to the side. Let's grab it quick before it's taken."

I got there quickly and sat down while my new acquaintance caught up then sat across from me. She held out her hand.

"My name's Sharon."

We shook.

"Molloy."

From this point on she did most of the talking. I am generally shy around girls, but I initially enjoyed sitting with and having the attention of an attractive older woman. She mainly talked about her troubles, past and present, and her philosophy in dealing with the ups and downs life offered. After a while I began to find the way she monopolized the conversation and talked about her issues a little tiresome and I do not remember many details. She was more than happy to carry on the conversation without me for the most part. I tried to at least make occasional eye contact with her when my attention began to waver.

Finally she said, "You're awfully quiet. Are you shy, the strong silent type, or just a good listener?"

"A little of both," I said, although there had been three options.

She smiled and laughed softly.

"Interesting combination," she said.

I could not think of anything else to say. There was a bit of an awkward lull in the conversation before she reached into her purse and pulled forth a rectangle of cardboard.

"Anyway," she said, "I should get going, but who knows, maybe we will meet each other again someday. I like you. You're sweet."

She handed the cardboard rectangle over to me.

"If you ever feel at your wit's end or just feel like you need someone to talk to, you can visit the address on the card. The people I met at a similar place were able to help me when I needed it...and they are still helping me. Who knows? We might even bump into each other there."

The card had a silhouette of a red tiger with three stylized black stripes and an address at the bottom. For some reason, perhaps intrigued by this coincidental second reference to the red tiger to me by strangers, I held onto the card. It was loose in my wallet among my paper money, but I noticed it occasionally and wondered if I should throw it out. I did not toss it away and eventually I made my way to the address on the card, but I do not recall ever seeing Sharon again.

Less Well Remembered

There were a couple of other unusual encounters like these included in earlier drafts of my diary, however, as I reviewed my thoughts and writing I noticed inconsistencies in the way I remembered these other events. Because of this, in the end, I edited them out altogether. I feel this is a relatively inconsequential matter. I include it only, once again, to highlight the fact that this is an extensively edited diary and to acknowledge and accept any negative connotations this may entail.

I carried the card with the red tiger silhouette with me for several months before visiting the address it advertised. Winter was beginning to end, but there were still plenty of snow heaps around. They were soggy piles of snow, but big enough to remain for weeks since the nights and parts of the day were still below zero. Most afternoons little rivers of melted snowbank trickled into the sewer. It was an afternoon like this when I decided to go for a long walk in the direction of the red tiger address. My idea was to see if I could find the place. The plan did not extend past what I might do if I happened to find it.

I spent the months between my chance encounters and my walk to find the red tiger address much the way I have described after Todd disappeared. I worked at Groovier's, put away some money, wrote and edited my diary, tried to exercise and eat healthy, and generally just lay low.

In retrospect it may have been simple loneliness that directed me to the red tiger address. The encounters that brought this mysterious red cat to my attention were unusual, perhaps even coincidental enough to make them

suspicious, but they were also friendly, interesting interactions with individuals who were not associated with my
employment at Groovier's. I think maybe I needed this
form of human contact more than I realized at the time.

27

Red Tiger Hunt

It was three months or so before I visited the address
on the card that Sharon gave to me. I had considered
tossing out the card on several occasions; however, I
seldom even noticed it and I never did get around to re-
moving it from my wallet. I had the day off from Groovier's
and was making a trip to a bank machine to get some
cash. My empty wallet made the red tiger business card
more noticeable than usual and I wondered if the place
even existed. It was a pleasant late summer day and on a
whim I decided to get a coffee, take a walk, and see if I
could find the address on my card.

In many ways I would have to describe my experience
after I left home as successful. I had become a valuable
employee at Groovier's and able to handle just about any
task required.

Though safety and survival had been my primary
concern when I got off the train in Ottawa I had actually
made and saved good money. Twenty percent of my earn-
ings, including tips, went into my savings account that I
vowed not to touch until I could come up with a practical
long-term use for it. Until then it was an emergency fund
in case of unforeseen difficulty.

It could be argued that I did not have a particularly
eventful life and I would not refute that, but I was not
wanting for anything. The pastimes I had become involved
with, reading, running, writing, and thinking, were not
expensive hobbies, but neither were they very social

activities. My work at Groovier's was the closest thing I had to a social life and that was really a business experience with remnants of friendship dangling off here and there.

In retrospect, I was somewhat lonely and I think that may have been a deciding factor in my eventual stroll to see if I could find the red tiger address.

28

Red Tiger House

The address was ninety-seven Orchard Street. I found it more easily than I had expected. From the outside the place did not look like anything special. If anything, it looked a little less well kept than the neighbouring houses. It needed a new paint job, the lawn was a little weedy and unevenly cut, the front walkway was covered with grit and pebbles, and the eaves-trough needed reattachment at one of the front corners. I was surprised by the ramshackle look of the place. For no logical reason, I had been expecting the location to appear anything but slightly drabber than average.

Initially, there was no indication I had come to the address of anything more than the living space of unmotivated occupants. Only upon closer scrutiny did I notice a white rectangle a little larger than the one in my wallet, about the size of a playing card, tucked into a bottom corner of one of the front windows. Upon it was the red silhouette of a tiger. I stood in front of the house silently for about two minutes, conflicted whether to investigate further or walk away. I decided to walk around the block and think about it.

I was confronted with a question I had not let myself think about previously. Why was I here? If I was simply out exploring to see if I could locate the place why did my breath catch and my mind go blank for a few seconds when I found it? Curiosity? The tug of fate? For some reason my tattoo itched and tingled for the first time in months. It would be simple enough to walk away and not to knock on the door, but I was still mysteriously tempted to give it a go. When I returned to the red tiger card in the window I extended my detour around the block once again, circling my decision. I went around the block a third time when I finished the second go round.

As if I had no other choice, I walked until I found the courage to knock at the red tiger door.

A young lady answered. I think she was younger than me. She was skinny and cute in a waif-like way with straight shoulder length blonde hair and big brown eyes in a small face.

"Hi." she said, "Can I help you?"

"Hi. Someone gave me this a while ago and said I might want to check this address out."

I gave her the business card.

"Is this the right place?" I asked.

She took the card and examined it, turning it over and around as if it were almost familiar, but not quite. After a few seconds she handed it back to me and smiled.

"I'm glad you stopped by. Come on in. There are only two of us here now, but I will call a few more to come over so you can meet more of the group. My name is Hope. I'll make some tea."

"Thanks. My name is Molloy."

"Hi, Molloy."

Hope held the door open for me to come in.

I came in, but stopped just inside the door. Hope walked over to the bottom of the stairs and called up.

"Jared, we have company."

She looked over at me.

"Make yourself comfortable. I'll start making tea."

I took off my shoes and looked through the doorway to what looked like a living room. There was a pinkish beige couch against the wall and a pair of matching chairs facing each other across a wooden, rectangular coffee table. The house appeared much tidier inside than out. It was fairly bare bones in terms of furniture and décor, but it was clean and neat. It reminded me of my own apartment in those ways.

I felt odd standing alone in the doorway of the living room, but I felt equally odd about the idea of sitting alone in the living room of a strange house. I chose to sit because I figured that was what was expected of me. Jared soon came downstairs. He had black hair, olive skin, and was slightly chubby. His eyes were grayish green and nervous, but also friendly and intelligent. He was maybe a year or two older than me. He smiled immediately once our eyes met.

"I'm Jared. It's a pleasure to meet you."

"Hi, I'm Molloy. Nice to meet you too."

"So what brings you to this neck of the woods, Molloy?"

"To be honest, I've been kind of wondering that myself. I met some people a while ago who thought it would be a good idea for me to check it out. It took a while, but eventually I decided to drop by. I know that's not the best reason, but it's all I've got."

Jared shrugged and smirked.

"It was basically the same for me. Anyway, I'm glad you did. Can't do any harm I suppose."

I smiled and shrugged back.

"That's what I figured."

Jared nodded.

"Some others will be here soon who can better explain what we're all about. Hope and I are fairly new, especially me, so other people might be able to answer any questions you have better than us. I still have more questions than answers to be honest."

Jared sounded almost ashamed of his last admission. It made me curious.

I asked, "What's this all about anyway? What do you think about what you've seen so far? I'm kind of clueless about the whole thing."

Jared smirked again and laughed quietly. He even rolled his eyes a bit.

"I'll try to explain what I know, but it's not much. *The People* are a big organization, and I guess they work on a bunch of different levels. I don't really think I have much of a grasp of it myself yet, but apparently that's normal. I'm told it takes quite a while to even begin to get a grasp of the whole thing."

The People? Jared seemed a little nervous, but also a nice guy. He seemed overwhelmed somehow even though not a lot appeared to be going on.

I asked, "What people?"

When he did not answer, the next question just kind of popped out of my mouth.

"Are you glad you came here, Jared?"

Jared looked briefly stunned by the question. Since I had not consciously planned to ask it I felt a little stunned too. We both recovered quickly and went on as if it were just a natural pause in the conversation.

"Oh yes," he said. "I am quite content."

He smiled at me and continued.

"I admit the whole thing takes some getting used to. The group is a big endeavour; big enough that it is generally difficult to see the whole scope of it from the point of view of our individual actions. I admit I have not got my head completely around it yet. I suppose for now we simply must trust our small efforts sum up to make the world a better place."

I was confused.

"I'm not sure I follow."

"Yes. The problem, for me at least, has been to see how my tiny roll fits into the larger scheme. But perhaps it's just me. Hope seems to take more intuitively to it than I."

"How do you mean?"

Jared looked vaguely worried and looked around.

"I really should let the others speak to you about it. I know so little at this point. I probably should not have said anything at all. If I am confused myself how am I supposed to enlighten you?"

Jared was acting a little odd, but I was warming up to him a little for some reason. He was well spoken. He seemed honest and thoughtful. I bet he liked to read books. He also seemed a little lost and lonely and maybe reminded me of myself in that way.

"I'm new too," Jared explained. "I haven't done…"

Hope interrupted.

"Tea is ready. Come on into the kitchen and see the meeting room."

The kitchen was compact, tidy, and bright. It was well lit despite having only a single average size window on one wall. Opposite the door we entered from the living room to the kitchen was a door to a large bright room that extended across the whole back end of the house. Several large windows looked onto the backyard with thick brown curtains that could be pulled if privacy were required. The room was mostly taken up with a long, dark brown wooden table running the length of the room with ten to twelve matching chairs around it. An odd looking chandelier with a few very small light bulbs hung above the table. I doubt it added much light unless the curtains were drawn tight.

I said, "You called this the meeting room?"

"Yes," said Hope. "We sometimes have meetings here, but usually they're at other places. This is really the only room where more than just a few people can sit together and talk. Others should be here shortly."

I felt a little freaked out because it almost seemed as if a meeting had been suddenly called together simply because I happened to arrive here on my spur of the moment notion to take a walk a find the red tiger house. It gave me a dreamlike, disjointed feeling as if what was happening was not real.

We went back into the kitchen and sat around a small table near a corner that was out of the way of the appliances and the doorways. The kitchen appliances, cupboards, and paint on the walls were predominantly white. Although I had never been to one, sitting quietly in the corner of all the whiteness brought psychiatric hospitals to my mind.

The tea Hope made had a nice, slightly spicy scent. It tasted great too. The tea eased away the edge that had crept into me due to the upcoming meeting and my self-inflicted images of being in a psych ward. In fact, once the three of us were settled at the table the edge melted completely away for a while. The sun shone in the perfect location, brightening the room without glaring our eyes. I was sitting at the kitchen table with two other people, enjoying tea and making light, friendly conversation. It was nearly family-like. I had been away from home for quite a bit more than a year now. It seemed a lot longer.

I said, "I've never had anything quite like this tea before. It's great."

"Thank you," said Hope. "It's Chai tea."

Hope looked at me and smiled like a small, excited child.

"I love having visitors," she said.

"Thank you. I couldn't ask for better hosts."

I smiled at both of them in turn. They smiled back, pleased with the compliment.

I drained my cup of tea before the others were even half finished. Jared noticed.

"May I refill your cup?"

"Yes, thank you. I really gulped that down. I must be a bit thirsty from my walk over here. Plus, it's delicious. I don't know much about tea. I'm more a coffee guy."

Hope jumped up.

"Goodness," she exclaimed. "Can I get you a glass of cold water with a squirt of lemon juice in it perhaps? We have coffee too!"

"No, no. Please sit down. The tea is great. I like the feel of the aftertaste in my mouth. I'll stick with tea. You've already done more for me than I deserve."

The tea was very relaxing. I was starting to appreciate the whiteness of the kitchen more as well, nice and clean looking. I felt like just sitting there peacefully and vegging out, but I always felt like I should say something. Hope saved me the trouble of coming up with something.

"I noticed you have your tea without anything in it. Have you always had it like that?"

"To be honest, this is the first time I have ever had tea. My family were coffee drinkers. I didn't know what I was missing. I usually have my coffee black though."

Hope said, "I like this kind of tea with a tiny bit of milk and sugar and a squirt of lemon. You should try it."

Jared said, "It is tasty the way Hope has it, but I usually have mine black as well."

I shrugged.

"It's tasty just the way it is, but I don't want to be a spoil sport. I'll try Hope's way this time."

"You're going to loooovvve it," Hope sang.

It was different with the stuff added, sweet from the sugar and the sour from the lemon. Even the spices tasted a bit different. I liked it.

"I like it. Different tastes, but they go well together."

Hope looked pleased.

Jared interrupted.

"You want a couple of tips on the pouring and mixing of tea?"

"Sure," I said. "Why not?"

Hope rolled her eyes.

"Oh, here we go."

I could tell they had had this conversation before. Jared purposefully ignored Hope and focused his attention on me. I could tell he was playing around a little. I think Hope knew it too although she seemed slightly more serious about it.

Jared said, "Okay, watch closely. First you put the sugar in the empty cup...to taste, of course. I use one teaspoon. Next, squeeze an average sized lemon wedge over the sugar and allow the juice to seep in and partially dissolve the sugar. Naturally, you add the lemon to taste as well. I try to get as much as I can out of the lemon wedge without making too much of a mess. Next comes the milk or the cream or whatever you use. Again, let the sugar sop it up and dissolve in it for a few seconds. Lastly, we pour the tea slowly and gently over the concoction and it mixes itself."

Jared smiled over at me looking genuinely pleased with himself. He pushed the cup over to me.

"Please take it. I'll pour myself another. Compare the two and see what you think."

I did and then took the diplomatic route.

"It's a new taste for me so it is hard to distinguish and judge the subtle differences in flavour. They're both great."

Jared and Hope both giggled and said at the same time, "Good answer".

Jared commented, "Just wait until you get to the bottom of the cup though, Molloy. That's where the difference in indisputable. You get a nice final jolt of cream, sweetness, and lemon at the end."

Hope rolled her eyes again.

"Whatever," she said.

As we sipped our tea and chatted, waiting for the others, Jared kept craning his neck to look into my cup and see how close I was to the bottom. At one point he spoke up.

"That's just about right. Tip the last gulp into your mouth all at once. It's a concentrated mixture of all the ingredients. It gives you an explosion of flavour to finish off. You'll love it."

I could not tell if he was being entirely serious or just trying to aggravate Hope. I tipped it back.

"Not bad," I said. "To be honest though it tastes mostly like sugar."

Hope stood up with her arms over her head.

"Yes. You got it, Molloy. I've been telling him that all along."

"It's definitely good though," I said, not wanting to take sides.

Jared smiled

"Don't worry about it, Molloy. It's my fault. I must not have mixed it right. It is a very delicate procedure and being off just a little can make a big difference. I even mess up making my own sometimes, but I'm getting better, more consistent."

Hope groaned, "Give it up. It's just sugar right, Molloy?"

I was determined not to get involved in their little game by leaning toward either side.

"I'll reserve my decision until I get more familiar with the tea and give Jared a chance to perfect his technique. I don't know enough about it yet."

Jared looked pleased.

"Good man, Molloy. I won't disappoint you."

Hope shook her head.

"Oh brother."

Not long after the doorbell rang. Hope jumped up immediately.

"It must be them. I'll get it."

Nervousness settled over me. I had reached an enjoyable, even keel sipping tea and chatting about silly things with Hope and Jared, but now unknown others were joining us, ones authorized to give me more information about the Red Tiger Club or *The People* as Jared had called them. The biggest problem was I knew everything might come down to a question I was not sure I could adequately answer. Why was I here?

The bustle of excited noise at the front of the house drew Jared and I toward it. We stood in the kitchen doorway watching the commotion of cheeriness, greetings, and hugs that were mainly centred on Hope. She looked to be in heaven. As the guests moved into the house and the distance between them and us narrowed glad shouts of "Jared" began and we were drawn into the fray. I wondered why everyone arrived at the same time. Did they come together in a bus or something?

Nobody recognized me, of course, but between handshakes and smiles Jared began to introduce me. Five to ten minutes of this non-descript mingling occurred before a man of somewhat more distinguished bearing, perhaps in his early fifties caught my eye and signalled to me from across the room. He began to ease his way through the fifteen or so guests toward me.

As he drew closer and I studied him, Santa Claus crossed my mind. He looked the part somewhat, slightly stout yet solid looking with a white-silver head of hair complete with beard, and a cheery, ruddy face. The beard was much shorter than Santa's and trimmed neater. He had on a sharp navy blue suit instead of the usual Christmas gear.

When he was within reach he held out his hand and shook mine firmly when I offered it. His eyes were warm, intelligent, and blue.

"You must be Molloy," he said, "since you are the only one here I don't recognize."

I was slightly put at ease by the man's friendly nature, but that he sought me out right away and called me by name set off little alerts cascading through my blood stream. Again I wondered...was it actually possible that this meeting was arranged simply because I showed up here?

I nodded in answer to his question.

"Yes, I'm Molloy."

The gentleman kept eye contact as he relinquished our handshake.

"My name is Duncan. It is a pleasure to meet you, Molloy. I'm glad you came by. If you let me know what you hoped to accomplish by stopping by here today I will do my best to see if we can accommodate you. I do not mean to pry unnecessarily, only to let you know that I will help you out if I can."

This was the difficult question I had been expecting. While I had walked around outside before ringing the bell I had gone over a variety of answers in my head and practiced the ones I thought were best, but in the end what came out was a short, honest answer that sounded unintentionally disinterested, as if I were interviewing for a job I was not sure I wanted.

"Hard for me to say really; a few coincidences, bumping into some people, and maybe feeling a little aimless and alone in some ways...if that makes sense."

Duncan chuckled and looked as if he understood.

"That's good enough for me. I think all of us have gone through periods like that in our lives. I also think it is possible we might be able to help you out. Mind if I take you around and introduce you? See what you think of us, how it feels?"

Duncan then looked at me knowingly with a smile and a little chuckle.

"Feel free to escape any time you like, sir. If it doesn't feel right, I mean."

I was glad he said that because that very notion to make a run for it had been shifting around in the back of my mind the whole time. It took some of the pressure off. It also felt nice that he called me sir.

Duncan's demeanour partially soothed my nerves. He exuded a mirthful state of mind as if none of what was happening around us needed to be taken too seriously.

"I think I can handle visiting a little more," I said.

Duncan gave me a short bow and a brief smile.

"As you wish, Molloy. May I offer you a word to the wise as an official spokesman for *The People for a Better World*?"

I believe Duncan noticed the title startled me a little.

"I agree the title is a bit ostentatious, however, we appear to be stuck with it for the time being. May I give you my pearl of wisdom?"

"Sure."

"First I want to say whatever the reason you decided to come here today we are very glad you did. The pearl is, nothing happens by coincidence. It follows that you are here for a reason. The key is to discover that reason. Make sense?"

"Kind of, I guess."

Duncan patted me on the back and laughed.

"That is about the best review I could give it as well. It is not even really my pearl. It is one of the mottos for... here it comes again, *The People for a Better World*. And it is not their pearl either. The pearl is ancient and has been spoken by millions of people for centuries. I am trying to get some of these stuffy titles and ideas out in the open quickly so they don't come as a shock to you when somebody else mentions them.

"Okay, thanks," I said. "It's probably a good idea."

Duncan took me around and introduced me to pretty much everyone in the house. Juice, tea, sandwiches, and cookies were put out so people could help themselves. I do not remember much about the exchanges I had with the members Duncan brought me around to see. It was mostly general pleasantries.

It was fun watching Duncan. It was obvious he was the leading actor in this Meeting *for a Better World*. The atmosphere changed within a group whenever he drew near. The gathering huddled in small groups chatting contentedly until Duncan arrived at their group and the scene shifted. Members seemed to become more alert and focused when he came into their group.

After about twenty minutes of this general mingling and guided introduction, Duncan looked at his watch then patted me on the shoulder again.

"Molloy, business calls. It was nice to meet you and I hope to see you many times again, but now I must go. There is lots of food and drink left and many good people to get to know. You are welcome to stay as long as you like."

Duncan then bellowed a deep short laugh.

"You can stay forever if you like. *The People for a Better World* can be a lifelong adventure if you want it to be."

I was surprised and a little disappointed to hear of Duncan's sudden departure. It was helpful and reassuring to have him anchor me as I was introduced to everyone. I had been safe and tucked in like a pilot fish attached to a large shark as he smoothly merged into groups of people who flowed like water around him when he came their way.

"Okay," I said. "Nice meeting you. Thanks for showing me around."

Duncan nodded graciously toward me.

"It was a pleasure."

He withdrew an item from his back pant pocket.

"Here is my card. I would be happy to clear up any uncertainties you have as best I can should you want to know more about...umm...let's just say *The People* for simplicities sake."

We both chuckled. Then Duncan shook my hand a final time and saluted me with the forefinger of his other hand. Afterward he made his way to the front door saying quick goodbyes along the way.

I shuffled around the room a bit until I caught sight of Hope and Jared. They seemed like the best bet for me to feel comfortable with while I regained my bearings. I contemplated leaving, but decided to try and stick it out for at least another short stretch after Duncan left.

I spent only another thirty minutes or so at the house and most of that time I was in the kitchen with Hope and Jared. It worked out pretty well. It was relatively cozy and familiar in there with the two people I had already met and become comfortable around. Others popped their heads around the corner once in a while to greet me and say a few friendly words.

I felt I would like to get to know Jared better. Hope was very nice too, but Jared seemed more sceptical and thoughtful about the whole People thing and my intuition trusted his opinion more. I don't remember the exact context, but Hope actually described her feelings about membership to *The People for a Better World* as an honour to be a part of the big machine that silently and gradually changes the world in a positive way. Maybe that was true, but Jared's hesitations sounded more reasonable and objective.

I immediately looked over at Jared to see his reaction when she said this, but he looked down at his teacup pretending (I suspect) to try to rub some sort of debris from the rim. Despite sensing his discomfort I could not resist trying to dig up more information.

"What do you think about this whole *People for a Better World* thing, Jared?"

Hope looked at him and smiled as if my question was naïve and the answer was obvious.

Jared said, "The group has been nothing but extremely kind to me. I have to admit I'm still pretty new and I'm still trying to understand certain things, but I'm getting the hang of it. I certainly have no complaints, that's for sure."

"What are the things you find hardest to understand? I'm asking because I feel like I might have to make a decision soon and I really don't know anything. I'm finding almost everything hard to understand."

Jared started, "Well that's just it. Even..."

Hope cut him off.

"A certain element of faith and trust are required," she said. "Everyone does their little part and the founders bring it together as a whole. That's how I see it."

Jared nodded.

"It's like she says, I suppose. At first I guess it is just hard to see the forest for the trees as they say."

I wished I could get Jared alone and talk to him, but it looked as though I would have to wait for another time. I felt like I should go. One last try.

"Is there anything else either of you can tell me?"

Hope answered, "Not really. There is an element of faith in joining, like I said. You find out more by doing and experiencing it first hand. If you don't like it you can just quit and leave, but I'm not leaving. Are you, Jared?"

Jared looked mildly embarrassed.

"Of course not. I am definitely better off here than I was before I joined and I am grateful for that. I am just a naturally inquisitive person."

Hope looked at him and smiled tenderly like an understanding parent although Jared was obviously older than her.

"I know you are," she said kindly.

That was enough for me. I left my phone number so they could call me to see if I wanted to take part in any future meetings that came up. I was spooked a little, but also intrigued. Just like my encounters with the characters who first brought *The People* to my attention, these new interactions were unsettling in a way, but interesting. And no matter how unusual the circumstances of our meeting, I could not fault any of them regarding their pleasantness or their willingness to connect in potential friendship.

29

Long Walk

Going for walks is a part of my routine when I have to make a tough decision. I walked around Brockville to help me decide whether to get my tattoo, and also walked as I wondered whether to leave home. I walked more than three hours contemplating whether to join *The People for a Better World*.

By the time I took this long walk I had participated in two more People meetings similar to the first one I described. Hope invited me by phone to one of them and for the other Duncan called me himself. The meeting Hope invited me to was at the same house. Jared was still there as well. Unfortunately, much of Jared's scepticism regarding *The People* had faded. When I had him alone I prodded him a little trying to determine the reasons for his earlier doubts, but his mind seemed changed, less individual.

He said, "At some point you have to trust something. For no reason I can think, they trusted in me and saw me valuable to their group. I should at least give them a fair trial if nothing else."

There was not much I could do to persuade him from this line of reasoning. Our discussion seemed closed before it started.

Hope was exactly the same as she was before and Duncan again made a similar, but briefer appearance.

The meeting Duncan invited me to was at a different house. Hope and Jared were not there. This place was more elegant than the other house and the average guest was older and better dressed. I may have been wearing exactly the same clothes as I wore to the first meeting for all I remember. I had not been told to dress any differently. In any case, nobody appeared to notice or disapprove of my casual attire.

This better dressed meeting was different than the other two I attended. Aside from the guest demographics,

Duncan was not as available to hold my hand and introduce me around. My intuition was these guests required Duncan's unencumbered attention more than those at the other house. He did not abandon me entirely. Several times he stopped to speak with me and introduce me to a person or two nearby.

At this meeting there was also a presentation. The lights in a large room were dimmed, and a man I had not been introduced to spoke and showed some slides. Apparently, *The People for a Better World* were involved in attaining basic rights for people such as food and water and also in trying to ensure technological advantages between social classes and different world economies did not get out of hand. The speaker seemed to imply that *The People* played a role in trying to maintain a balance of power not only within Canada, but in other countries around the world. I admit much of the rhetoric was over my head, but that is how it sounded to me at the time. I found the whole thing a little overwhelming, and I told Duncan soon after the presentation that I had to go.

"No problem, Molloy. I just thought I would let you see another level of meeting that goes on among us and maybe give you a better overall feel for what we do. Feel free to call me any time if there is anything you think I might be able to help clarify. Sound good?"

"Sounds good," I replied.

Duncan's clean straight smile parted his slightly unkempt beard and moustache. He was always fairly well groomed, but I sensed the spirit of a friendly mutt underneath, eager to play in the rain and mud if only one knew the secret signal.

As he shook my hand to say goodnight Duncan looked me warmly in the eye.

"I feel you are a special person, Molloy. Whatever decision you make will be the correct one. Your path is always your own. Call me if you need me."

I have to admit Duncan's last words lifted my spirits that evening.

Thus the reader has the background for my long walk to think and decide whether my future would be tied to

The People for a Better World. Hopefully, the reader might be able to sympathize with the ideas and images of *The People* that sank, rose, twisted and turned in my mind as I wandered for hours along the Ottawa River.

It is a beautiful place to walk. The river path is not at all city-like, insulated on one side by the river and on the other side by significant land and trees that block most of civilization from view. There are cattails, bushes, small forests, flowering weeds, and landscaped, treed paths stretching for miles. The river itself is a minor wonder in its own right; shallow enough in spots to challenge kayakers with its rapids and spotted with several tiny islands where noisy gulls and nearly silent ducks rest and socialize. The geese that appeared in large numbers seemed too dependent on human charity. They lingered on the strip of land between the water and the path. Many took hopeful steps toward me as I walked past, then averted their attention quickly when it was apparent I would not be providing food.

Across the river lay Quebec, the Gatineau Hills rolling and fading down the distance. The long Champlain Bridge connected the provinces over the water. I considered walking across the bridge to another province as a minor adventure, but chose to walk under the bridge and stayed on the Ontario path in the end.

I cannot say exactly how far or how long I walked, but I remember I went past Westboro Beach. I stopped there and watched for several minutes. It was very peaceful. The sand stretched and flattened until it was pulled down even with the water before sliding beneath to yield an unobstructed view of the settling sun. The scene continuously shifted as the Earth blocked more of the sunlight and the remaining rays were refracted and reflected at different angles. The wind and the clouds moved as well, doing their part in the creation of an evolving natural artwork. I stood for a long while, but then moved on before everything dissolved into gray, then black.

Time wise, I can only say with certainty it was light when I left and dark long before I returned. In the end, I could not find a good reason not to allow *The People for a*

Better World to tell more of their story, or as Jared put it, to give them a fair trial. The next day I called the number on Duncan's card and arranged for a meeting in his downtown office.

30

First Official Business

Duncan's office was in a building near The Market only a few blocks from the Rideau Centre Mall. The Rideau Centre was huge compared to anything in Brockville with at least two of every genre of store. The board in the lobby did not mention anything about a better world, only Duncan Kinlin, room seven hundred and thirty one.

It was a clean, quiet lobby with very shiny elevators. I wondered if it was a new construction. There was a man in uniform at a desk I figured I had to see before I went up.

"I have an appointment at ten o'clock in room seven-thirty-one."

The man smiled.

"It's only nine-forty, but you can go up whenever you are ready."

"Thanks."

I figured since the guy mentioned it maybe I was too early. I was afraid I would get lost so I left lots of margin for error whenever I was going somewhere for the first time. I sat in a comfortable brown leather chair and flipped through a business magazine to kill a few minutes. I did not really understand it, but I made an attempt to comprehend some general concepts in a short article before I put it down and walked to the elevator.

The elevator delivered me to the seventh floor where I followed the signs past identical dark wood doors with gold coloured metal numbers until I got to seven-hundred and thirty-one. I knocked.

Duncan's friendly voice said, "Come in".

Duncan always looked the same; smiling blue eyes, finely lined face, a stout, solid stature, and silver hair, beard, and moustache which was always neatly trimmed yet slightly unkempt at the same time.

He stood and reached his hand over the desk for me to shake.

"Hello, Molloy. You are exactly on time. Tremendous. Have a seat."

Duncan's office was nothing exceptional. It was fairly small with a plain L-shaped wooden desk covered with papers, files, a cylindrical container holding writing instruments, and a phone. On the other arm of the L were a computer and a small printer/fax machine. There were two wooden chairs opposite the side of the desk where Duncan sat. I sat down in one of them. I was a little surprised at the office's lack of glamour and sophistication, but Duncan seemed content.

"Hi, Duncan. I thought you had a secretary for when you weren't here."

"I do, but she is shared by a few of us. She mostly takes messages and arranges meetings for us. She sits in a separate office."

"Oh."

"I take it you've been doing some hard thinking," he said.

I nodded.

Duncan opened his eyes wide and smiled.

"Well, don't keep me in suspense. Tell me about it."

"Can I ask a question first?"

"Of course."

"Well," I said, "what if after joining *The People for a Better World* I decide it's not for me? Is there a problem quitting? I ask because, as you have even said yourself, details are pretty hard to come by. I can't help but be a little nervous about what I'm getting into."

Duncan looked at me seriously and nodded.

"As you should, my boy, as you should. But I am happy to inform you that at no time, under no circumstances are you obligated to remain a member of *The People* for even a day longer than you wish. In fact, that is a large part of the reason why details are so hard to come by. The organization is not for everyone and the initial secrecy is a system whereby individuals have the freedom to try us out and leave if they so choose without *The People* having to fear about ex-members taking...trade secrets, for lack of a better term...with them when they go."

Duncan raised his eyebrows and asked, "Does that explain things a little, Molloy?"

"Kind of."

Duncan laughed.

"I know it is a bit of a mind twist, this whole thing. As crazy as it sounds there are actually forces that oppose our efforts to make the world a better place. Our methods may interfere with their interests, they may have what we consider to be bad intentions, or they may even feel they have a better method of making the world a better place. The point is we feel it is best to keep our work and our methods as under the radar as possible to decrease the likelihood that anyone would interfere with our efforts."

He continued

"I'm sure this all may sound a little conspiratorial and secretive, but unfortunately, that is the status of things at this time. I know I have already said this, but every important endeavour requires an element of faith. You either have it or you don't. We have tried to set things up in a manner where an individual does not have much to lose if they give us a try."

I suspected I had all the information I was going to get. Faith aside, I was either going to do it or I was not. I had basically already decided to give *The People* a try, but something had kept me scurrying along the edge of a decision until it was all but forced from me.

"In that case, Duncan, I will take a chance and give *The People for a Better World* a try if you still want me."

Duncan's smile appeared genuine.

"I assure you that I do. I should really say we are honoured to have you among us."

I felt a wave of relief that the decision was finally made, over, and done.

"Thanks, Duncan."

What else could I say?

Duncan laughed. He too looked relieved it was done.

"You are most welcome. I hope and believe you will not regret your decision."

He held out his hand and we shook once again. There did not seem to be much else for me to say or do, but it seemed as if there should be. Duncan spoke and saved me from having to ponder what to say for long.

"Within the next day or two I will get in touch with you to arrange a meeting to give you a little orientation and set up some more training before your first assignment as a member of *The People*."

"Alright," I said.

"Terrific. I will talk to you soon."

It appeared the meeting was over and though it seemed sudden, I was relieved it was not prolonged unnecessarily. Duncan still held my gaze and smiled warmly, but I sensed he was trying to determine what he would do the moment I shut his office door behind me.

I shrugged and waved.

"Okay, bye for now. I'll talk to you soon."

"Take care, Molloy. Thank you for coming to the meeting right on time. I admire that quality in a man. As you will see, it is important in our work."

It felt good to be referred to as a man by another man, especially one that was unquestionably a grownup.

31

Introductory Training

Duncan phoned me the next day and we arranged a meeting time that fit into my work schedule. We would meet for training Sunday at nine o'clock in the morning in the same building as Duncan's office.

Near the end of the call Duncan said, "I should let you know there will be two other rookies with you at the same time for introductory training. It's much more time efficient in small groups rather than train every person individually. As well, I think having the company of others in the same situation is less stressful for the newcomers. The training will be in room two-nineteen. The desk clerk can help you find your way."

"Okay, see you Sunday."

"See you then, Molloy."

Sunday morning I arrived at room two-nineteen several minutes early, but the other two trainees were already seated, ready, and waiting when I arrived. I worried I might look less enthusiastic than the others, but there was no one else but us three there to notice. I hung my jacket on one of the hooks that lined the back wall of the room and took a seat four chairs from the others since they were four seats from each other.

The room seemed like a larger, newer, and quieter version of a high-school classroom. The chairs were the kind with a flat wooden piece that can be swung up to lock in front for use as a desk for writing upon. There was even a chalkboard and large desk at the front of the room.

Duncan entered shortly after I did, but from a different door near the blackboard. He hung his jacket on the chair behind the large desk. His desk faced the rest of the room like a teacher's desk. Bowing and waving what I suppose were his lecture notes at each of us in turn, Duncan greeted us.

"Greetings, Molloy. Greetings, Richard. Greetings, Agnes."

"I prefer Aggie."

"My apologies, Aggie. You told me that already. I should have remembered."

"No worries."

Richard was a tall slim Oriental man around my age. He raised his hand to offer me a short wave and smile.

"Howdy," he said.

Aggie made a bemused face I doubt anyone else could see. She looked like she wondered what she was doing here. She was trim and fairly tall with straight, dark-brown hair to the bottom of her neck. She wore slightly Gothish makeup. I guessed she was around my age as well, maybe a little older. She was cute in an unusual sort of way.

She said, "Hi, Molloy".

"Hey guys," I said. "Nice to meet you both."

Duncan sat on the edge of his desk facing us rather than on the chair behind it. He shuffled his notes in his lap for a few seconds before looking up at us.

"Well, here we are," he said. "Are you ready for the spiel?"

"Bring it on," laughed Richard.

Duncan nodded.

"Yes. May as well get started, I suppose."

He stood up.

"Today's session is primarily to give you a basic idea what to expect during your work with *The People for a Better World*. It is important for you to know straight away that no matter what I or anyone else tells you, in the end, your satisfaction with this work will require an element of faith on your part."

"Sometimes the tasks we assign you will seem to have more in common with throwing feathers at the wind than with making the world a better place, but you will have to set those doubts aside and trust that the big picture is clearer even if it is very difficult to see the big picture from your vantage point."

"I realize this is not an inspiring message, but it is something all of us have to deal with at some point. I want to have that out in the open from the very beginning."

I raised my hand.

"Yes, Molloy."

"Will things become clearer at some point?"

"That is a reasonable, straight-forward question, but unfortunately, the answer is less straight-forward. It depends on your state of mind. Trainees and employees have experienced a wide variety of personal answers to your question. Some feel they know what we do is great and are able to put tremendous effort and emotion behind their work. Others find the experience totally unintuitive and it just never clicks with them. These people often leave. Most people fall somewhere between these two extremes. To be completely honest with you, I myself lie somewhere between these polar viewpoints."

Richard asked, "Have things become clearer with time and your higher position within *The People*?"

Duncan nodded as if to acknowledge the question as a good one. He was silent a few moments as he paced in front of his desk and thought about it. He stopped and looked at us with honest, soulful, blue eyes as if he were the unfortunate bearer of disappointing news.

"In all honesty, probably not that much. You may find it hard to believe, but I doubt I have a much clearer vision of the big picture than the hundred plus new members such as yourselves that I supervise. Perhaps this is my own failing, my own lack of vision, but in that case why did I find myself promoted one day? I suspect you will gain some insight after a few weeks on the job and a little more after a few months, but I cannot say anything for sure. Again, it seems to vary greatly between individuals. Please let me know your experiences in this regard as you evolve through your work. I would like to know your experience so I may add it to my own knowledge when others ask this same question. It is a question that is often asked."

Duncan paused for a few seconds before continuing.

"The point is, the mindset you will need to succeed at this work will take some practice to get accustomed. It is difficult for most. It was difficult for me."

Richard put up his hand again.

"Yes, my friend?"

"I'm a bit confused. Will we never know anything about what we are doing?"

Duncan shook his head and smiled, reminding me of that rare breed of school teacher I had once, eager to listen to the questions and patiently share what he knew.

"Otherwise would be just plain cruel. Once or twice each year we will get together for a celebration and a presentation showing the great achievements we all played a role in making happen. The difficulty is in connecting the tasks you performed with these tremendous achievements. Let me assure you it will be difficult for all of you to fathom. Faith will be required, my colleagues. There is no other way."

Duncan took a big breath and smiled.

"It is not too late to leave before we go into any further training. It has happened before and there is no shame in it."

Nobody moved to get up, but I think all of us felt a little weird about the situation. I certainly felt that way although the cryptic talk also pricked my curiosity.

Duncan clapped his hands together.

"Okay then, if we are all staying we might as well get on with it. Despite what I have told you everything is not all gloom and garbage. If you can get your mind to accept that *The People* are indeed trying to make the world a better place you can work hard at your daily tasks, make decent money, and know it's all for a worthy cause. Anymore questions before we get started?"

There were none.

Duncan gave Richard three pieces of paper and asked him to pass them along so we each had one.

"Your initial work with *The People for a Better World* will be to perform a list of tasks that shall be delivered to you early each morning. The tasks will be listed in chronological order with the time the task is to be performed in a column at the left of the page and a description of the necessary details of the task on the right hand side."

"The list of rules I have given you are meant to be firm guidelines on how to perform your duties to get the best results. They are also meant to ensure your safety. Read them several times each day until they are memorized in the same way you have memorized how to breathe and they simply become the way you behave naturally when at work. You may as well get your first reading of the rules now. I will leave you to it and even give you enough time to read them twice."

Duncan then sat quietly at his desk reading some papers and occasionally writing notes on them.

This is a list of the rules he gave us.

Be sure to approach the target(s) of your task as close to the stated time on your list as possible.

Do not place yourself into ANY perceived danger at ANY time during your tasks.

The following are reasons to abandon your tasks without completing them:

Any perceived danger to yourself or others resulting from continuing with the task including:

Any illness or injury that may negatively affect your performance, health, or safety on the job.

Targets are not at or close to their identified place, at or close to the identified time when they should be there.

Any clear sense of strangeness or the unusual during a task situation. This could be live targets acting in a very unusual, unexpected, or threatening manner. Strangeness may also apply to extenuating circumstances unrelated to your task such as coincidental, emergency situation in the area where your task is to be performed.

Be EXTREMELY CAREFUL during data entry. Accuracy is a MUST.

I had more than enough time to read the handout twice before Duncan stood up and moved to the front of his desk.

"Allow me to clarify some of the terms on the handout I gave you.

"Target refers to the subject you must act upon or interact with to perform your task. The target may be a person, plant, animal or an inanimate object. Your actions may involve speaking with someone, moving an object, or some combination of things. Your task might be as simple as saying hello to a particular person at a particular time or it might be something much more involved. You might have to purchase an item somewhere, make small talk of a particular nature with the staff, then take your purchase and put it in a particular place at a particular time. As you might well imagine there is no limit to the arrangement of such tasks that might be assembled. It will be difficult to see the point in many of your tasks. We will do some role playing of possible tasks at future training sessions."

I have trimmed details of our first day of training significantly, but the above summary contains the key elements of my introductory training.

When Duncan's session wound down he stopped and smiled at us.

He said, "Your first training session is essentially over. Can I answer any questions?"

Richard raised his hand.

"Yes, Richard?"

"How do we get paid?"

Duncan chuckled.

"Always question number one or close to it after the first session and I don't blame you one bit. I believe you would also like to know 'how much', am I right?"

We all laughed and nodded.

"Here is how it works. We give you a debit card that is attached to an account of *The People*. You can pay for your day-to-day expenses out of this account including your rent. Normally, rent is paid by post-dated checks and we will provide you with checks for this purpose. As long as your day-to-day expenses are not out of line, access to the account will not be denied. If things get out of hand the transaction will be declined. On the other hand, should your expenses be well managed, an amount of money above and beyond your expenses shall be credited to an account of your own for you to do with what you like. Of course, *The People for a Better World* would like to keep their costs under control leaving more money available to make the world a better place. If you manage to keep your costs low, reasonable even, *The People* will share the savings with you in the form of bonuses. Bonuses may also be awarded if it is felt a member is doing a particularly good job in consistently performing their daily tasks well and efficiently."

Aggie spoke up.

"What if we can't or don't keep our costs low?"

"Well, in addition to having suspicious Interact transactions declined, member privileges may be suspended and the member asked to come in for additional training. It has even happened on rare occasions where the situation was declared to be unworkable and the persons involved were released as members of *The People for a Better World.* The more common situation of this kind is the member never becomes good at managing their money and they wind up with very little savings or bonus money. Perhaps in the end these members are simply spenders versus savers, and they choose to spend whatever they can instead of keeping something in reserve for a rainy day or future purchases. My own belief is those that manage their money wisely receive more in total compensation in a variety of ways, but to each their own. Everyone is different. Everyone is special. Usually, we can find a mutually acceptable arrangement with each member."

I had a question.

"Are we allowed to have another job at the same time?"

Duncan pointed at me.

"Thank you, Molloy. It is normally part of my routine to touch upon that very topic during my spiel. I must be going soft. Thank you for reminding me.

"Here is how it works. We try to treat our members like mature adults and avoid outright telling our members what they can and cannot do. However, we do insist that your work with *The People* is your number one priority job.

"The pay we provide you should be enough to pay your living expenses, as well save some if you choose, to treat yourselves to occasional treats, and even occasional luxuries. That aside, if for some reason you wish to pursue a part-time job in addition to your work with us we will not stand in your way as long as it does not interfere with your work with us. This is important and I want to make it very clear."

"Your other job would have to be quite flexible because once you are fully up to speed in the schedule you will be working approximately one in four weekends as well as one in four weeks of evenings, two in the afternoon until ten at night. We have select night members for the midnight shift, but it is possible you might be called upon to work one of these shifts in a pinch. If you can find employment flexible enough to allow you to perform your duties to *The People* unencumbered, it is allowed."

I gave Duncan a thumb up and asked another question.

"Will we know our evening and weekend schedules fairly far in advance?"

Duncan did not hesitate.

"Yes."

"Okay, thanks for explaining those things."

I planned to continue to work at Groovier's some, at least in the beginning.

Duncan looked back and forth between us to see if there were any more questions. When it appeared there were not, he clapped his hands together to signal the end of the session.

"There, I've told you all I know. I want you to think about what I've said for three days and decide if this sort of arrangement with *The People for a Better World* sounds like something you would like to be a part of, or more like something that would drive you out of your mind. I repeat, give yourself three days to think about it. It is an unusual system and it is not for everyone. Either answer to the question is acceptable. If you decide you want to give it a go call me and we will get the ball rolling. If not, you may also call me to let me know, but you also have the option to walk away quietly. If I do not hear from you in a few days I will assume your answer is no."

Duncan was finished speaking. He gathered his papers before asking us for permission to leave.

"Any other items I can attempt to shed some light upon for the lady and you gents before I go?"

We were silent.

"Great," said Duncan. "Once last thing then; should you decide to join our group you will need to fill in the information requested on this form."

He passed them around.

"With this information we can set you up a bank account linked up with *The People*'s group account to ensure you get paid and have access to the group's funds for living expenses and the like. It will also allow us to do a quick background check to make sure you are a suitable candidate to join *The People for a Better World*. As long as you have nothing overtly criminal hidden away, I assure you there is nothing to worry about."

Duncan gazed at us, smiling for several seconds.

"Nothing else? Are you sure?"

When there was not a peep from us, Duncan scooped up his coat from the desk and strode for the exit near his desk where he had come in.

"As always, duty calls. I hope to hear from all of you soon. Thank you for your time, my friends, and be well."

He was gone.

Perhaps Duncan suspected the rookies might like to be alone to speculate about the potential membership and what we would each do. Perhaps he knew it would be easier without him around. This possibility did not occur to me at the time, only upon further reflection.

Our conversation centered upon the vague nature of everything we learned. Even our pay and hours were only hazily outlined. It did not take long until there was nothing left to say since we did not have a lot of clear details to build a conversation around. Aggie asked the only important question we had the power to answer.

"So, you guys going to do it?"

No one knew for positive, but we all indicated we were leaning toward giving it a try. No one really said it outright, but I think we all figured maybe we did not have a lot to lose.

I had been holding off going to the bathroom for a lot of our training session.

"Anyone know the quickest way to a bathroom?"

Richard did.

"Turn right outside this room until you get to the lobby, then diagonal across the lobby near the corner across from the entrance."

"Thanks."

By the time I returned from my quick pee and hand rinse the other two had already left. I had been thinking I might ask them to go out for a coffee together, but it would have to wait for another time.

I spent that evening and following day thinking a lot. The two days afterward were primarily spent reorganizing my life.

32

Demoted at Groovier's

I went into Groovier's on one of my days off and told Mr. Iaello I had something important to speak with him about. I had tried to choose a time when things were generally quieter, but the restaurant was busier than I hoped.

My Iaello said, "Give me some time, Molloy. Go into my office and I will speak with you when I can, okay?"

"Okay, boss."

I went into his cramped office and squeezed myself into one of the chairs against the wall across from Mr. Iaello's desk. My knees were about two inches from the front of his desk. In my head I practiced what I planned to say while I waited.

It did not seem long before Mr. Iaello came into the office. He tucked himself in behind his desk. He looked calm, but serious when he sat down, like he did not want to prolong our talk with idle chatter. Some other matter going on within Groovier's might well have required his attention

"You wanted to speak with me about something, Molloy, so please speak."

I took a deep breath and got it over and done in as few words as I could manage.

"A friend of mine has offered me a unique job I would like to try. I'm not sure about it, but Groovier's is the only job I've ever had and even though I like it a lot and I'm really grateful for it, I feel like maybe I should try a few things before I decide what's best for me. Is that okay?"

I sensed a momentary glimpse of disappointment within Mr. Iaello. I say sensed because his face or body language never showed me anything. I just felt it. It was gone almost as fast as I sensed it, so maybe it was just wishful thinking on my part that Mr. Iaello would miss me if I left. Mr. Iaello's voice and gestures were calm and measured when he replied after a few seconds thought. He cut right to the heart and conclusion of the situation.

"Ah well, Molloy, what can I say? You are a good worker, but you are also young and the pilot of your own fate as we all must be. If you have to go, you have to go. How much notice can you give me to work you out of the schedule?"

"Two weeks. And I would like to stay on part time if I could."

He raised his eyebrows and looked thoughtful. I knew what came next. I had heard it before when other staff moved on, but wanted to keep their toes in the pool at Groovier's while they got a feel for their new job. I saved my boss the trouble of making the speech and said it myself.

"I know I go right to the bottom of the pecking order; worst shifts, worst duties and all that. I'll give you my availability and you can put me wherever you want up to two shifts per week."

Mr. Iaello nodded.

"Fair enough. Give me your availability when you have it and I will see what I can do."

"Thanks, boss."

We shook hands.

Mr. Iaello said, "Just to make certain, you're sure your scheduled shifts can stay the same for the next two weeks?"

"Definitely."

I was relieved everything had gone so smoothly, but I felt kind of empty inside, as if I expected, even needed the occasion to be a bit more emotional.

I felt I should say something more and I tried, but it did not come out well.

"I'm sorry to have to do this...I mean, I know I don't have to do it...I mean I hope you realize I appreciate..."

Mr. Iaello shook his head.

"No, no, Molloy. You are going and you are right to go. If you don't try things you will never know what is best for you. I think it is almost impossible to be satisfied with your life if you do not at least try some different things and taking some chances."

I smiled at him.

"Thank you. I really do..."

"Let's not talk about it anymore. We already did well enough. You are working tomorrow and I will see you then."

I nodded and went home without another word.

33

First List

I was nervous in bed the night before my first real day on the job with *The People for a Better World*. I thought every creak and bump in the night might be my first list of tasks dropping through the mail slot downstairs. The meetings, the training, the role-playing, and the whole drawn out experience seemed so strange and unlikely, it was almost hard to believe I was a single night's sleep away from the surreal becoming real. My thoughts flipped and spun and I woke up several times through the night, but in spite of it all I managed to get a reasonable night's rest.

Like a child at Christmas, I imagined forcing myself to stay awake to watch someone deliver the list to my door. Like most children I did not have the will or the desire to follow through on the dare, knowing silently it would spoil any hope that benevolent magic might truly exist.

The first instant I awoke when it was actually morning I went to the top of my stairs and looked down toward the door at the bottom of them. The envelope was there on the bottom step below the mail slot. I brought it upstairs to the kitchen and opened it carefully with a knife, making sure not to tear the contents within. I am embarrassed to write that I trembled slightly in anticipation. Role-playing training never gave the impression that performing the tasks would be overly difficult or complicated. I had no logical reason to be nervous, yet I trembled.

When I got the envelope open I was surprised to see my list of tasks for the day was very short. I supposed they were easing me into the job.

This was how my first day at the new job unfolded:

At 08:30 I arrived at the Bayview O-Train Station. As described, there was a middle-aged man with thinning, gray-blonde shoulder length hair. True to the task list description he also wore sunglasses and a hooded, red sweatshirt. As instructed, I asked this man the time and complimented him on his sunglasses. The man simply nodded to me in a semi-friendly manner which I figured was a gesture of thanks for the compliment. However, when I then, as instructed, asked the man if he knew what time it was he did not respond at all. I then walked home, also as per my instructions. My first official task was complete. Supposedly, the world was a little better.

Next on the list was two hours of data entry. Even being painstakingly careful and triple-checking my work the entries took less than one hour.

Training had taught me I could do anything I wished between tasks as long as I was on time and focused for the next task on the list. However, on my first day I did not feel comfortable letting my mind or body stray too far from the next task even though it was an hour away. I sat reading at the kitchen table within clear view of the stove's clock which I checked about once per page. After a little reading I switched over to jotting down some points about my day so far for my diary.

I was having difficulty concentrating on either my reading or my diary so I picked up my list of tasks and studied the next one I was to perform. I paced around the apartment trying to envision how it might play out.

When the time arrived I walked about eight blocks to a new take-out pizza shop, Pizza-Plus. I was to enter the shop at 11:30. I left my apartment a little early in case I bumped into any unexpected delays on route to the pizza place. I did not meet any resistance so I extended my walk a couple of extra blocks to fill in the time. It was a pleasant fall day with only scattered clouds and plenty of sunshine. The air was just below skin temperature and the world felt still.

My watch read exactly 11:30 when I entered the Pizza-Plus and followed my script. I was the only customer.

"One Hawaiian slice, please, and could you throw some hot peppers on top for me?"

"Yes, sir."

The guy sprinkled a few slices of pickled banana pepper onto my slice then slid it into the oven. His hands were sanitized with a pair of thin rubber gloves he pulled in a wad from his pants pocket as I was telling him my order.

"Will that be everything?"

"Yes."

"Two fifty, please, sir."

I gave him three loonies.

"Keep it," I said.

"Thank you, sir."

"No problem. Say, you might be able to help me out with something if you don't mind. You seen Dean today?"

The guy shrugged.

"Dean?"

"Yeah, pretty big fellah. Usually wears a baseball cap, leather jacket, and maybe sunglasses. Scruffy type. Generally says as little as possible."

I thought I might see a glimpse of recognition in the man's eyes, but nothing clear enough to be certain. What did I care anyway? My job is done no matter what he said or what he is thinking. Who the hell was Dean anyway?

The pizza guy said, "That kind of describes a lot of guys around here."

134

He takes my slice out of the oven and passes it over to me.

I say, "Ah well, thanks anyway."

"Thank you too, sir. Take care."

I ate the slice on the way home. I was not sure about the banana-peppers, but I was hungry enough to give it a try. I was pleasantly surprised and made a mental note to give hot banana-peppers another go.

Back home I had around forty minutes to kill before my final task. Afterward, there is a bit of optional data entry if we had time. How could we possibly not have enough time? I tried to read some more to pass the time, but I was not in the mood. Writing did not work either although I managed to scribble down a few more points about my day for the diary.

I paced the apartment. My mind was stimulated, but unable to find anything to grasp onto. I assumed our first day was unusually easy to give us a chance to ease into the process of completing our list of tasks. Was it even possible any of this had anything to do with making the world a better place? If not, what was the purpose?

Eventually, I paced and fidgeted long enough that it was time for the last task. I took another walk, approximately one kilometre and then simply stood in front of the Scotiabank entrance on the corner of Preston Avenue and Norman Street for fifteen minutes. If anyone should ask me a question I was not to give them any information of any kind. Examples are given: If someone should ask me the time, I do not have a watch. If someone should ask me directions, I do not know the way. How am I doing? All right, I guess. What am I up to? Not much.

Once again, I leave my apartment allowing myself a little extra time. There are no delays so I do an extra loop to arrive exactly on time. As it turned out, not a single person looked at me let alone asked me a question. After fifteen minutes of standing I retraced my steps back home then carefully performed my optional data entry.

I was finished my first day at the new job and although I had done next to nothing I felt bushed. I did not have the internal energy required to continue to question the validity of my new role in the universe. Enough was enough. I had been doing that all day. Duncan had warned us this would be a part of the job at first and he was right. I would either grow into the position or I would not. It would be a matter of faith in the end. So far I was not feeling the faith, but Duncan told us these feelings were common in the beginning.

Though it was getting into fall it was a decent temperature outside. I opened some of the windows in my apartment to let a breeze blow through to freshen the air. I decided to go for a run to clear my head. I was weary, but running often boosted my spirits and my energy level.

34

Nudged Toward The Brink

The lists did not get more coherent, intuitive, or comforting with each day of practice. Through the fall and deep into the winter I could not come to terms with my position as a *Person for a Better World*. It was beyond my power to conceive how the trivial, ridiculous tasks I performed made a positive difference in the universe. If anything, it was slightly easier to conceive of a conspiracy theory and imagine my tasks as a complicated series of planned, subtle manipulations designed to influence the reins of fortune and power. Admittedly, the conspiracy theory is no saner, but nonetheless it felt more believable to me. Then again, I may have been nudging toward the brink at the time.

During winter, struggling and slipping through the snow, cold, and slush to complete my inane duties made the experience feel even more steeped in futility.

The mystery of *The People* was something I could not get out of my mind. Even though I knew I had been over it from every angle many times I still tried to make sense of the phenomenon. Even the previous oasis of my long walks and runs were often invaded by hallucinatory visions of *The People*'s convoluted web weaving through my thoughts. My dreams were often nonsense, paranoid streams of consciousness that my sleeping mind felt compelled to make sensible. But awake or asleep it never made sense. The mystery of *The People* was breaking me down.

My crumbling mental state would have been evident to the reader had they seen my original, unedited diary during these months, but the read would have been a very tedious process. Even I was a little startled as I took up the chore to reread and edit the original pages; repetitive, mistrustful, and untethered as they were. I thought it better to hope the reader take me at my word rather than test their resolve and patience with the original prose.

During days off from my regular, mind-eroding duties with *The People*, I often checked in for rehab by doing shifts at Groovier's and reconnecting with my previous, more rational existence. It helped me get my feet temporarily back on the ground to refortify my defences.

I wondered many times, the obvious question, whether enough was enough and I should except that *The People for a Better World* was simple not for me, but something kept me going. I was barely sane at the time, but trying to find possible clues as to the motives of *The People* buried within the words of daily lists of my duties kept me struggling along. And the compensation was good. I suppose a combination of these factors kept me hanging on during my initial months with *The People*.

Also, Duncan had drilled into us from the beginning that what I was going through was typical and that we could often work through these doubts, make peace with them, and be successful in our new careers. His words did not prepare me for how excruciating my doubts could be, but he warned us several times nonetheless and I felt that counted for something, gave me hope my doubts would subside. Besides, I always sensed Duncan liked me. He even said he thought I was a special fellow and I did not want to let him down if I could avoid it.

I have called Duncan twice with my concerns and neither time did he express disappointment. He only assured me I was not alone in my struggles, not the only member calling him with similar troubles. In fact, both times Duncan reminded me that leaving *The People* was something that sometimes happened when a member could not get comfortable with the philosophy and the routine. It was as if he was holding the door open for me to quit if that is what I wanted.

I had been tempted to speak with Mr. Iaello about my work with *The People*, but I was unable to bring myself to do it for a number of reasons. It was against the rules to discuss People work with non-People. Also, it was difficult for me to imagine an honest conversation with Mr. Iaello about my work with *The People* without him believing I had gone insane. Then, if I managed to convince him I was telling the truth, how would I explain why I had not quit the idiotic job if quitting was an option?

I was paranoid as well. Even to myself, as I edited my diary, the paranoia sometimes leapt off the page as I read and drastically rewrote this tangled section of my diary. I worried quitting might only be a code name for being reclassified in a less voluntary manner. As I mentioned, conspiracy theories were sometimes easier for me to swallow than the beneficent theory of *The People*.

Lastly, I would be dishonest if I did not mention that old-fashioned greed was a factor in me going above and beyond the call of duty to salvage my career with *The People*. I was putting away significantly more money with *The People* than I was at Groovier's, plus I still had my part time Groovier's pay and tips. In addition, it seems *The People* felt I kept my expenses low enough to deserve a significant expenses bonus tagged to every pay deposit. *The People* covered my basic living expenses so my paycheck was essentially free cash flow. Since I was working so much with two jobs I had little time or desire to spend cash on entertainment. On my rare days off it felt luxurious enough just to lounge around the apartment drinking coffee. My savings were becoming impressive.

Further, despite my scepticism of the whole operation, my pay stubs indicated I had earned three performance bonuses during these initial months. Apparently, as long as one performed the discombobulating, yet relatively simple tasks as they were described, this was enough to merit a performance bonus. Apparently, my heart did not need to be in my work.

So my best guess as to what kept me plugging along with *The People* was some strange mix of going crazy, making more money than I ever dreamed, maybe looking for a father figure in Duncan, and still hoping to belong to some noble group of individuals. I seemed to attain just the right balance of things to keep me from quitting, and also to barely avoid going completely out of my mind.

I am not proud to say that I think pride was also involved. Even though the nonsense I performed in the disguise of making the world a better place angered me and insulted my common sense, I did not want to let *The People* beat me. If I could just hang on long enough maybe I could witness the collapse of *The People*'s mirage under the weight of its own lies. After all, how could such a thing endure indefinitely? But perhaps this notion was only another symptom of being nudged toward the brink.

And in the end, despite these venomous declarations, a kernel within me trusted Duncan. This small part of me hoped for the opposite of my paranoid madness, that with dedication and effort I might understand or at least accept the ways of *The People* and join them in spirit as well as duty. My life so far had programmed me to believe that nothing worth having came without a fight. Maybe this was just another spiritual battle I had not yet won.

Anyway, I stayed on. I kicked an empty can into a sewer. I told someone he looked like someone I knew from Oakville. I applied for part time work as a meat cutter with a false identity, qualifications, and contact information. I bought a small bag of Harvest Cheddar Sun Chips and left them in someone's mailbox. And so on. And so on. To make a better world.

Mostly, I tried to cling to my sanity.

35

Moon Dreams

The moon was alive. It was with me, floating just above me out of my reach, much smaller than the real moon with a soothing, pale yellow glow. It was beautiful, radiant, and benevolent. The moon spoke to me and sought my help. It believed in me.

I was in my room in Brockville as a younger child. The moon's smiling face loomed large in the window urging me to be its teammate. The moon wanted me to move a shell I kept on my desk onto a higher shelf in the corner of my room. It wanted me to close the curtains a little bit. I did both and the moon was extremely happy. Its face smiled and beamed a brighter yellow.

Then the moon wondered if the room might look better with a grey pillow instead of a beige pillow.

I said, "I don't think it really matters too much."

The moon laughed and lifted its face to the sky.

"Maybe not," it laughed. "Maybe not, but for some reason I think it might though...do you mind to give it a try?"

It was a harmless request and the moon was very friendly and polite so I did it.

"Thank you so much for humouring me...and I do think it fits in a tiny bit better there. You've made me very happy."

~

The moon again. This time it was outside with me at what seemed to be a well-groomed campsite on an island. The moon was as glowing, friendly, and benevolent as before. This time the moon had no chores for me. We were only there to celebrate the wondrous beauty of the night and the joy of life itself. And wondrous it was with a comfortable, refreshing and crystal clear night sky.

We danced together and everything seemed right. The moon could fly, of course, and I almost could too. My feet barely touched the earth as I spun with the moon smiling in front of me keeping perfect step. The moon was formally dressed in that vague, dream-like way, lacking fine detail. It wore a black vest, pants, and shoes. A small black hat was dwarfed by the smiling, glowing, pale yellow face.

With my light, nimble step I thought to get behind the moon and look at its back to see if my hallucination of a living moon was complete enough to retain the formal attire from a rear view. But no matter how I danced, leapt, or negotiated our movements I could not get behind the moon for a look. The moon would only smile fondly at me and encourage me face to face.

~

I decided it was time that the moon and I lay our cards on the table. I felt a profound attraction to the moon and desired its well-being, but something about it did not seem quite right. What could be wrong with the moon? It was just the moon. It could not be any other way. Still, I could not be content with the moon exactly how it was unless it could clear some issues up for me.

To its credit the moon had no problem meeting face to face to set things straight. I was relieved and happy to find this out. I felt buoyed with light and hope on my way to the first meeting with the moon to set matters straight. But the moon did not show up. It said it showed up at the agreed upon time which was later than the time I believed we agreed to meet. We carefully arranged the next meeting time, but still one of us got the meeting place mixed up and we did not meet.

Somehow or another busy schedules, miscommunications, and untimely events continued to keep us from sitting together and setting matters to rest.

I had this type of dream on several occasions and they never ended...I simply woke up frustrated in between futile attempts to meet with the moon and set my mind at ease.

36

Paranoid

I write this chapter for the same reason I felt compelled to write a brief summary of my recurrent moon dreams. I have mentioned that while rereading and editing my diary I encountered frequent passages where I was disturbed by the haunted, paranoid view that described my daily interactions in connection with *The People for a Better World*. Below are a few collected excerpts, a small set of episodes I remember when I must have been closest to the edge.

Today, on the way home from my last task for *The People*, slowly rolling three oranges, one at a time, down the center isle of a small, independent grocery store on Wellington Avenue, every person I walked pass seemed to have a hidden agenda. In the back of my mind I knew this was unlikely to be true, but the notion that each person was taking careful record of every movement I made was much stronger than the quiet voice within me whispering not to be ridiculous. At the peak of my paranoia I would have sworn my thoughts were being separated, analyzed, and judged. The records were then swiftly transferred to People headquarters for further analysis.

As I got closer to home the feelings gradually dissipated, but it was several minutes before the flushed tingling upon my flesh subsided and my breathing slowed to normal. Days later, even with no further similar episodes, just the memory of that state of mind made me nervous for my sanity.

~

In a rare effort to entertain myself at the movie theatre I went alone to a screening of The Sixth Sense. The movie was getting a lot of buzz and I had an unusual evening off from both my jobs, when the itch to see the movie built up inside me enough to make the effort to go.

I had been to the movies few enough times that anticipation was a strong, positive thrill within me as I tucked down in the darkness with my popcorn and waited for the ads to end. I had a good spot just off center near an aisle with nobody on either seat beside me despite the fact the showing was well attended.

Unfortunately, just as the movie started, I became gradually convinced one person in the audience was an agent for *The People for a Better World* sent to observe how I reacted to certain events that would happen during the movie.

Underneath the stress I suspected the paranoia was all in my mind, but the feeling remained. I could barely concentrate on the movie. I spent the majority of the time crouched down in my seat behind my popcorn using my peripheral vision to attempt to discern which moviegoer was keeping an eye on me. Without success in noticing any suspicious behaviour, but also unable to enjoy the film, I left long before the movie ended.

~

I had another day working through my tasks, convinced *The People* were watching my every move. The air felt thick with invisible eyeballs. My skin was warm and clammy all day despite a moderate temperature. I worried the persistent perception of being watched would affect the performance of my tasks and then the eyes would have something negative to report back to *The People*. This was no way to live.

The feeling persisted well past work hours in my apartment. I imagined peepholes and electronic spy devices in the walls, ceilings, computer, and appliances. Eventually, around dusk, I decided to leave the apartment to see if I could shake off the awful sensations within me by walking along the river.

Gradually, it worked.

The quiet, persistent murmur of the river, the fading light from the sky above me, and the city behind me, the solitude. All these things seemed to quell and push back the turmoil in my head and free my mind. I was a different man.

Gradually, these episodes were happening more regularly. It scared me. I was not sure what to do. Leaving *The People* was the most obvious choice, but I could not escape the notion that they would not let me leave so easily despite what Duncan had told us. More selfishly, it was difficult to deny I was earning and saving more money than I ever dreamed possible with *The People* and my additional work at Groovier's. Was it wise just to let it all go? What would I do?

For the moment I just kept walking; finally, at the end of the day, I was enjoying the freedom of a quiet mind. I went three miles at least, feeling less tethered to the Earth the farther I went until something snapped. As I entered a narrow archway of thick trees that darkened the sky, I felt (more likely hallucinated) the detection devices of *The People* leave me completely. It had been many minutes during my walk since I had even thought about the prying eyes of *The People*, but still I felt a distinct and sudden disappearance of any trace of their surveillance.

Relief swept through my being, literally taking my breath away for a couple of seconds. I stopped in my tracks and nearly sank to my knees, momentarily beginning to weep tears of joy before I realized what I was doing.

I realized I needed help.

Part 5

Refuge

37

More of the Same,
Then a Friendly Face

Initially, it was just another day at the office. During the morning I performed four tasks. I approached a bearded, dirty-looking fellow who looked about thirty years old and walked with a pronounced limp. He stood beside the highway off-ramp leading from The Queensway to Parkdale Avenue. He carried a cardboard sign with large printed words written in black marker.

```
Sick
No Money
No Job
No Food
Please Help
```

As instructed, I handed him the bag holding the six apples I picked up at a convenience store on the way. I spoke to him as instructed.

"Judy wants you to call her."

He took the apples from me, but did not seem impressed with them. He was more interested in Judy.

"Judy? How do you know her? Where is she?"

As instructed, I replied, "I don't know anything. I don't even know Judy. I was only asked to pass the message and to give you the apples".

"You can fuck your apples," he shouted, handing them back to me.

Then he dropped his cardboard sign and strode purposefully away with an obviously less pronounced limp.

My other chores were less eventful.

I smiled at a frumpy, middle-aged woman in a green jacket pulling a wheeled suitcase behind her on Bell Avenue.

I purchased a get-well card and envelope in a stationary store on Sparks Avenue then left the card on the counter just out of view of the cashier. As instructed, I left the receipt in the envelope with the card.

I sat in a Chinese café of some sort on Somerset Avenue and drank a mango bubble tea with pearls at the corner table furthest from the street. As instructed, I sat facing the corner and did not look around as I drank my bubble tea with pearls. The bubble tea was new to me. It seems to be a slushy/smoothie type drink and the pearls were slimy, spherical jujubes that got sucked up in the wide straw. I had never heard of such a thing and the pearls freaked me out a little when the first one shot into my mouth until I realized it was just slimy candy.

Afterward I had three hours to eat my lunch and perform less than two hours of data entry. The data entry still never took nearly as long as the estimated time on the task list.

My last task of the day required I travel to the Ottawa Civic Hospital on Carling Avenue to deliver something to my target without knowing the sender or anything about the target except for his name and hospital room number. The target was Christopher Jubien in ward D2-Trauma, room seventeen, bed two. My package was not really wrapped. It was in a Styrofoam, take-out soup dish and lid held shut with clear plastic wrap secured by an elastic around the Styrofoam.

My delivery looked to be some sort of electronic gadget that I suspected to be information technology. Even though information technology is not a particularly specific guess I am not sure why I even bothered guessing at all since I am useless regarding that sort of thing. It took me hours just to get my computer hooked up to the Internet the first time I tried.

None of this mattered; the patient was alone and unconscious in their room when I dropped off the package. He was hooked up to a bunch of needles, lines,

IV bags, and large monitors with shifting numbers and graphs. I did not understand what any of the readouts meant, but if I had to guess the outcome, things looked grim. I put the package on the bedside table as near to him as I could. My work was done.

Back down on the main floor on my way out I noticed Aggie in line at the Second Cup coffee shop, one of about ten small stores in the hospital mall. It surprised me how happy I felt to see her. I had not really thought about her except briefly over the past months. It made me realize that this People stuff was a lonely business. I was thrilled to see someone I recognized. I was nervous to approach her, but I forced myself knowing I would regret not even trying to say hello.

"Is that you, Aggie?"

"Molloy, hey, how's it going?"

"Alright, I guess. I just finished my last task for today. What about you?"

"Yeah, me too. Want to sit for a bit?"

"Sure. Ever had a red eye mocha?"

"No, what is it?"

"It's awesome. I'll treat. It's like a mixed drink for coffee. Espresso shot, mixed with coffee, and chocolate syrup for flavour and sweetness."

"Sounds pretty strong. I better have a small. I've already had a lot of coffee today."

"Me too. Two small red eyes, please."

"Anything to eat with that?"

"Not me. You, Aggie?"

"Nah, I'm good."

"Okay, they'll be ready for you on the side in a couple of minutes. That'll be six-forty-eight, sir."

"Okay. Aggie, see if you can find us a good spot and I'll bring the drinks over when they're done."

"Alright."

She grabbed a corner table and I followed her there when the coffees were ready.

"They better be good. Pretty expensive for a couple of smalls."

"I just get them once in a while for a treat or if I'm really tired. It's like three coffees in one."

She smiled and lifted her cup toward me.

"Cheers."

"Cheers."

We were only quiet for a few seconds before I asked her what I absolutely had to ask her. I kept my voice low. The hospital was a busy place and we were forbidden to speak with non-People about *The People*. I had to be sure not to be overheard.

"Are you getting used to this People thing...the tasks, the data entry, the ongoing mystery or whatever you want to call it?"

Aggie studied me for a few moments.

"Not really. You?"

"Not at all. Sometimes it makes me feel like I'm going crazy."

"Any improvement from the beginning like Duncan said might happen?"

"Honestly, no. At least I don't think so. Sometimes it's hard to remember how I feel one day to the next let alone over weeks and months. I guess some days are better than others, but I haven't noticed a clear progression. You?"

"Maybe. I do have occasional days where I don't wonder what the fuck I'm doing with my life. Some days I manage just to do my tasks and not think about it much and those days are okay."

"I guess I've had a few of those too, but not many lately."

Aggie smiled.

"It's nice to hear another opinion from a *Person*."

We laughed a bit before she continued.

"Even if we wanted to we're not supposed to talk about it with regular people and you're the only *Person* I've seen since we graduated."

I was a relief to hear I was not completely alone upon the Sea of Confusion.

"Same with me."

"Any news about Richard?"

"Nothing. You?"

Aggie shook her head.

"Not from you either until now. I even wondered a couple of times if the training was even real. I thought maybe you and Richard were in on the joke."

I laughed. More relief. It was not just me going out of my mind.

"I know; the whole thing really screws with your mind, eh?"

Aggie put her hands on her head and scrunched up her face. She flipped her hands off her head and made a soft kind of kaboom noise as if her skull were exploding.

"Crazy," she whispered.

With the smile she showed afterward it appeared Aggie was also relieved to discover she was not the only one struggling. Small talk flowed easily between us so that *The People* and our work did not continue to dominate the conversation.

As we talked I got the impression Aggie did not have an overwhelming social life, though it was doubtless fuller than my own. This hopeful observation, along with the fear that this enjoyable companionship might fade forever when we separated, gave me the courage to be more forward that I had ever been with a woman in my life. This amounted to a single sentence.

I said, "We should exchange numbers so we can meet up again if we want to sometime."

Thankfully, Aggie said, "For sure."

38

New Attitude

It was remarkable what a hint of potential interest from a female did for my frame of mind. Work was still a ridiculous, nonsensical chore, but it did not worry me nearly as much. I concentrated enough to be certain I completed my tasks accurately, but otherwise I wondered how Aggie really felt about me. I wondered if she might call or whether I was expected to be the one to call her. I fussed about my appearance and healthy living habits way more than usual. *The People* workdays were still a drag, but it no longer felt like they were chewing a hole in my spirit. Compared to before I bumped into Aggie, they passed quickly.

Aggie had me, a total noob, and a child when it came to relationships with the opposite sex, emotionally twisted from the beginning. I was elated at the prospect we might like each other, worried she might not reciprocate my interest, and confused as to what I was expected to do about it. Initially, I was content with only the glow of possibility, but each day that passed I figured I might be letting a potential window of opportunity close. My greatest wish was that it was her responsibility to contact me if she was interested, but I knew the reverse to be the norm.

After four days I decided I had to either call or just forget about it. I spent any time that was not spent concentrating on my tasks trying to get up the nerve to call and practicing what I might say.

I did manage to get my courage together enough to make the call. The anxious build up in my own mind turned out to be only a petty, local storm. This is how it happened after hours of stressful plotting.

"Hello?"

"Hi Aggie, it's Molloy."

"Hey Molloy. I was wondering if you were going to call me."

"Yeah, I kept thinking about it then I finally did."

"Good, so what's up?"

"Well, like we said when we exchanged numbers, I wondered if maybe you wanted to do something together."

"Sure, what'd you have in mind?"

"It might be a weird idea, but I thought since it's been pretty warm outside maybe we should go for a walk and chat after work someday. While we're doing that, if we feel like it, we can decide what else to do together."

"That's not weird. Sounds like a good plan. When?"

I had not planned that far ahead, but we worked it out and went for a walk together the next day after work.

39

Walk and Talk

The next day, Aggie and I met for a walk at Dow's Lake after work. We decided to walk around the canal since it allowed the journey to be flexible in time and distance. To walk around the whole thing would take hours, but there were many convenient turning points along the way so our walk could be as long or as short as we wanted. Also, around the canal were pedestrian paths with no motorized traffic. The fall weather was cooling, but it was still relatively mild and we were still snow free. It dipped below zero some nights, but no frost had stayed into the day.

"How's People work treating you?" Aggie asked.

"A bit better actually. I think it relieved a lot of stress just bumping into you at the hospital and finding out I wasn't the only one afraid I was losing my mind."

Aggie giggled.

"Me too. Thanks for accidentally bumping into me."

It was nice to see she had a sense of humour.

"It was no accident. It was on my task list."

Aggie's face looked briefly horrified before she realized I was messing with her. She laughed, but looked a little mad as she punched me in the arm.

"Don't even joke about it. You had me for a sec. I guess *The People* still have a grip on my brain, making me feel paranoid."

I smiled.

"Sorry, it just came out. I've spent so much time worrying about *The People*, and the weird shit we do, I probably have a thousand remarks like that stored up. I think in words, if that makes sense."

"I'm not sure."

"I guess I mean if I see or feel something that gets to me in some way, good or bad, my first instinct is to find the best words to describe what I feel or see."

"I think I get what you mean. I don't do that."

"What do you do?"

"Hmm. I never really thought about it...pictures more, I guess, and feelings. Words too, I suppose, but not how you said."

It got dark earlier now. It was not long into our walk before the sun began to fade. As always, I am condensing what happened and what was said to move the reader along, spare them the lulls in conversation, the minor sights, sounds, and activities that happen incessantly around us. For the reader I describe how it was for me at the time, mainly Aggie in focus by my side and the general surroundings blurred and distant in the background.

"Look over there," said Aggie.

Toward the West the sun was heading down over the horizon. Over the Experimental Farm where there were few buildings, we could see the horizon below a brilliant sky. It had a small band of rich red over the edge of the top of the sun, then a larger band of bright pink, then whitish orange, then clear, royal blue that gradually darkened as it distanced itself from the sun. I had never seen a sunset that way.

"Beautiful," I said.

The structured, perfect bands of colours seemed to blur and dissolve as we watched.

"Didn't last long," said Aggie.

"But we saw it."

"Yeah, don't you wonder how stuff like that happens?"

"I do, but I worry finding out might spoil it."

"What's that supposed to mean? Way to spoil a beautiful moment, Dinkus."

I suppose it was kind of a Dinkus thing to say. "Sorry. Thanks for pointing out the colours. It made the day worthwhile."

"Much better response."

We walked, outlining the canal while negotiating the other pedestrians, bicycles, and descending gloom. We negotiated silences too, but not too awkwardly.

Aggie asked, "So what do you do for fun?"

"Hmm, I read a lot. I jog some. I write a bit. I work a lot. I have another non-People job at a restaurant."

"Waiter?"

"Yeah, mostly, I guess. I help out however I can."

"I've waitressed before."

"Like it?"

"No. People are dicks to waitresses. Not just the guys either."

"It doesn't seem too bad where I am, but there are exceptions sometimes."

"My place was a sleazy, boozy place; I got treated like garbage by people who were garbage, customers and staff. I really didn't like it."

"My place is mostly a diner, not much drinking to get drunk. You know Groovier's?"

"On Gladstone? I've seen it. Never been inside. It looks freaky."

"It's only a little freaky in a laid back way, almost like they're retired party-goers."

"You like working there?"

"Yeah, I think so. Sometimes it feels kind of low level, but it makes a lot more sense than this People bullshit. At least you know what you're doing and why. Pay and tips are decent, but not as good pay overall as *The People*."

"I know, eh. When you take in all the expenses they pay for us, we get a lot for basically nothing as far as I can tell."

"I know. It drives me crazy trying to figure it out."

After we negotiated some more gloom and silence, Aggie asked me another question.

"So, any social hobbies? You said jog, work, and read."

"And write a little."

"Socially?"

"No."

"Anything else?"

"I guess not really."

"No friends?"

"No major friends anyway. I think I might be a bit of a loner or something. I kind of had a friend when I first moved to Ottawa, but they disappeared."

"Disappeared?"

"Vanished. It might have been drug related. I really don't know, they really did just disappear."

"Guy or girl?"

"Guy. Just someone I bumped into and hung out with a bit. We didn't really even have a lot in common. It just happened. I more wonder what happened to him rather than really miss him to be honest."

"That happened to me once too."

"Friend disappeared?"

"Yeah, I think it was drugs too, but I'll never know for sure."

"Good friend?"

"I thought so at the time, but not now. After a few days I felt better with her gone."

"It's weird, eh?"

Aggie nodded.

"It is."

I asked her, "Do you have any non-disappeared friends?"

"I suppose. It seems like most of my friends have moved on with careers or relationships and kind of left me behind. I still see them now and again, but less often and when we do it seems there's less in common and less to talk about."

Aggie seemed to become slightly sad at this turn in our conversation. I felt sorry for her though I expected I was more of a social outcast than her. Maybe she felt worse because she knew what she was missing. The only thing I could think to say that might make her feel better was that I had never really had a close friend, but I was too embarrassed. I did not want her to think too strangely of me. Instinctively, I knew friendlessness was weird.

She said, "It doesn't sound like you have a girlfriend."

"No. You?"

She laughed a little.

"I don't have a girlfriend either."

"That's not what I meant, but you never know."

"True...and why not?"

"Yeah, why not? Whatever. Do your thing."

"What's your thing?"

"I'll assume you mean what's important to me or my goal in life rather than whether I like boys or girls. I don't know. I'm pretty dedicated to my hobbies, running, writing, and reading. I'm working a lot trying to save up money to give me some freedom and options. The true answer is I don't have a clue. You?"

"That is what I meant."

She thought a few more seconds, then answered, "I'm also undecided."

We smiled at each other and shook our heads in unison; two mostly blank slates that were probably not gay.

Aggie said, "You can probably tell I don't have a boy-friend."

I was glad it was dark. Due to that simple comment I could feel the blood rush into my face like a five-year-old boy. I could barely think straight or respond.

I only managed to basically whisper, "I'm glad."

She took my hand and we soon turned to head back. We did not say much, but we did not have to say any-thing. We had figured it out for the most part. We could relax a little.

40

The Date

On a Friday night, only a couple of days after our walk by the canal, I walked to Aggie's apartment to pick her up. The late fall season was experiencing a cold snap with temperatures hovering near zero. It was early evening, overcast and almost dark. I was comfortable in a light jacket, but that may have been because I was wearing my only dress jacket underneath. I also had on my newest looking shirt with a collar and my seldom-used best pants. I also wore my best shoes, but they looked more past their prime than I remembered. I was a little regretful of them.

Toward the end of our canal walk Aggie and I had decided our date would be out for dinner. She wanted me to pick the place so she might be surprised. I put a significant amount of effort into the matter with Internet and door-to-door research. I had chosen Som Rudee's, a Japanese steakhouse where the elegance seemed friendly and laid-back rather than upscale and formal. I reserved a large comfortable half-circle booth. I also spoke with the waiter and advanced him half of his respectable tip as a reward for excellent service during our date.

I surprised even myself with the focus and dedication I put into trying to ensure our evening together was special. I did not have to think much further about it or put in a super-human effort. I just started planning and getting things started as soon as the date was set. The effort came to me naturally though it was unlike anything I had ever done, as if some friendly spirit decided to jump into my skin and help me along.

The time had arrived. I rang the doorbell at Aggie's apartment.

Aggie opened the door and her beauty actually surprised me a little, stupid as that sounds. She looked better than ever and I couldn't imagine why she would want to hang around with a guy like me. She was not super dressed up, just perfectly dressed. Her hair went with her top, which went with her light touch of gray eye shadow, which went with the length of her skirt, which went with the colour of her eyes, which went with her perfume, which went with the temperature of the evening air. I may have been delirious, but that is how I felt at the time.

I did not even try to say much, knowing I would blow it.

I managed a barely audible, "Hi."

She seemed to know what I meant.

"Well, thank you. You look nice too."

She put a hand on one of my cheeks, pulled the other cheek toward her, and kissed it. Then she walked to the edge of the porch and lifted her forearm into the night to gauge the temperature and the breeze.

She asked, "Without spoiling the surprise, about how far is the walk?"

"Around a kilometre."

"I better grab my winter coat even though it doesn't go with my outfit."

"Yeah, especially to keep warm for the walk home."

"What about you?"

"I have another jacket on underneath, but I might wish I wore a warmer coat later."

Aggie shook her head.

"Boys."

It was already getting noticeably cooler, but I saw no point in being a wimp about it at this point.

"I'll be fine. I don't get cold that easily."

In truth, the chilly air did not bother me at all. I was more intent upon Aggie's presence and letting the night unfold naturally without me getting in the way by saying or doing something stupid. That was my primary goal.

Other than the chill it was perfect outside for walking to a nice restaurant. It was quiet, the air was still, the sky was clear, and the moon was nearly full. Every few blocks the scent of burning fireplace wood livened our senses. We did not say a lot, just walked close and held hands. Aggie radiated warmth and smelled faintly tropical.

She asked, "So are you going to tell me which restaurant we're going too?"

"Nope. Let's do it like we planned. I've got everything arranged and we'll just see how it goes."

I was sorely tempted to tell her this was my first date, but it did not feel right somehow. It was the truth, but a confession should have been made earlier if that is what I intended. Now it would just be an excuse in case the date was a failure.

We did not talk as much as one might expect considering we were alone during a fairly long walk to the restaurant. It was a pleasant quiet walk, tucked close together and breathing air that smelled faintly fresh with a hint of excitement, and perhaps with the scent of encroaching winter. However, I was not secure enough to let the silence drag on indefinitely. I tried to think of something to say that was not too stupid.

"Beautiful night, eh?"

Not stupid, just inane.

She squeezed my hand.

"It's beautiful."

After a moment she added, "Can I at least try to guess where we're going tonight?"

"Sure."

"We seem to be headed toward Preston Street. Are we going to Little Italy?"

"Yes we are."

"Oh, I love Italian."

"Tsk, tsk. Don't get ahead of yourself. Just relax a see what happens."

She looked at me sceptically, thinking.

"Little Italy, but not Italian?"

"I didn't say that."

She laughed.

"Now you're just trying to mess with me."

"We'll be there in no time and the mystery will be solved."

I had noticed Som Rudee's a couple of times before I even imagined having a date with anyone. Besides being a non-Italian restaurant in Little Italy, the corner building had an unpretentious, elegant charm that caught my eye whenever I passed. I never seriously considered dining there before now because I was generally cheap with my personal expenses.

Visiting the restaurant at an off-hour time when it was not busy, I discovered the same charm within the building as without. I was shown around the place. The atmosphere, the music, the staff, and the menu all seemed just right. I hoped Som Rudee's understated elegance would not intimidate a pair of well-meaning pawns trying to pass as upscale for a couple of hours. Soft, jazzy, nightclub music played gently in the background. The lighting was intimate, but warm and not overly dim. The colours were rich; a lot of browns, greens, and pinks mostly in soft shades with a few deeper hues for contrast. There were a number of large paintings or prints upon the walls that were willing to melt into the background, but kindled interest if one's focus lingered.

While being given a quick, preliminary tour of the restaurant I connected well with two staff members. The hostess, who I presumed to be Japanese, gave me the impression she was at least co-owner of the establishment. The gentleman I met was a waiter with a mild, interesting accent that might have been Jamaican.

Both of them were very attentive and helpful when I explained my plan and described how I hoped the date would go. They had even volunteered small touches to my plan that sounded good and let me know they were on the same wavelength. Their attentiveness put my fears of appearing foolish at ease. I reserved a half-circle booth that could have comfortably seated four, before I left. I also made some arrangements with the waiter.

The hostess noticed us and recognized me as soon as we arrived. She saved me the embarrassment of acknowledging I had forgotten her name. She came near and gently bowed her head as we hung our coats in the small lobby near the dining room entrance.

"Good evening Mr. O'Grady. Your reservation is ready. This must be the lovely date you mentioned."

She looked at Aggie.

"I am Anika. I am honoured to be your hostess tonight."

Aggie surprised me a little with her graciousness.

"Thank you, Anika. I'm Aggie. This is a beautiful place. Probably the nicest restaurant I've ever been inside."

Anika smiled.

"Very kind of you to say."

We were shown to our table and slid into the booth. The curved coral-pink upholstery was plush and very comfortable. It was well cushioned, but firm enough to allow us to sit well at the table. I could tell by Aggie's demeanour she was impressed. This gave me a needed shot of confidence. We smiled at each other across the table.

When we were settled, Anika asked, "Do you have any questions for me?"

"I don't think so," said Aggie.

I shook my head.

"Everything's great."

"Very well, I will leave you to get a feel for the place and I will have Lewis drop by in a little while to assist you. He will be your server. Thank you for coming. I hope you have a wonderful evening."

In unison, we said, "Thank you."

Lewis. I was thankful Anika said his name. Once again I had failed to commit it to memory. I could see his face clearly in my mind and remember most of the details about our conversation. For some reason it was always names that gave me trouble.

I took a deep breath and looked around. Everything felt perfect; the lighting, the music, the spacing of the tables. Apparently, my date felt the same way.

"I love it here already. Great choice. And definitely a surprise. I had guessed a lot of places in my mind, but not this one."

I smiled.

"Only the best for the best, as they say."

"Do they say that?"

"I don't think so actually, but it sounds like something they would say."

Aggie smiled back.

"You're sweet."

Suddenly, I was much less nervous. It seemed I had done a good job at arranging the date. We sat like children waiting to go downstairs to the living room on Christmas morning. We made small talk and soaked in the atmosphere until Lewis arrived.

"Mr. O'Grady, welcome. Who is this lovely lady accompanying you this evening?"

"Hi, Lewis. This beautiful lady is Aggie. Aggie, meet Lewis."

"Nice to meet you, Lewis."

"The pleasure is all mine, miss. Thank you for coming."

Lewis cut an impressive figure. He was taller than average and large in a reasonably fit kind of way. He wore his tuxedo well. He was late-middle aged and had a smooth, dark-chocolate complexion. His voice was soft, but he had a deep, cutting tone where his words always came through sharply. His accent was subtle and difficult to pinpoint. I kept thinking Jamaican, but it could easily have been something completely different. I have very little experience with accents since Brockville has very few of them. I had already been exposed to a hundred times more accents in my relatively short stay in Ottawa than the rest of my life combined. I decided to ask him.

"I like your accent, Lewis, but I can't place it. Do you mind telling me? I keep wondering."

"Of course, it's no secret. A long time ago I grew up in Ghana. Around the time I became a man, I came to Canada."

"Thanks, Lewis. I never would have guessed Ghana so I'm glad I didn't try."

"Yes, Ghana is far from here and not spoken about much in this part of the world. It has been so long since I visited I suspect I would no longer know the country. However, we are celebrating something else entirely tonight and we should not let ourselves be led astray. May I get you two anything to drink while you look over the menu? We have several kinds of juice or pop. Or perhaps I could interest you in a nice glass of wine to toast your special night?"

I think Lewis suspected we might be underage, but was willing to overlook it. I knew nothing about wine. I was afraid to speak and make an ass of myself. I spoke up anyway since I had to say something.

"I will have a glass of wine, please, but I think I would have better luck if you picked it for me. My wine knowledge is pretty limited to be honest."

"All right, sir. Will you be having steak tonight?"

"Yes."

"Fine, I will choose a nice red for you to go with your steak. And the lady?"

"Hmmm. I'd like you to pick a glass for me as well please, Lewis, but I would prefer a dry, white wine even though I will probably be having steak too. I've had better luck with white wine in the past. Whichever you think will work out the best."

"Very well. I am sure I can come up with something. I will ask the chef's opinion as well."

Aggie looked pleased smiling.

"You're the best, Lewis," she said.

Lewis smiled back and gave us a small bow before he left.

"I shall return," he said.

We were magically alone, temporarily accepted into a world that was normally beyond our means. I felt happy, special, and in love. Could that be true? Was it even possible an inexperienced yokel like me, completely out of his element, was in love? Maybe not, but it was a great feeling, one I wanted to enjoy without thinking about it too much for the moment. Could Aggie be feeling anything similar? The answer almost did not matter for several minutes. Everything glowed from within and Lewis was our spiritual guide in a new frontier. Our new frontier might just be a dream balloon in my mind, but it was a pleasant, harmless one if the air was not let out too quickly.

With Lewis' aid we were not embarrassed by our initial confusion regarding the menu. The layout and descriptions on the menu were different from those I was accustomed to, but in the end we managed to order a small filet mignon for each of us and share a multitude of other things; a lobster tail, crab rolls, buttery seasoned mushrooms, and a collected variety of perfectly steamed vegetables.

We both nursed and savoured our wine. I was not keen on it at first, but gently it grew on me as I sipped down the glass. I could feel the wine in my head before I was even half finished. The effects amplified certain things and left others in the background.

Our meal was exquisitely paced, never rushed, and never awkwardly empty. Romance was in the air more than I had previously even imagined possible. If our lower limbs accidentally bumped under the table we smiled and lingered. I believe we secretly sought this hidden contact a couple of times. We shared everything except our separate steaks. We talked about everything except our work for *The People*. By unspoken agreement that was forgotten and put aside for the time. I ate roughly twice as much as Aggie of everything we shared. We both felt too full for dessert.

At times I had to rein myself in from talking excitedly about some book I was reading or how I was getting into running. These things were too solitary for our intimate meeting of sharing and finding common ground. I was simply eager to share myself with Aggie now that she seemed open to the idea. Still, I tried to keep these outbursts to a minimum and check them before they went on too long.

Shortly after I managed to quiet one of these outbursts near the end of our meal, Aggie offered her hand across the table to hold mine. She squeezed and rubbed my fingers a little, watching me quizzically a few seconds before speaking.

She said, "You seem like a very honest person... naturally, I mean."

I was not sure how to reply. It seemed the kind of statement where she might be saying something other than what the words said. I shrugged.

"I try."

She laughed and rolled her eyes a little.

"Of course," she said.

Again I felt as if I was missing something.

"Don't you try to be?" I asked.

She thought for a few seconds.

"Yeah, I guess. You just don't seem to have to think about it as much as some people. That's all I meant. That's how it seems anyway. Maybe I was just thinking out loud."

Then she chuckled and said, "Or maybe you're just a great liar."

"Or maybe I'm a vampire."

"Don't be...too trendy."

"Alien?"

"Also trendy. Just you is fine. Being honest is a good thing. It's a compliment."

"I do take it as a compliment. Thanks. Now that you mention it, I do think about things like that quite a bit."

"What, being honest?"

"Not exactly. More like what's true. Try to figure out how I really feel about things."

I did not mean it in any particular way, but Aggie took it as a cue. She tickled my palm with her fingertips.

"How do you feel about me? Thought about that any?"

"I suppose you seem to be fairly awesome."

"Pretty?"

"Very."

"Sexy?"

"Yep."

"Smart?"

"A genius."

She took her hand away.

"Now I know you're lying, Mr. Honesty."

She pretended hurt feelings.

"I guess you're right. I don't know you well enough to know if you are a genius, but you seem pretty smart."

She gave her hand back and smiled at me.

"That's more believable anyway."

Aggie continued, "You seem smart for sure in a quiet way. I think you're a bit younger than me, but sometimes it's hard to tell. You seem younger in some ways, but more mature in others. What do you think?"

"I don't know. I've never really thought about it much. I read a lot, so I guess I'm smart in that way. I'm probably a bit of a social doofus, so maybe young in that way. I did okay in school. Not super, but better than average. I usually did my homework and studied for tests, didn't go out much. I guess it all fits together. Otherwise, I figured we were around the same age. Aren't we?"

Aggie winked at me across the table.

"I just wondered if you wondered how old I was, since I wondered how old you were sometimes. That's all."

I pointed at the wine glass.

"Technically, I'm not quite old enough to be drinking this quite yet. You?"

"Recently legal."

"See, pretty close."

For some reason I did not like talking about our ages. I was glad Lewis appeared to check in on us.

"Looks like a certain fashionable young couple have good appetites. You've done well."

Aggie complimented everything.

"The food, the service, the atmosphere, everything is awesome."

I nodded in agreement.

"That's nice to hear folks. Thanks very much."

Lewis then rubbed his hands together in front of his chest mischievously. His Ghanaian accent became slightly more pronounced as he lost himself in whatever plan he had cooked up. He spoke quietly so the other guests would not hear. This was not difficult as the occupied tables had generous space between them.

"Now you may not know it, honoured guests, because I have been trying to stay out of the way to allow you to enjoy each other's company, but I have been keeping an eye on you two this evening. Seeing your young romance get its start has pulled me in, and I would like to contribute to it."

Our waiter's enthusiasm was his own, not something we had planned together when I made arrangements at the restaurant. He seemed genuine and his manner was contagious. Aggie looked slightly incredulous, but also looked bright and alert as if she were watching a magic trick she could not figure out. I felt the same way.

"First," asked Lewis, "may I confirm that neither of you are driving tonight?"

"We're walking."

"I thought so. I would like to offer both of you a special coffee that I invented myself as well as a dessert for the two of you to share. The special coffee is wonderful, but it does have alcohol in it. If you prefer, I can do the same thing for you with high quality regular coffee. Either way it is my gift to you to wish you the best in your new relationship. What can I say? For whatever reason you two take me back to when I was young, makes me nostalgic, and makes me want to put something in. What do you say?"

I was a little dumbfounded and touched by the gesture. I replied quickly to avoid becoming choked up.

"It sounds great, Lewis, but we'll pay for our whole dinner. We were going to get something any..."

Lewis interrupted.

"No, no, no. The Lewis Special is a secret recipe that is not on the menu. The only way to receive the Lewis Special is by a rare gift that only appears during moments of weakness in the giver."

Lewis giggled softly as if he was amused by his own words. I chuckled with him. His behaviour was pleasant, but surreal.

I said, "Okay, fine, but the dessert..."

Lewis's voice was quiet and friendly, but firm.

"It is all part of the same package. Will you accept it?"

He looked back and forth between us. Aggie and I looked at each other.

Together we said, "Yes."

Aggie added, "Thank you, Lewis."

She looked a little emotional and very beautiful.

"It is my pleasure," replied Lewis. "Now just relax. It won't take too long."

Lewis left our table, but the warm glow of his special attention remained. Aggie and I smiled at each other. She pointed at me and screwed up her face as if to ask if I had something to do with this sudden offer. I shook my head, "No".

As Lewis stepped away from our table he seemed to instantly regain his formal waiter's dignity as he approached another group. I was amazed at his seamless transformation from intimate, almost naughty, playfulness with us to a much more reserved yet equally attentive demeanour as he neared the older, better dressed patrons.

I looked back to Aggie. She had been watching me watching Lewis. There was affection in her eyes and I tried to project the same sentiment toward her. Something happened to me in those few short seconds we looked at each other. I wished I could give myself to her somehow, make her world better, but I did not know what to do. I was paralyzed by the gap between what I longed to achieve and my skill set.

After several long seconds I managed, "You look really nice tonight."

She reached across the table for my hand again.

"I feel nice. This is by far the best date I've ever been on, Molloy. Thank you."

That was exactly what I needed to hear. Before, I was nervous, feeling in love, and fascinated by what was going on around and within me, but now I was happy, sure I had finally landed in the right place at the right time.

"I'm glad you came. I'm pretty shy. I really had to work up the nerve to call you."

Aggie laughed.

"I'm glad you did. I wondered what you thought about me. It was hard to tell."

"Same for me. I wondered what you thought about me. Being on my own, this crazy Better World job, plus having another part-time job on top of that with unpredictable hours. My mind has been unsettled to say the least."

I did not want to blather on about my troubles and spoil the mood. I squeezed her hand and changed the direction of the conversation.

"Anyway, we made it here together and it's been better than I had even hoped. It's the best date I've been on by a mile too even though I have to admit I haven't been on too many."

None to be exact.

Aggie smiled.

"In a way, I'm not surprised. You kind of seem like a thoughtful, loner type a lot of the time. That's another reason I thought you might not ask me out even if you sort of wanted to."

I felt as if our conversation might be sneaking up on my past personal life and I was not sure I was ready to go there at that particular time. Once again, magical Lewis saved the day. He appeared with a polished silver trolley that shone even in the quiet light of the room. Coffee and dessert had arrived.

"Come on you two. You are in one of the lovebird booths with no chairs. You can shift along and sit as close together as you like. Dinner is over and dessert-a-la Lewis is on. It will be easier to share if you are sitting close together."

We barely hesitated before shifting around the booth toward one another until our hips touched. A rich bouquet of scents gathered over the table as Lewis served out his special treat. He produced and lit a candle smelling faintly of rose. It mixed with the smells of the coffee, the rich, sweet dessert, and the light perfume Aggie wore. I would have been content to sit there inhaling quietly for a long while.

Aggie knew what to do. She raised her coffee in a salute of honour toward Lewis. I followed her lead.

She said, "To our amazing night and waiter. To Lewis and to us."

I could only nod and glance back and forth thankfully between the two people responsible for my amazing night. I felt strangely separated from our little group for a few seconds, unable to do anything but bask in the glow of my good fortune. In retrospect, I may have simply relaxed for the first time during the date, as if the point had been reached where there was nothing I could do to completely ruin the evening. It had been a success.

Lewis replied, "Thank you. I am going to leave you now to enjoy yourselves and I'm not coming back until I'm sure you're finished. Take your time. You cannot rush the Lewis special."

When Lewis left it really felt like we were suddenly all alone. One of the tables nearest us had finished and left. Apparently, they had been the noisiest group of guests. The restaurant was almost silent except for the background music. We enjoyed a long, luxurious, and intimate dessert with alcohol and spice infused coffee. We held hands, leaned against each other, and made little noises of approval over the tastes.

The coffee was strong and rich with heavy whipped cream on top. The liquor and spices in the coffee reminded me of liquorice as well as hints of citrus. The chocolate dessert was so moist and rich it felt nearly liquid in my mouth. Banana and some unfamiliar spice mingled around the primary chocolate flavour. Though we were very full, we each ate as close to half as we could manage to divide it up. I remember our dessert together mostly as a pleasant, delicious blur.

By the time Lewis poked his head back to check in on us I was tipsy, happy, comfortable, and a bit delirious. I focused on complimenting Lewis quickly so I did not have to follow Aggie's lead for once.

"That was by far the best dessert and best coffee I've ever tasted...and I've had a lot of coffee."

I noticed I was talking too loud and toned it down before continuing.

"Thanks very much, Lewis."

Aggie squeezed my knee.

"Yes, thank you, Lewis. You made the night perfect."

"No. If I had been here doing exactly the same thing and it had just been one of you here the night would not have been what it was. I saw something in you two that made me want to help out and take part. All I may have done is help ease the flow. You did everything yourselves. It is your night, not mine."

Lewis's words made me feel choked up again. I felt like punching myself in the stomach for being such a wuss. What was wrong with me? I could not be that drunk from two drinks. I focused on words and speaking to separate myself from my emotional tangle.

"Whatever it was, Lewis, it wouldn't have been as good without you. That's for sure."

Lewis put his hand over his heart.

"I appreciate it. Now is there anything else I can do for you this evening?"

I looked at Aggie. She shook her head slightly. I agreed.

"I think we'll just take this perfect ending for what it is and head home. Just the bill please."

"I will be right back, Sir, Madam."

I let out a deep breath. I was feeling a little sweaty under my clothes and my head was still a stew of thoughts and emotions. Since we had moved close together in the booth I had been forced to fight off occasional erections. More recently I had been more like a shrivelled husk of a man on the verge of tears because the waiter thought we were a nice couple. I was a mess.

Aggie noticed.

"You alright, sweetheart?"

I leaned into her. I liked that she called me sweetheart.

"Yeah, I feel good. I'm just a bit of a lightweight when it comes to booze, I guess."

She laughed and punched me very gently on the chin.

"You big baby. Actually, I'm feeling pretty lightheaded too. Good, but more than I would expect from two drinks over a pretty long period of time. Must be the Lewis Special."

Lewis brought the bill and I tipped him enough extra to make up for his gift. The cynical part of me could not help wondering if this might have been figured into our exceptional waiter's calculations, but I shut those thoughts down quickly. Why spoil a good thing? We thanked our hosts for the wonderful evening and headed back out into the now much cooler night air. Aggie took my arm and pulled me tight so I did not regret my lack of a coat. We walked slowly and quietly, only commenting occasionally on how great the dinner was and thanking each other.

It may be in poor taste to kiss and tell, but this is a diary and despite the admitted liberties I have taken with its presentation my aim has always been at the center of the truth.

I do not remember how or why we decided, but we ended up at Aggie's place instead of mine in the end, probably because it was cold out and her apartment was closer. Without saying more than necessary, we made love twice, my first and second times. Aggie took control for most of the first time, and I played an improved role the second. Both were unbelievably great, but the second may have been a little more satisfying overall; I felt more useful.

Aggie fell asleep before I did. I lay awake for some time feeling calm, amazed, and entirely different than before. It seemed as if Aggie somehow realized I was awake even as she slept. She raised herself and looked drowsily at me before bumping down again with her arm across my chest.

"Humgnh?" she asked.

"Thank you," I whispered.

"Gungh," she said.

While waiting to drift off to sleep, among other things, I contemplated her words of wisdom and what they might mean within the new contexts of my rapidly changing world.

41

Opposing Forces

The following months with Aggie were the most peaceful, happy, fulfilling months of my life so far. *The People*'s antics were still annoying wraiths floating through my mind, but Aggie's light pushed their pain to the edge of my consciousness. I could wade through the murk knowing at the end of the day her company would refresh and cleanse me.

We spent more time together at her place than mine. Her place had a television, an audio system, and more comfortable furniture that two people could sit on together. She also had her own bathroom. My place seemed bigger and more open, but it was probably just because she had more furniture and décor. Also, whenever I was at her place there were two people occupying space instead of one. If I could compare the apartments in one sentence I would say hers was more fashionable, more comfortable, and had more amenities, while mine had better lighting from outdoors and seemed more solidly constructed. Her place was definitely better when a couple wanted to hang out inside.

Aggie expanded my universe. I tried new foods, I saw several movies, and my ears were opened to many different kinds of music. I shared affection, made love, and actually went out in public to do things with another human being. We discussed and decided what we would do together. I experimented (modestly) with my hair and wardrobe. I had my first best friend.

I think I helped Aggie in some ways as well. She told me I was the most reliable person she had ever met, the most trustworthy. She would not go into details, and I did not press, but she told me I helped her let go of some hidden grudges she held against the world. I got her to read a book or two I thought she would enjoy. It worked to the extent at least that she picked out, bought, and read one for herself. She started putting money aside for future opportunities. We started an entertainment fund: we put an equal amount of money into it each week to fund our "together" expenses. She even went jogging with me a few times.

I was sure we were soul mates and sometimes Aggie reluctantly agreed. She did not like to talk about it, feeling it was tempting the fates to say it aloud. She *would* say she was happy we found each other.

It was closer to bliss than I had ever even remotely considered.

But gradually, stealthily, inexorably, *The People* started to wear me down and turn the tide in my mind. I could describe the details of my agitating, incomprehensible tasks I did supposedly in the name of the greater good, and the gradually progressive decay of my state of mind, but you have already heard this story. The only thing different this time was that the inane and mundane tasks of *The People* had to gnaw through the protective, hopeful barrier of Aggie's companionship. It took time, but over months the slow grind of the tasks, bit by bit, made progress in dampening my spirits. I could feel my inner peace and control slipping again.

I tried to fight off the feelings and concentrate on the good things I had in my life, but before long I admitted I was not going to win the battle and approached Aggie about it.

"I have a confession to make. You know how you've been asking if something's bothering me?"

"Yeah, I thought so. I *do* know you, ya' know."

"I know. I was trying to handle it myself, but I'm having a tough time and I guess it's time to let you know."

"I'm listening."

"The tasks, *The People*, The Better World; all that stuff's all getting to me again. I just can't seem to find peace with it. It grates on me."

"I thought so. Have you even considered just quitting?"

"I've thought about it, of course. I don't know why, but something in me wants to keep holding on. Probably the people I feel a connection with, you and Duncan mostly. I don't want to lose that connection. But really we don't see Duncan much anymore anyway."

"There are other ways to stay connected than *The People for a Better World* you know. Other people do it."

"I know. It's just a subconscious feeling I'm trying to put into words. Why I don't just quit I mean."

"And the money and paid expenses."

We both laughed at that. It was true, but I only mentioned the moral ambiguity that was troubling me, not that I enjoyed the compensation.

"I do like the money and expenses, but it's been going on long enough I'm starting to think about admitting defeat."

"Duncan said from the start this might happen and he repeated it several times so obviously you're nowhere near the first *Person* to have this problem, right?"

"Yeah."

We were quiet a few seconds before I finally asked the question to which I was nervous to hear the answer.

"What about you? How are you dealing with everything these days? We haven't talked about it much."

"I'm actually doing better. I guess the good vibes I got from us coming together is still working for me. You're not trying to tell me something are you? Is my good vibe wearing off?"

I assumed she was joking by her tone.

"You're by far the best thing that's ever happened to me. I just cannot get in sync with this People shit. I thought I had it beat for a while, but I was wrong. You were just covering up the smell. Have you really started to figure it out? Please tell me about it. Maybe you can help me get my mind straight."

"I haven't figured anything out. I've just been able to put it aside more often. Sometimes the crazy feelings do start edging back into my brain and I still have the occasional edgy dream, but the money's good. They tell me exactly what they want me to do and I can follow instructions and complete my job generally without too much problem. They seem to appreciate what I do and don't bother me if I do what I'm paid to do. In my job experience that's a pretty good arrangement; clear manageable duties and a nice, liveable wage in return. I don't have to understand every little detail. That's not my job."

Just like Aggie had suspected the negative turn in my relationship with my People duties, I had suspected a positive turn in Aggie's mind. It put a crimp in one of the several plans I was trying to decide among. I asked anyway, maybe in desperation.

"Would you ever consider running away from *The People* with me? We have decent savings and some other work experience. We could start a new life together somewhere else, a new adventure."

"I don't think it's right to quit just when I feel like I might be easing into the job. It's very good pay and I'm somewhat relaxed in my life for the first time in ages. Don't forget Duncan also said some of us will get our head around the seeming contradictions of *The People*'s work and come to terms with it, not just that some of us will never come to terms."

Hearing her say the words made me realize my disappointment in them was selfish. I was disappointed that her view of her position had taken a positive turn because I wanted her to share my negative feelings. I tried to counteract my destructive attitude. My lingering, intuitive fear that I could not have one without the other, Aggie without *The People*, would not leave me.

"You should definitely keep at it if it's starting to work for you. I'm sorry to try and pressure you into my way of thinking. I think I was starting to panic a bit once I started to feel myself slip back to the creepy way it was after such an awesome time away from it."

Aggie smiled.

"I can sympathize with that, I think."

After a pause she said, "What about a compromise?"

"What do you mean?"

"Why not try a break before quitting?"

"What would I do?"

"Whatever you want, I suppose. You want my honest opinion?"

"Of course."

"Why don't you go away for a few weeks and see how it feels?"

"Away where?"

"Away from *The People*, from Ottawa, from me; see what happens to you?"

"What about Groovier's?"

"Couldn't you get a leave of absence there too? You're only part time."

"What about you?"

"I'll be here. Maybe it's time we spent a little time apart to see how it feels."

Was Aggie breaking up with me? I felt a little sick. "You want to spend some time apart?"

"I don't necessarily want to, but it might be a good idea. You were talking about quitting our jobs and running away to start a new life together. That implies some things I don't know if we're ready for. We haven't been together that long really. I love our time together, but if that sort of thing is coming up in conversation now maybe

176

it's time we try some stress tests on our relationship. It just so happens your trouble with *The People* lets you test two things at once."

I was struck sort of dumb. Was Aggie saying in a roundabout way that I had asked her to marry me? Had I? Could I really just take a break from *The People*? It seemed unlikely somehow. I thought I could do it with Groovier's, although I expected a silent trace of disappointment from Mr. Iaello. To an extent, it was the nature of restaurant work that the staff was in a constant state of flux so they were used to working around personnel changes.

"I guess it's a decent idea. It's a little overwhelming to think of walking away from all those things at once. Especially you."

"I'll still be here. I don't think you'll be gone for years."

"How long do you think I should go, if I go?"

"What do you think? You can think about it while you see if it's even possible to take a break from your two jobs. See what's possible first."

"Alright, I'll think about it and see how it settles over the next day or two."

42

Preparation

I decided to go on a leave of absence or at least try. *The People* thing just wasn't working for me and asking for a leave of absence would, if nothing else, be a good test for my paranoid fear that it might not be so easy to leave. I had no evidence this was the case, but the feeling stayed with me and leave of absence might be a safer way to test it out rather than outright quitting.

Preparing to leave two jobs, my first apartment, my first girlfriend, and go away somewhere for several weeks sounds like an overwhelming endeavour to achieve on short notice. However, the idea of leaving *The People* had been fluttering around in my mind on one level or another for a long time. I was mentally prepared enough when the time came to get a running start.

I had enough money saved to be able to miss work for a while without major consequence. I even decided to keep my apartment and pay for it while I was away. I doubted I would find a better value. Taking into account the expense and hassle of moving, and the fact I was only going for a relatively short time, the decision was a no-brainer. Not to mention I loved my place. I had been there long enough and been through enough during my time there that it truly felt like a home, a sanctuary.

My talk with Mr. Iaello at Groovier's was very similar to the talk we had when I cut back my hours to work with *The People*. He kept a poker face and told me I had to make my own decisions in life and face their consequences. I thought he might be secretly glad I was stepping away from *The People*. I never told the boss any details, but I think he was as perplexed and suspicious about the general concept as I was. As usual with Mr. Iaello, I could never say what was on his mind for certain.

I also made sure to spend quality time with Aggie. Now that I would be stepping away, it once again became easier to put aside my suspicious frustrations with *The People* and concentrate on how she made my life much better and fuller than it had been without her. I think Aggie felt it too. We went out of our way to make the time before departure as sweet as possible.

If all went according to plan I would be away from *The People* and their tasks for a while, but I would also be without Aggie. Instead of taking the bad with the good I would be leaving the good with the bad. It was screwy how the negative seemed to encroach on the positive no matter which way I turned it. Knowing I would be temporarily leaving her reminded me how lonely it would be away from Aggie's charms regardless of how peaceful it might be away from the pompous idiocy of *The People*.

But things could not remain as they were. My biggest challenges before my departure remained; figuring out where I was going and letting *The People* know I needed time away from them.

43

Farewell Duncan

Before deciding where I was going I figured I should deal with *The People* first. I felt unsure what would happen when I asked for time away and I did not want to make any more plans with this still hanging over my head. I phoned Duncan and left a message. He called me back within minutes, much quicker than usual.

"Hi, Molloy, it's Duncan. I got your call. What can I do for you?"

"To be brief, Duncan, something has come up, and I would like to take about a month's leave from my duties with *The People*...without pay, of course."

Duncan chuckled.

"Really? That's interesting. A bit of a coincidence."

Duncan sounded quite pleased for some reason.

"Coincidence? What do you mean?"

"I'll talk with you about it over lunch; my treat. Your month leave should not be a big problem. We can arrange that over lunch as well. I'll bring the paperwork. Is there a good time for you to meet me tomorrow during the work day?"

"It always depends on when and where the tasks are, but if I was going to take a guess based on how things usually work out I would say one o'clock might be a good time."

"Perfect. I'll see if there's anything I can do to ensure it works out time-wise with your tasks tomorrow. Meet me at my office around one and we'll get things sorted out."

"Okay, great. Thanks."

It was nice that something went much smoother and easier than I expected for a change...so far, at, at least.

Duncan took me to a place in the market he called a tapas bar. Apparently, a friend of his ran the place as a separate business, yet he shared rent and food preparation equipment with the restaurant next door. I did not understand the arrangement precisely, but that is the gist as I could follow.

The tapas that Duncan took me to did not even have a name and was probably considered by most customers to be another section of the larger restaurant that shared the same building. I would have thought as much had Duncan not told me differently.

It was a beautiful early fall day perfectly suited for the indoor patio area where one outer wall was open to the outside. There were also skylights in the mostly glass ceiling which were cracked open to allow circulation of fresh air. It was heated just enough to keep the chill out of the room.

The place had a South American feel. I have never been to South America, of course, but whenever I think back to this occasion I am reminded of our continental neighbour. Perhaps it is something I have read or I am simply remembering how Duncan described the restaurant to me.

The staff recognized Duncan immediately. Several appetizers and a pitcher of beer were ordered before I even had a chance to look around. The appetizers can generally be described as spicy, crispy, and cheesy. They were delicious and mostly unique to me.

"Hey, Duncan," I said. "I don't know about the beer. I still have some tasks to do."

"Not to worry, my boy. I've arranged for you to have the rest of the day off. You're tasks will be taken care of by another and your pay will not be affected. A small celebration is in order."

"What's the good news?"

"You remember that coincidence I mentioned on the phone? It turns out that not long before you called requesting your leave I notified *The People for a Better World* that I would be retiring early. I'll be gone before you are back from your leave, assuming you do come back that is."

"What do you mean?"

"Let's be honest with each other. Your faith in the motives and ways of *The People* is not without doubt is it?"

Duncan's gaze was so clear, honest, and knowing I could not bother to consider lying.

"No."

"Is your leave of absence related to these doubts?"

"Yes."

"So then, after some soul searching you may or may not come back to *The People*. Am I right?"

"I guess so."

"Well, that is what I mean. I will be gone before you come back, assuming you do come back."

"Okay. Why are you retiring and why are we celebrating?"

"I have tried to hint a few times to you that I might have some doubts of my own. Initially necessity and perhaps later cowardice kept me from walking away or even taking a leave of absence as you are doing. I can honestly say that the doubts I have today are not one bit less than the doubts I had at your age. Then suddenly I was promoted, given better compensation and benefits and I have never looked back."

"*The People* have been around that long?"

"Longer."

"Okay, but what exactly are we celebrating? I think I missed it."

"We are celebrating me finally getting the balls to step away while I am still young enough to think critically and independently. I may even rediscover myself. I procrastinated a long time, but as a company man I have benefits and a pension with *The People* that would improve if I stayed on and retired later. By leaving early I am at least leaving something on the table. It may not be much, but it is a small piece of mind I can salvage.

"I believe we should also celebrate your leave of absence. Whatever you decide in the end, I applaud your decision to step away and think it through."

"So you've never believed the whole time?"

"Not really. Sometimes I wondered if maybe I was starting to, but in retrospect I think those were just times when I stopped thinking about it altogether."

"Why did you keep doing it?"

"Nothing to be proud of; mainly money, security."

"Nothing really wrong with that, I guess."

"Maybe not. It is probably the same with most people and their jobs to a large degree. Nothing right in it either though. It grates quietly away at one's moral fibre I think."

"Could it be true...the *for a Better World* stuff?"

"Ah, yes, the hook, the possibility we are helping our fellow beings. The only thing I can honestly say after many, many years of work and thought is that I have no proof for-or-against the claim."

I shook my head. I was a little amazed, but deep down I was not blown away. I would have been more surprised if Duncan produced clear evidence of *The People*'s good deeds and intentions.

I said, "You told us before that even with your elevated position you did not know much more than any of us. To be honest, I didn't really believe you."

"I don't blame you for being sceptical. I would be too in your place. I was sceptical when I was in your place many moons ago. But sadly, it is true."

"Don't you think the whole thing is a little crazy?"

"It's insane. Sometimes I can hardly believe I was a part of it for so long."

I was speechless for a little while and Duncan must have thought I was in shock.

"Cheer up, boy. Don't forget there is a bright side to not having a clue what is really going on with *The People for a Better World*, not knowing what is right or wrong, true or false."

"What's that?"

"They have no good reason to keep us from getting the hell out of here if we want. We have no secrets to tell, no bridges to burn. We're not a threat to them even if the whole thing is a big scam. What could we tell anyone?"

"So I take it my leave of absence isn't going to be a problem."

"You just have to pick your starting date. I can arrange it so the end of your leave is left open. You can come back whenever you want to, and if you decide you don't want to come back, you don't have to do anything. Simply never return to *The People.*"

"Is that allowed?"

"It is a little irregular, but it is not the first time such a thing has occurred."

He pulled an envelope from an inside jacket pocket and passed it to me.

"You simply have to return this form to whomever takes my place when your leave of absence is finished. If it never finishes just don't return it, throw it away."

I could not help but laugh.

"What's so amusing?"

"I just can't believe how easily I got my leave of absence. I agonized for days about how to go about it, and what would happen if I tried to leave."

Duncan laughed as well.

"I hear you. Everything is so strange, secret, and incomprehensible you cannot help but have paranoid feelings sometimes. It's happened to me several times over the years...less as I became accustomed to the way things work, but I have to admit I felt a little nervous about asking for early retirement. I couldn't help but feel people higher up than I might frown upon my act, people hidden in the shadows whom I had never met. However, just like you, it turned out to be no problem at all.

"Now how about a starting date for this leave so we can put this business behind us and enjoy ourselves."

Duncan pulled another neatly folded paper from his jacket while I considered a starting date. I had been so preoccupied with the problem of obtaining the leave I had not thought much about exactly when I wanted it to start. It did not take much thought. Things seemed to be going so much smoother than I planned. I decided not to get in the way.

"I'll finish off the week then start my leave after that if it's not too soon."

Duncan gave me a thumb up, pulled out a pen, and bent over the document.

"I had it all set out except the starting date. Here's your copy if you want one, and I'll handle the rest."

"I might as well take it, I guess. Thanks very much, Duncan. You made this a lot easier than I expected."

Around this time the appetizers started arriving one after the other. I ate about twice as much as I normally would. I also got pretty tipsy as the afternoon wore on. We shared two pitchers before we had a last pint for the road. Duncan had more of each pitcher than I did, but I certainly had enough to feel it.

He was responsible enough to ask, "You're not driving are you?"

"Nope. No car."

"Good. Me neither. I didn't think you were driving, but it is nice to be sure."

I had a great time with Duncan. We got along very well despite our age difference. The fact that he was my boss did not create any static between us. I suppose any tension of that sort was dissolved in the coincidence that we were both in the process of leaving our mutual place of employment.

We chatted and goofed around quite a bit, sharing occasional sarcastic barbs aimed at our experience with *The People for a Better World*. What follows are the pertinent details of the conversation we shared beneath the transparent roof and next to the open outer wall of the tapas bar, indoors, yet bathed in the fall sunshine.

I asked, "What are you going to do when you're done? Relax? Start a new career?"

"I'm not planning on starting a new career, but one never knows, I suppose. I've got enough put away to live a satisfactory life if I do not get extravagant. I've heard retirement can be boring for some. I golf. I do some charity work. I like to read and hike and putter around doing little jobs around the house. I've often thought I'd like to live in a nice cottage-type of place in the wilderness somewhat.

Not too wild, but nothing trendy or crowded either. Maybe now's the time to look into it. We'll see how I feel once the dust starts to settle."

"Is there a Mrs. Kinlin?"

"Not anymore. We went our separate ways some time ago and we haven't kept in touch."

"Seems pretty common these days. My folks split up too."

"Yes, I hear there is a less than a fifty-fifty chance of keeping a marriage together these days. It makes me wonder if people need to invent another method of defining relationships. The old style of marriage just doesn't seem to be holding up to the stress of the times or something. The world, of course, is a different place nowadays and I even wonder sometimes if we humans aren't exactly the same species we used to be either. Sounds crazy, I know, but the idea's crossed my mind more than a few of times over the years. Living things evolve and there's no reason to believe human beings have stopped evolving."

I got a little quiet and thoughtful there for a few seconds thinking about Mom and Dad, Duncan with his broken marriage, and Aggie and I, and whatever future lay in store for us. Duncan snapped me out of it.

"What about you? I suspect you're not married, but is there a special someone?"

"Yeah, actually there is. That's partly what this leave thing is all about."

"Oh, going away somewhere together?"

"No, kind of the opposite. We're taking a break from each other to see how it feels to be apart, and maybe get an idea for how serious we want to be."

"Thinking of going steady?"

"Umm, well actually we are going steady. I guess we're trying to figure out how steady and for how long. It's kind of complicated."

"Love is always complicated. I'll resist the temptation to try and give you advice since I have not had enough long-term success to be considered wise on the subject. Listen to your heart, and try to be still and quiet when you listen so you hear everything correctly. That's all I feel confident enough to say except good luck."

It sounded like good advice, but it also reminded me I was going to be very alone soon. I had been alone plenty before, but not for a while. What would it be like? Where should I go? What would I do?

I said, "I hadn't thought of it that way, but maybe that is part of what the leave is for...to go somewhere quiet and be still and listen."

Duncan nodded and looked me in the eye.

"Perhaps," he said. "And I'll say it again, best of luck to you."

I could tell he meant it. I smiled.

"And to you as well, Duncan."

We both ran out of words for a few moments. We just sipped our beer, looked around, and settled our nerves. Eventually, I broke the lull.

"Are you seeing anyone these days?"

"I am as a matter of fact, but it is very early, too early to tell how things might play out. She tells me she is thinking about retiring soon as well, so I suppose you never know. Maybe the timing is right. I just don't have a clue to be honest, but there is hope."

"What about kids? Do you have any?"

Duncan barely flinched, but I could tell I poked a tender spot.

"Yes, I have a son. He is his own man now, full grown. I see him once or twice a year, but we are not as close as I would like. As you may know, things are very tense when parents split up. The children suffer every bit as much if not more than the parents, but we are too busy fighting for our lives, so to speak, to notice. I could have done better. I am trying to slowly knit things back together, but it is slow and tough going."

"Yeah, I haven't seen my Dad since I left home or my Mom since she left home before me."

I felt bad for Duncan. I could see traces of pain in his eyes. I looked away and fiddled with something to give him a little privacy. I guess we got ourselves under control with a few deep breaths and large swallows of beer.

Duncan said, "I probably shouldn't be giving advice with my poor record, but you might be glad later on if you don't let the family ties sever completely unless the situation is completely unmanageable. However, if you must stay out of harm's way by all means do so. I don't pretend to know your situation."

"It wasn't all bad," I said. "I wasn't done real physical harm. I might visit. I'll at least think about it. I'm not sure where Mom is now."

"Yes, that is the best idea. Think about it and decide for yourself."

By silent consensus after that we agreed to stick with more cheerful, less serious chatter until we parted ways. We ended by exchanging best wishes and fond farewells over a final pint. Then I walked home. I wondered if I would ever see Duncan again. He was in my thoughts most of the way home. Though all along I had an instinctual, if wary, trust of him, I was still amazed by what an unexpectedly kindred spirit he turned out to be.

It seemed now as if Duncan had known, or at least suspected, our connection of disbelief all along, but it had never occurred to me. That in the end things were so arranged that we could speak openly from a somewhat common viewpoint before going our separate ways, and thus seal the bond between us was almost enough to make a sceptical, young man believe in destiny.

I passed an empty paper-recycling bin that had not been brought in from the front of someone's home. I leaned over it and tore up my copies of the documents regarding the beginning and end of my leave of absence. I knew it was not just the beer that made me sure I was not coming back to *The People*.

I cried a little on the way home remembering how obvious it was that Duncan badly missed his son. I thought about how I might be going to lose Aggie and have to start all over again. I realized how many months it had been since I had even thought of my own father. I hoped he was not all alone.

Part 6

S elf E xile

44

ALONE AGAIN

The title is melodramatic, but that is how it feels lying in bed my first night at the cottage away from Ottawa, away from Aggie, *The People*, and Groovier's.

The closest town where the train stops is Cobourg, Ontario. That is where I met up with the kind old gentleman, Mr. Kwapisinski, who rented me this place. We first came into contact through the Internet where I came across his extremely brief rental listing.

Very private, peaceful cottage with all basic amenities and a wonderful view of Lake Ontario. Great off-season rates.

We managed to reach an agreement on the financial and logistical details after exchanging four emails between us. He sent me a few pictures in one of his replies. In all my dealings with Mr. Kwapisinski I have found him to be almost painfully slow, deliberate and methodical. However, his pleasant, straightforward honesty and obvious unselfishness made up for his lack of efficiency.

Our email negotiations offer an excellent example. In these exchanges I would generally reply within an hour of receiving his email and in turn his responses would come around forty-eight hours after mine. Twice I wondered if he had rented to someone else and forgotten about me. To be fair, when his replies came, any questions I had asked were answered completely and even contained useful information I had not thought to ask. Mr. Kwapisinski was slow and meticulous, but we were able to come to an agreement without a lot of difficulty in the end. He was more than fair.

According to our agreement, Mr. Kwapisinski met me at the Cobourg train station, took me to the grocery store to stock up on supplies, and drove me out to the cottage. This arrangement made me realize at some point I would have to work on getting a driver's license. I was very lucky this elderly landlord was so accommodating.

Cobourg is a town of about 18,000 people. The train station is quite small and we had no trouble recognizing each other among the handful of people that were there when I arrived. In an email he mentioned that he was in his eighties. It was not difficult to pick him out. Although it was a cool, early fall day, I did not feel any need to zip up my light jacket. Mr. Kwapisinski was decked out for winter. All the outer clothes he wore, except perhaps his pants, were fur lined, including his hat and gloves. This outfit made him look bigger. At the cottage when he took off his outer gear I discovered him to be a much slighter and frailer looking man.

Mr. Kwapisinski spoke at a slow and measured pace, but his tone was generally cheerful, and a seasoned, reserved mirth often played about his lips and eyes while he spoke. He had what I guessed was an Eastern European accent of some kind.

"You must be Molloy."

"Mr. Kwapisinski?"

"Of course. How was your journey?"

"Good. I got to see some of the countryside, read a bit, and drank some coffee. It was relaxing. The train wasn't too busy."

My host nodded. "It only fills up on the weekends and holidays. I have always found the train to be the most relaxing way to travel."

"I haven't traveled a lot, but so far I agree with you."

He laughed and patted me on the shoulder.

"Okay. Let's go to the grocery store, get your supplies, then I will take you out to the cottage."

We shook hands and he led me to his car.

At the grocery store, Mr. K was quite helpful in making suggestions for what I might need and what I definitely did not need. He seemed to know every item that was stocked in the cottage down to the minute details. The most vague he ever was regarding his inventory was to say, "I am not sure which drawer I put it in, but I am sure it is there and I am sure I can find it when we get there." He saved me some time and money as we went through my list and filled the shopping cart.

On the way from the grocery store to the cottage, Mr. Kwapisinski asked, "If you don't mind me asking, why is a young man such as yourself going out to such a secluded place all by yourself for more than a month?"

"I can see why it seems a bit odd."

He nodded, but kept his eyes on the road. "To be honest, it bothers me a little to rent it out at such a low rate, but it is that or it sits empty only giving me the cost of its upkeep. My wife and I are too old to enjoy it anymore and my daughter, grandchildren, and great-grandchildren have no interest. Perhaps I should have foreseen they would need a little more excitement, especially the young ones. The view and the property are nice, but it is very quiet and the water access is mediocre at best."

"I wasn't planning on swimming that's for sure."

Mr. K laughed and slapped the steering wheel.

"No, I suppose not at this time of year."

There was a little silence between us then and it occurred to me he was still waiting for an answer to his recent question. I had no reason to hide anything from him.

"I think I might be at a big turning point in my life, and I have a couple of big decisions to make. Career and relationship things mostly."

"I see," he said. "Those things are certainly important."

He looked thoughtful and drove in silence for a while before he spoke up.

"I understand these are big decisions and why you would want to get away from it all and think about it. I don't mean to intrude, but shouldn't your girlfriend be here to think and talk about it with you? At least the relationship part. Also, maybe it's not my place, but you seem almost too young for big problems like this. I realize everyone's situation is different. I honestly do not mean to pry. You do not have to tell me anything you don't want to, of course."

I thought about it and wondered if he were right. Maybe Aggie should be here with me. She had not mentioned anything either and I got the feeling she would not have wanted to ask for a leave of absence. But also, some part of me thought I should do this alone.

"I don't know. I certainly didn't expect to be where I am now a couple of years ago, that's for sure. Things changed so quickly I barely got used to one big change before another hit me. I guess there's no reason it can't happen again too."

Mr. Kwapisinski seemed to find this very humorous.

"Tell me about it," he said. "I was just thinking the same thing about my life a couple of days ago and it's not the first time in my life I thought it. It seems sometimes like the young and old don't have a lot in common, but I guess some things are the same for everyone."

After that we were both fairly quiet. I thought about the similarities and differences that might exist between the driver and I until he said, "The cottage is just up the road from here. I hope you've been paying attention in case you need to find your way back to town."

I had not even thought about it.

"Probably not as much as I should have been," I said.

"Don't worry. I'll draw you a little map in the cottage. It's pretty far, but it's only three turns all the way back to Cobourg."

"Okay, thanks."

Mr. K helped me bring my stuff in from the car. He even helped me unpack. He mostly unpacked my grocery load into the kitchen and I took care of the rest. I chose the bedroom that looked the roomiest and easiest to unpack into quickly. I decided to wait until I was alone and got a feel for the place, before more carefully arranging my things for the month. It took only a short time to get everything unpacked.

"Thanks for the help, Mr. Kwapisinski. That went way easier than I was expecting."

"You're very welcome, Molloy. Are you ready to learn how to open and close the cottage as we talked about? Make sure I tell you about the garbage as well."

As it turned out, Mr. Kwapisinski was going to be out of the country when it came time for me to leave. It was agreed he would show me what to do and I would close up the cottage for the winter before I left.

"Okay. I'm ready."

There were essentially three simple things I had to know about opening, closing, and the general operation of the cottage. From my perspective, the complete instructions for all three duties could have been clearly written on a half-sheet of standard paper. From Mr. K's perspective, the successful transfer of this knowledge from himself to myself took almost two hours. In retrospect it is comical, but at the time I seriously wondered if he was perversely and knowingly tormenting me with his extended, repetitive instructions.

To give one example I will briefly explain how he taught me the simplest task of the three; how to manage the garbage collection. He showed me where the garbage bags were kept, where all the garbage cans were in the cottage, how to best put the bag in the can to ensure an excellent seal, where the community dumpster was (25 meters away), and that early Thursday morning was the pick up day by the garbage collector. He emphasized all these things several times over and even made me go through each step, even insisting I pretend to take the trash from the cottage to the dumpster to be certain I had it all straight. He even produced a calendar and showed me how to utilize it to keep track of what day it was. He insisted on leaving it at the cottage to help me out.

The turning on and off of the water was the most complicated issue. Mr. K seemed to be extremely concerned about potential pipe leaking. Apparently, five separate faucets had to be turned in a particular order to safely turn on or off the taps.

Even after memorizing the order and demonstrating as much by twisting the taps in their proper order in both directions, one way to turn the water on and the reverse to turn it off, I could still sense his obvious unease. He looked quietly beside himself in angst. I offered to write the instructions down complete with a little diagram to remind me of the correct sequence. I saw the idea pleased him. I got a pen and a piece of paper, wrote everything down, and stuck it up with a dart on a dartboard that hung in the basement near the taps. For whatever reason this act seemed to press exactly the right psychological button in Mr. K, and from that point on he became noticeably more relaxed with the notion of leaving the cottage in my care.

Mr. K's lesson in operating the cottage ended soon after, but not before I was taken on a detailed tour of every room, cupboard, closet and drawer to point out where various items I might need could be found. As a single example, he showed me a yellow cloth pouch hanging on a nail on the door on the inside of a closet in the smallest bedroom that was furthest from the cottage entrance.

He withdrew a little sewing kit.

He said, "This will come in handy if you need to replace a button that has come off your trousers or you tear your clothes."

Mr. Kwapisinski's final act was to give me a brief tour of the outside grounds. There is nothing out of the ordinary to mention except that at the end of the brief tour he took me to the back end of the property to show me the view that had been mentioned in his online ad for the cottage.

"Have a look," he said.

He had not stretched the truth. The view was striking, though not in the way I had idly imagined with picturesque pines around a deep green lake bordered by a setting sun, cottony clouds, and perhaps some sailboats and water birds. The view was beautiful, but it was stark.

The closely cropped lawn led to a clear drop-off guarded by two scrawny, nearly leafless maple trees on one side and a small pine with skinny, twisting branches on the other. Between the trees, over an unfenced cliff, was the view. Below the cliff was a very narrow, rocky beach followed by endless water on which it was hard to discern even a ripple. There were no islands, boats, or ships and not even the slimmest hint of a shore on the other side. The lighting, atmosphere, sun position, and clouds were such that the sky was a homogenous smear of blue-gray-white over dark water that appeared to absorb rather than reflect the light above. Only water and sky forever with two tiny creatures, one old and one young, watching silently at the edge of it all. We both seemed to feel it and said nothing for a minute or two.

Eventually, Mr. K said, "If I added up all the minutes over the years I spent looking over this ledge and contemplated my past, present, and future I bet it would add up to two or three months in total...no joke. I feel like I have put in a week or two here in the last half-year alone."

He sounded a little sad.

I asked, "A lot to think about lately?"

"Yes. I have a lot of time to think now that I am old. It may seem pointless, but I mostly think about the past because that is where most of my life is. I don't have a lot up ahead of me. I do not mean to be morbid or seek pity. It is only a fact."

I was not sure what to say, but he sounded like he wanted to talk.

"Any regrets?"

The question made him very still and silent for several moments before he spoke. "I suppose not," he said. "My life has taken a lot of unexpected twists and turns, but I survived and prospered for the most part. I wish some things were different at the moment, but they are not and I don't think it is my fault. I hope not."

"Is it something you want to talk about?"

"A little, yes. My wife is gone to me, not dead, but gone. It is like she hates me now, and it seems as if in her mind she always has. The doctors call it dementia, a common aging process, but it is hard not to wonder if it is true. You know, how they say where there is smoke there is fire. How can it be that only just recently she came to believe she has always hated me? Wouldn't there have to be some seed for this idea to grow from? I never see her now. She is in an old person's home in a dementia ward. It is too painful to visit, for when I do I receive only her curses. But then sometimes I feel guilty not going to see her. I told the staff at the hospital to let me know if she asks about me or wants to see me. I have not received any calls."

Mr. Kwapisinski seemed somewhat dejected, but resigned as if he had made peace with the situation as much as was possible. I thought maybe I should say something in the pause, but I did not. He continued.

"My children and my grandchildren come to visit when they can and I love to see them, but I see it is more a duty than a joy. I understand. They have more life ahead than behind."

He looked at me. There were no tears in his eyes, only weariness.

"I am sorry to tell you these things, but it is nice to let it out to another. This view always seems to make me look inside myself, and it has been a long time since I have looked out this way with someone else nearby."

I kind of knew what he meant. I was half-tempted to pour out my own tale of woe, but it seemed like it was his time for that, not mine.

I said, "It may be hard to believe, but I think I understand how you're feeling at least a bit."

The old man was slightly teary eyed now. It might have been partly the chilly wind. He laughed with watery eyes.

"I do believe you. We all have our challenges. I hope you believe I was telling the truth when I said I had no regrets. I don't think we humans are designed for perfect endings. Still, for some reason, I expected things would tie up a little more neatly toward the end than they seem to be heading. That's all. There was no reason for me to expect it to tie up neatly, but I did and I'm still trying to get a handle on it. Sometimes it seems as if the end drifts along and there is no clear direction to go."

I took the agreed upon rental sum in cash from my inside coat pocket and shook his hand as I gave it to him.

"I wish there was something I could do to make it easier."

Mr. K nodded. "In a small way maybe you have. I wish you the best of luck and wisdom with your big decisions."

I nodded back. "You too. Good luck."

"Good luck."

We shook hands again and he walked back to his car. I waved and watched him pull away, tires crunching along the gravel out to the paved road. For a few seconds as I watched the tail lights disappear, I felt as if I been visited by the ghost of my future self come both to wish me well and warn me. I felt hollow, see-through.

Before going inside I stayed and looked out at the view for a while. The view made my thoughts turn inward as well. I watched the shifting monochromes, the parallel divide of dark water and lighter, yet darkening sky. They did not seem to end and I briefly longed to join them in their infinite dispersal. The silence was a secret and profoundly beautiful heart-wrenching song I somehow failed to notice before.

I walked up the lawn and went inside.

45

Three Days In

I have been at the cottage for three days and three nights. I have worked on my diary at least three concentrated uninterrupted hours each day, more than I ever have before. Admittedly, most of this time has been spent reviewing and editing rather than writing new entries. I figure I spend another two hours per day thinking about and digesting my diary as I reread and edit it. It has been written little bits at a time over years where sometimes the context has changed tremendously. It had direction, but it was scattered. The diary needed to be reined-in, distilled, and shaped into its essence.

I have run every day so far. I am working up to running into the town of Cobourg. I figure it is around fifteen kilometres. I am pretty sure I can do it. I plan to pick up a few things in town and take a taxi back to the cottage. I think one of the reasons I am focused on running to

Cobourg is simply for a bit of company, even just to be in the presence of other humans and exchange trivial pleasantries. I have not seen another person during any of my jogs along the rocky beach or utility trails I found in some nearby woods. Running along the road one day only a single truck passed me the entire time, which was about an hour including my cool down walk. Maybe in some ways I have always been a bit of a loner, but now I have taken it to an advanced level that leaves even me a little unsettled.

I have begun to experiment with meditation. I have been curious about it and it has crossed my mind several times to try it, but I never bothered, feeling that I already spend enough time alone to take it on as an official hobby. However, I did pick up a used paperback introduction to meditation while perusing a second hand bookshop a while back. If now was not the right time to dabble with it, the time was never going to happen.

I suspect whatever I am doing meditation-wise, I am likely not doing it right, but I am giving it an honest try for a short time each day. I try to use what I have learned to focus and dwell upon Aggie and I, my old family, *The People for a Better World*, Groovier's, and my possible futures.

I will avoid going into detail for now. It is early yet. My retreat has only begun.

46

Two Weeks

I am fourteen days into my cottage stay, but there has not been a lot to write about. I have been doing all the things I planned, but they almost seem like something to pass the time in order to let the fragments of my mind shift and settle behind the scenes. I keep my diary notebook on the bedside table and force myself to jot things down at night before I sleep even if I do not feel like it. However, as I look over these entries they are rather bland and repetitive, certainly not each worth separate sections in the diary. This two-week review is a more appropriate synopsis of what has happened.

It has been a very calm holiday. I feel as though I was correct to come here. With the peace from nearly zero responsibilities, except those I set for myself, it feels as if my tangled desires and emotions are spreading out, un-ravelling, and untangling themselves without much effort on my part. I am hesitant to disturb their progress by thinking about them too much.

For now it seems best to summarize all the things I have worked on since my arrival at the cottage two weeks ago, revealing my experience and state of mind thus far.

Cooking

While exploring the cottage I came across two cook-books on a small, portable bookshelf in a large closet. They are: An Introduction to Ethnic Cuisine and The Student's Budget Cookbook. With their aid I have begun to experiment with cooking. I am lacking many of the ingredients necessary for the ethnic cookbook, but I in-tend to make at least one trip into town to try and gather some. The student's guide is more fitting for the initial supplies I brought and also for my level of expertise. This cooking hobby is an unexpected development, but it is a welcome change of pace to occupy my time once in a while.

Running

I have run every day except one since I have been here. It is a way of exploring the surroundings and I have found a number of pleasant, interesting spots. There is a rocky beach that continues much farther than I care to follow. The terrain is very interesting, littered with both natural and manmade debris, as well as multitudes of living scavengers lurking around the contours of the shore, but the going is rough on both the lungs and legs.

I also found a path through the forest and a field that leads to what seems to be a summer camp of some kind with an outdoor pool and posts in the sand where it looks like a volleyball net would be set up. Many of the signs around the camp are not in English and I wonder if the language in which they are written is the language of Mr. Kwapisinski's country of origin. I could probably Google some of the words as well as the name Kwapisinski and come up with something, but Internet access is not one of the basic amenities at the cottage.

The roads are very quiet, however, by observing small clues yielded by whatever meager flows of traffic I noticed, I was lucky enough to discover a very small town at the top of a long hill north of the lake. A small sign upon entering the town reads Grafton. It even has a decent sized general store. I looked, but as expected, the store did not have any of the ingredients I would need for the ethnic cookbook recipes. Soon, I will attempt to make the long jog to Cobourg and try my luck there.

Meditation

I have read the meditation book I brought once all the way through. Since I have no experience and am essentially interpreting and making it up as I go along I will not attempt to explain or describe it in detail. My explanation would surely be inaccurate. It is also a very personal experience and so far has changed each day I have practiced, trying to refine what I do and what I am trying to achieve. It is a work in progress, but I believe it may be something I end up liking and find useful.

This short meditation section could easily have been merged into the running section. I almost always do the two together. The rare occasion I do not run I meditate walking through the woods. The book I brought describes sitting positions generally considered to be the best techniques to enhance meditation, but it does allow for personal preference and experimentation. In my experience so far I definitely prefer meditation in motion.

At this point the best way I can describe what I am trying to achieve with my meditation is this: By focusing and concentrating on what I believe to be a correct, worthy, and useful life, I can breathe reality into my visualization and perhaps even make it so. Again, so far my concept of this sort of life has changed a little each day. I hope this makes a little bit of sense, but it is personal, incomplete, and at this point difficult for me to explain; again, a work in progress.

The Diary

I have continued to spend a lot of time rewriting, editing, and tightening my diary. I am really getting into it. My primary concern with these rewrites is whether I have crossed the line and blurred my diary into a work of fiction. I hope not, but to be honest I cannot be absolutely sure. I suspect life itself can be a blur at times, especially when viewed through the warped atmosphere of memory. I can only say I did my very best to display the true heart of the matter.

Unexpected Reading Material

I did not plan to spend a lot of time reading at the cottage. I only brought my book on meditation and my diary as distractions hoping to spend as much time as I could figuring out what to do with my life. The logic worked, but I have to admit I am somewhat shocked at the amount of free time I have on my hands. For some reason I did not realize what a huge percentage of my life and thoughts were taken up with two jobs and a steady girlfriend. Time is thick in the air and together with the silence it is sometimes overwhelming.

Anyway, I expect most devoted readers would have a hard time trying to suddenly stop reading, and I am no exception. Diary revision and meditation by themselves were enough for a few days, but before long I decided to search the cottage for books and found the small, portable bookshelf I mentioned in a big closet.

The vast majority of the books were romances and religious stuff, but for lack of better options I have begun reading through some For Dummies books that were tucked away in the corner of the bookshelf. The ones that have got my attention are Economics for Dummies, The Stock Market for Dummies, and Physics for Dummies. I have a little experience in physics from high school, but until now I had never even thought about economics or the stock market. I am pleased with my unexpected interest in learning about new things. I realize now it has been a long while since I allowed my mind to be directed away from its well worn paths. I realize now this was likely a mistake.

My enjoyment of discovering new things through the Dummies books has got me wondering about my education. This cottage time has been allotted for other thinking, but my education is something I know I must revisit in the relatively near future.

Aggie

I expected contemplation of my relationship with Aggie would be one of my primary foci at the cottage since discussions with her on the topic is what precipitated my journey here. So far, however, I would have to say it has been only one of many issues on my mind.

Almost as soon as I had all my things packed, before I even set foot on the train, the fact that Aggie and I may not be together forever, or even much longer, became a very real, even reasonable, possibility. It was as if the idea appeared complete and fully formed in my mind with very little prelude. Maybe talking about difficult relationships with Duncan brought it on. Maybe I had struggled so much with the idea before I came to the cottage I felt worn out from worrying about it and just accepted the fact.

Also, I think I came to the realization that no matter how long I dwelled or what my thoughts and decisions turn out to be, they will only be part of the situation's eventual outcome. Aggie will have her own feelings and conclusions, and we will see what happens when we put our minds together.

I can still imagine a long and happy life together with Aggie, but within days of settling behind the walls of this cottage beside a cliff, it was no longer impossible to imagine a future without her. Isolated here with *The People* gone from my life and with Aggie at least possibly gone, suddenly my future seems wide open, vast and unknown. Even the relatively near future, when I leave the cottage, the details of my life are mostly unknown, but rife with potential. What will I do when I leave here and go back to Ottawa?

The main point is that simply leaving everything behind and coming out here has allowed me, even forced me, to glimpse many possible scenarios of my future with or without Aggie by my side. It is easy to imagine good and bad possibilities in both circumstances.

It makes me nervous sometimes because it was not what I expected to feel before I came here. I just do not know. There are so many factors beyond my control.

The Future

The nervous tension from not knowing what the near future holds in store for me has naturally led me to attempt some planning. With so many uncertainties, planning seems too strong a word. Sizing up potential opportunities and seeing what they feel like is a better description. It is nerve wracking to imagine returning to Ottawa without my main source of companionship and my biggest source of income. Once again, I could basically be starting over.

Despite this, I never had any doubt about my decision to leave *The People for a Better World*. They are not frequent tenants in my mind. It is primarily with relief that I reflect upon my split from the institution. I knew I was done with them for good after my last meeting with Duncan. I left them at the train station in Ottawa.

Groovier's and its crew on the other hand are in my thoughts more than I ever imagined. Realistically, I am going to have to ask for my old job back as soon as I return. Or at least whatever hours I can get. I have been pretty straightforward and dependable in all of my dealings with Mr. Iaello, so I am hopeful. Though I may have singed the bridge by reducing my duties at Groovier's twice now, I do not think I have burned it down. I gave fair notice both times and I did not expect any favours when I went back the first time. I will expect none this time.

I do not think any of my little hobbies are going to help me pay the bills. I doubt I will become a professional diarist, world-class runner, or meditation expert. If I do any cooking for money, more than likely it will be at Groovier's.

I have not given a lot of direct thought to my lost family. However, in the open, silent space around me these days I can sometimes feel Mom, Dad, and Kim floating around the outer edges of my active mind as if they were trying to ask me something. I suppose I will hear them when I am ready.

Two weeks is a significant amount of time and I feel I have barely turned over any stones that make up the relationship between Aggie and I. I have mainly managed to set it aside, stop obsessing, and let come what may. I struggle with this; it seems both right and wrong, but it just seemed to happen and I have no strong urge to fight against it. However, I will attempt to more urgently consider the matter. Aggie deserves it. We deserve it.

The future looms.

Part 7

Loose Ends

47

Home Again

I wrote every day my last two weeks at the cottage, but little of the work made it into the final draft. Instead, its essence was captured and included in my more encompassing rewrite of my previous diary entry after two weeks at the cottage. I am almost embarrassed to report no further significant revelations during the last part of my stay. I can only say I came to terms a little more with the things I wrote about after two weeks. I cooked, ran, and meditated a little better. I understood economics, the stock market, and physics slightly better than before. I did manage to run to Cobourg and gather enough ethnic supplies to try a few recipes from my ethnic cookbook.

I feel more capable of dealing with anything Aggie might have to say about our relationship. I believe it is mostly up to her since I think a lot of our future is tied up with her decision regarding her career with *The People for a Better World*. In my mind, on the train from Cobourg to Ottawa, I filtered through all things related to Aggie to try and prepare my mind for our reunion.

As soon as I was home and unpacked I called her.

"Hello?"

"Hi Aggie. I just got home."

"I thought it might be you. How'd it go?"

"Pretty well...different than I expected."

"How so?"

"Hmm...I guess I'd say more peace and quiet than I ever imagined."

"Is that good or bad?"

"Good, I think."

"Well, I guess we should get together and talk about it. I took today off since I knew you'd be getting back, but I wasn't sure when. I had it written down somewhere, but I lost it and could only remember the date. Where should we meet?"

Aggie made me think of *The People*, which brought Duncan to mind, which reminded me of the last time I saw Duncan. For some reason I did not tell Aggie everything Duncan and I talked about. Even though he had not sworn me to secrecy, I felt as if Duncan might have been letting me in on his leaving before it had been officially announced. I did not want to break his confidence in me.

"Have you ever been to a tapas bar not far from where Duncan's office was? I don't think it even has a sign or a name."

"No. Sounds posh. Is it like a hotdog stand type deal?"

"No. It's different and kind of cool. Duncan took me there on our last meeting before I left."

"I should tell you Duncan's not with *The People* anymore."

"I'm not surprised. He mentioned his plans to me at the meeting."

"Oh...hmm, okay. Well, where exactly is this place with no name?"

"I think I remember how to get there, but I don't know the names of the streets. Want to meet in front of the building where Duncan's office used to be and walk there together?"

"Sure, how about in one hour?"

"Great. How were you while I was away?"

"Pretty good. I guess my time was different than I was expecting too. It will be nicer to talk about everything in person."

"Alright. I'm having trouble describing my time at the cottage anyway. The land where time stood still keeps popping into my head."

"Sounds interesting. We'll talk soon. I missed you."

"I missed you too."

"See you soon."

"See you."

~

I was very happy to see Aggie, but it was kind of weird seeing her again, as if I'd been gone for years instead of a month. Aggie expressed a similar feeling. We hugged, kissed, and laughed about how strange it was we both felt that way. I thought I had resigned myself to living either with or without her at the cottage, but suddenly it was clear how different those two realities would be. The marriage vow, for better or for worse, was an equally high stakes decision if we chose to give up and not stay together. Aggie seemed nervous too. We walked arm-in-arm through the chilly breeze hoping to let the nervous energy radiate away into the air.

The tapas bar with no name was exactly as I left it when I was with Duncan, a little blip on one of many busy streets in The Market. It was neither packed nor empty, neither discovered nor undiscovered. It was simply there for the likeminded, the undecided.

"Cool place," Aggie said. "I'm surprised I've never heard about it. I like the way it lets in the light from the outside."

In the chilly fall the front was no longer open to the air except for a small vent space above the doors, but the front wall was mostly glass. A lot of light came in from the roof's skylights as well.

Coincidentally, we got the same waiter I had with Duncan. He seemed to recognize me, but he could well have been pretending. It is a common restaurant staff technique that I have used myself. Even more strangely, we got the exact same table I got with Duncan, or at least one situated very close to the same position. The coincidences spooked me briefly, but the light and atmosphere at the tapas would not let spooky feelings dwell for long. I noticed more plants dotted around the restaurant this time, perhaps to help customers forget about the looming winter freeze.

I described to Aggie the vast quantity of appetizers Duncan and I had. We chose a couple to share. Aggie only wanted a Diet Pepsi, but I was in the mood for a beer. I figured I deserved one after my self-inflicted exile, but I stopped after one since Aggie was not partaking.

"So tell me about the cottage. Did you have a good time?"

I thought about it for a few seconds.

"I guess so. It was definitely an interesting experience even though there was not a lot to do."

"So what did you do?"

"All the stuff we talked about. I ran a lot. I thought about the present and the future. I finally read that meditation book and practiced almost every day. I read. I even experimented with cooking some ethnic food."

"Did you make any new friends?"

I laughed.

"I had to go out of my way to even see another human being."

"Really?"

"Really. There was a tiny town about five or six kilometres away and a decent sized small town about fifteen kilometres away. The cottages are spaced pretty far apart and they seemed to be pretty much abandoned for the fall. Sometimes when I went running for an hour or so I didn't see a car on truck on the roads the whole time."

"Wow. Kind of what you were looking for, but even more so."

"Yeah, it was really something. A couple of times I pretended I was the last person on Earth and it wasn't hard to get into character. Not only did I try the meditation thing, I might have gone a little bit crazy without it."

Aggie was looking at me sort of fondly, but as if she was not really sure she knew me.

"I always thought meditation would suit you. I don't know much about it really. It was just a hunch I guess."

I have to admit Aggie always did encourage me to give it a try once I had expressed interest.

After more cottage talk I said, "Enough about me. What have you been up to?"

Aggie smiled. The smile looked proud, but a little sheepish as well.

"I got a promotion."

"With *The People*?"

"Yeah, just a couple of weeks ago."

I had imagined this conversation with Aggie a hundred times and ways, but once again, this particular scenario had never made an appearance in my mind.

I could only say, "Wow. Congratulations. I mean if... you are happy about it, right?"

Aggie rolled her eyes.

"Of course I am."

I was kind of stunned and words did not come easily.

I said, "What does this mean?"

It was a pretty lame thing to say in retrospect.

Aggie shrugged.

"Not a lot actually. I do pretty much the same things I always did except on Fridays. On Fridays I organize those little get-togethers for potential new members of *The People for a Better World*. So far I've only organized one."

I went a little numb; as if she had told me she had found a new guy while I was away.

"How do you like it," I asked, "so far, I mean?"

"I'm not really sure yet. I'm not comfortable or used to it yet, but I think it will be good."

It was my turn to say something, but what? Through a fog of vague disappointment I managed to see that Aggie had received recognition and reward for good work at something to which she had dedicated herself. That was the main point above and beyond anything I was feeling confused about. I tried to rise above my slightly hurt feelings.

"I don't doubt you'll figure it out and do a great job. You got through a lot to even get the promotion in the first place didn't you?"

Aggie put her hand across the table offering to hold mine. I accepted. She looked happy and a little sad at the same time, perhaps a little torn and unsure like I was feeling. I worried I saw a glint of pity in her eyes. We held hands quietly for several seconds until she started the conversation that needed to begin.

She said, "My promotion complicates things doesn't it?"

"I don't know. Maybe. I have to admit it wasn't something I was expecting."

Aggie snorted one of her little laughs.

"Me neither."

Then she took a deep breath, as if about to say something she wasn't sure she should.

"I heard through the grapevine that Duncan arranged things so you can come back if you want."

"That's what he told me."

I did not feel comfortable saying I threw away the paperwork soon after he gave it to me.

"I'm sure it's true then."

"Any word from Duncan?"

"No. It's like he just disappeared."

I nodded. For some reason I thought that was a good sign, a sign he made a clean escape. Unless Aggie could read my mind, my faced must have showed something.

She said, "*The People* just isn't your thing is it?"

"No. I just don't get it."

She squeezed my hand then let it go. I felt like I knew what was happening, and I just wanted go home, crawl into bed and start getting over it. But Aggie and I deserved a more dignified farewell. Neither of us said a lot until our appetizers started to arrive and broke the spell. The food was just a good as I remembered and it gave us something to talk happily about. Eventually I told her more of my cottage experience and she filled me in on new developments at *The People for a Better World*. We listened to each other, but I think we were each more attuned to the undertones suggesting we would not be a couple anymore. It was fascinating how we did not have to say any direct words on the subject to know what was happening. We loosened up over lunch, already taking the first little steps toward letting go.

Outside the tapas I asked Aggie, "Can I walk you home?"

"Sure. I live in a new place though. Same phone number obviously."

"Where do you live?"

"Not too far from here really. *The People* have a building a few blocks from where Duncan's office used to be. A perk of my promotion is I get to live in the low-level manager's building. We all pitch in to take care of the building and property in exchange for free room and board. It's a nice set-up. We have a swimming pool and we each have a good entertainment system. We get a little better pay, as well."

"That does sound pretty sweet. Is it actually called the low level manager's building?"

Aggie laughed.

"No. We just call it that because we are the only ones who live there, like they want to segregate us from the higher managers, the non-managers, and the non-People. We get a building management stipend for looking after the place as well. It makes a difference in overall expenses."

"I wonder if they have a middle management building as well. Maybe even lower-mid level and upper-middle management buildings too."

"Who knows?"

"Okay, well you lead the way."

Aggie pointed the direction we would be heading and we headed off that way. We held hands, but we did not speak a whole lot. It seemed as though we would be splitting up, but it did not feel as bad as I thought it would, perhaps because it was not entirely unexpected. Also, it had happened much more quietly and gently than I could have dreamed, almost telepathically. A lot had been tabled, motioned, and agreed upon behind the scenes. There had been no anger, no war, and no collateral damage to the good things that had happened between us. Who could ask for more in a break-up? Of course I did not think about it exactly this way as it was happening, but I think sensed the general gist of it.

With gentle turns, tugs, and pulls of my hand, Aggie led the way for the fifteen to twenty minute walk to her new place. It was cool, but sunny and windless enough to feel mild.

Her new place looked like a smaller version of the university residences I had seen at Carleton and Ottawa Universities. Tucked in behind a U-shaped driveway in front of the building and next to the building was a small parking lot that could hold about twenty cars. The lot was empty. Seemingly, the promotion to lower management did not provide enough extra money to comfortably buy a car.

We stopped at the base of the driveway and Aggie turned to me.

She said, "So what happened to you out there all by yourself. Any wild revelations? You haven't told me a lot."

I wondered. It did seem as if my time at the cottage had done something to me, but I was not sure what or how. I had to kind of wing it, thinking about it as I spoke. I had thought about it before, of course, which is why I was only kind of winging it.

"I guess so. Things really slowed down a lot. I had quite a bit of time to just be alive, I guess. It was difficult to get stressed out about anything or feel that anything was so important that it couldn't wait before I thought too much about it."

When I paused, Aggie looked as if she expected me to continue. I guess it was true that I had not really said much.

"I realized I had to get a job soon after I got back and that my best bet was Groovier's. I decided I should at least finish high school. I meditated while I ran. I wondered if we would be getting back together."

"Wondered? I didn't even know we broke up."

"I don't mean like that. I chose the wrong words. I guessed I wondered if we'd be staying together and for how long. I was trying to see the future, what was best for you and for me, and to not let my own internal strain block the view. It sounds weird I know, but it seemed less weird when I was isolated on a cliff by a giant lake."

"Those don't seem like major revelations, more like some basic decision making in suspended animation."

"I realized it was impossible for me to know what was best for us because I'm not us. I'm just me and it's not just my decision. I guess that's my revelation; that it doesn't particularly matter what I want."

Aggie smiled in what looked to me like an internal sort of smile.

"I suppose that is a revelation."

Then Aggie looked like she had suddenly learned meditation and sent her attention inside herself, leaving her outside unattended.

To try and bring back her attention I asked, "Did you have any?"

"Hmmm?'

"Any revelations for you while I was away?"

"I don't know. I guess I had a kind of revelation about my role with *The People*. In a way I felt as if I'd found a place where I belonged, but I also had some doubts I was finding really difficult to shake. I'm sure you can at least empathize with my doubts."

I smirked and nodded. I knew about the doubts.

"Anyway, when I got the promotion it felt like a sign that validated my feeling of belonging. It really allowed me to set my doubts off to the side where they don't constantly pester me. I think about them once in a while when I have time and a clear mind, but I'm sure my doubts are fading or at least becoming less important."

None of this was going how I imagined, but then again I had not tried too hard to imagine anything about this moment. I think my decision not to bother trying to imagine the future too precisely was another cottage revelation. Whatever was happening, it seemed to be flowing along fairly smoothly and naturally. I did not know what to say, but I thought I should try to be supportive.

"Cool. I'm glad things are working out for you."

Both saying it at the time, and writing it, now seems a bit lame, but that's what happened.

"Did you think about our relationship while you were away?"

"Of course. That was the main point of the whole thing wasn't it? But it was tough once I realized my own point of view wasn't enough."

"Yeah."

Aggie watched me for a while before she continued. I could not read anything in her eyes, but I was having difficulty even reading myself at the time.

She sighed, "I do know what you mean. It seemed almost stupid to try and make a decision on my own. I guess my idea to send you away so we could soul search had some flaws. In the end I started focusing on getting my own shit together. That's kind of what you were saying you did too, right?"

"Yeah, it's weird. It was tough to go and I really missed you when I left, but after a while it was just the way it was. With so much free time I ended up taking turns concentrating on different things and tried to make a little progress each day, but the hardest for me was to make progress on us. I don't think it was a bad idea at all though. Sometimes it felt ridiculous to be out there all alone, but even so it felt like the right thing to be doing most of the time."

"I hear you. It was basically like that for me too. But here we are and we're not alone anymore."

I smiled at her. It really was nice to see her, but it still felt odd for some reason. It was like we kept waiting for something inside us to thaw and loosen up.

As if trying to describe how I felt to Aggie I said, "It's a bit of a shock to the system coming downtown so soon after the cottage. I don't know if I can adequately describe how silent and empty of people the cottage area was; even little old Brockville was an absolute roar of activity in comparison. Even for me, and I was kind of a loner back then."

Aggie smiled and shook her head.

"I've got news for you, Molloy. You still are."

"What?"

"A bit of a loner."

That shut me up and left me hanging in my own mind. I did not think so, but mainly because I just had not thought about it at all. Even thinking about it for a few seconds after Aggie said the words was enough for me to see that it was true. I was kind of a loner. It struck me as profound, though I was not sure why. Loner. I had directed the concept at myself in thought occasionally, but hearing it in plain English from a close friend was haunting.

We talked, hugged, and played with the leaves on the ground for a little while, but once my loner status had been revealed I guess we were only putting in time until

we said our goodbyes. I think we both thought we deserved a little more time before the next and possibly final
separation.

However, when the time came neither of us cried
though it seemed like we might. We knew what was happening, but we did not want to say it. Maybe we just did
not understand it exactly or know how to put it into
words. Eventually, we ended up just hugging a long, silent
goodbye.

When it was done I said, "Good luck."

"Good luck. Call me if you ever need me...or *The
People*."

"Okay, thanks. I'm here for you too if you need
me...and if you need a hamburger, Groovier's has your
back."

We smiled, almost laughed.

It did not seem right to kiss her for some reason even
though I had already kissed her a couple times since we
met downtown. The long hug seemed more appropriate.

I did say, "I love you."

"I love you too. You made a difference for me."

Her words touched me. I nodded.

"Thanks, you too."

There were a few more hesitations and looks toward
one other, but it was done, and I soon was walking home.

48

Another R eunion

My life has gone pretty much back to the way it was
before I went to the cottage, except for Aggie and *The
People*. Then again, those are very significant changes.
Still, it seems not a lot has changed somehow, as if my
internal priorities and concerns were just housed within a

larger closet previously and now I have downsized. Maybe it has something to do with being a loner.

I have dealt with most of the issues that my mind explored while I was at the cottage. I am back at Groovier's. As fortune would have it my plea to Mr. Iaello for reemployment coincided with a time when employees left the restaurant on short notice. I am getting lots of hours.

I have not come up with any fantastic new ideas to improve Groovier's yet although I have been trying. At least not any I am confident enough with to put my neck out and suggest to Mr. Iaello. I am always thinking about it, but I have a lot to learn. That is what I am doing now, working my ass off to show Mr. Iaello I want to learn every aspect of the business.

I will be attempting to finish my last year of high school through a mostly online program that begins in the spring, only a few weeks away. Winter is beginning to loosen its grip on Ottawa.

I almost signed up for driver's education, but I backed out just before I went into the office to register. I cannot imagine buying a car soon, but it would be handy to be able to at least rent one if the need or desire arose. The problem is that for a period of the licensing procedure you need to practice driving with a licensed adult in a car with you. At the moment the only adult who fits the bill is Mr. Iaello and I do not feel it is appropriate to ask him to do this for me. The driver's license is on the back burner for now.

Aggie has not called me and I have not called her. I have been very tempted to call her more than once, but something in me suspects I need to get over her more than I need to speak with her. I have a tremendous urge to help her, but who says she needs my help? Every notion I have about my relationship with Aggie seems to have an equally valid, opposite possibility.

At the moment of this writing I am once again on the train. I am going to take care of another piece of business I conceived at the cottage, to visit my father in Brockville. I attempted to call first, but the old number did not work. I tried to discover the new number through the operator and the online directory, but Dad has either an unlisted number, is without a phone, or has moved away from Brockville. I decided to take one last shot and come down in person to see if I could find him. If he is gone at least I did what I could and can put the matter aside with a clearer conscience.

The train pulled into Brockville on schedule at 14:25. My return ticket is for 18:45. Mr. Iaello let me take today and tomorrow off work. He is glad I am going to visit my father.

It has been about two years, but Brockville is still much what it was when I left and fairly still fresh in my memory. Without effort I begin the walk toward what used to be my family home. It was as if by coming back I had unlocked the mental cellar where I imprisoned some of my memories, giving the ghosts of home permission to stir within me. I say ghosts because it truly felt like I was haunted for several minutes, spirits waking up and looking from my eyes and asking me what was going on. My answer was to keep walking and concentrate, as if to explain to them that the only way to find out was to watch, wait, and see what happened.

The ghosts gradually settled as I went forward, but memories kept popping up all over. Some were clear, others distorted, and some were only tugs and twists of emotion. The corner where I thought I saw my long lost sister screaming at the child I did not know she had. The street that led to the number two highway along which I traveled to get my tattoo. The high school where I never truly belonged and never graduated. And finally, the home where I grew up. I had to stop a few houses away before I approached to stare at it and pull myself together.

It hit me that much of what molded me was beyond my control. The house in front of me and what had happened within it directed my evolution. I had blocked it out for a couple of years and now I was nervous to confront it. As if by avoiding it I had betrayed it and now must skulk back seeking forgiveness, or at least acceptance and a joining of the paths. Still, I came for a reason.

My awe and my nervous helplessness did not change any-thing.

I forced my mind clear and walked quickly toward the front door. The property looked tidier, better kept than I remember. After I knocked a middle-aged woman with dark hair and a frumpy demeanour opened the door. I did not recognize her.

"Yes?"

"Is Mr. O'Grady here?"

She looked at me blankly.

"Pat O'Grady?" I repeated. "I'm his son."

Nothing registered in her expression and she started to move into a position where she could get her weight behind the door. Then something clicked in her eyes.

"Your father used to live here? Oh, he lives somewhere else now. I don't know where, but I see him sometimes. I think he's still in town. We bought this house."

It should not have been a total shock to me and it was not, but part of me reacted as if it were. It was a very strange sensation that is difficult to describe. On one level I did not even blink, thinking, 'It figures, I suppose. How was he going to pay for the place himself without a steady job or any inclination to get one? But now how do I find him?'

Another part of me felt as if it had been brutally torn away; my childhood, my past, my original connection to the Earth unpegged from the dirt and blown away.

The rest of me just watched the swirl of emotions and waited for the turmoil to settle down so I could think. I went silent and blank for several seconds.

The lady tried to help me.

"When I see him once in a while he is usually closer to downtown. My best guess is that he lives down that way."

"Okay. Thanks a lot. I'll check it out."

I left straight away, eager for some reason to be out of view of my old home, ashamed for some reason that my entire family had abandoned the house and confused by my shame.

The only place I could think of downtown that Dad used to go on occasional, social visits was a general store on the main street that had off-track horserace betting in the back. There were a few televisions there where clients could watch their wagers run. It was called Ritchie's. Maybe they knew where I could find my Dad.

I knew exactly how to get there. I was amazed how I knew my way around so well after hardly thinking about the place for so long. It was as if the Brockville map became integrated into my DNA while I grew up there.

It was a return to the past; a little kid hunting down Dad to tell him it was time for supper. That is how I thought of myself when I lived in Brockville, a little kid, even though it had only been two years ago. Then suddenly it seemed insane that I had come back. I stopped dead in the street and thought about whether I should continue or march back to the train station and see if I could exchange my ticket for the soonest available one back to Ottawa. It took less than a minute to unglue myself from the sidewalk and decide to finish what I started.

Like a lot of what I had seen so far, the general store with off-track betting in the back seemed hardly to have changed. Still, I could not help but notice how different this store was from the stores in Ottawa. The shelves were dark lacquered wood that would never look particularly clean even if they were. The store was relatively long and narrow, a long rectangle rather than a square. The lights were normal old bulb lights and there were not very many of them. That, combined with the fact there were few windows other than those at the front of the store, made the experience feel more like exploring an abandoned warehouse compared to the Quickies and Seven Elevens I visited in Ottawa. Still, at the back of my mind there was something vaguely comforting about the experience.

The man behind the counter looked very familiar as well.

"Hi there," I said.

"Evening, sir. Can I help ya?"

"Yeah. I'm Molloy O'Grady. I grew up here, but I haven't been back in a while. I dropped in to see my Dad, but he's not at the old place anymore. He used to come by here and I wondered if anyone might know where I can find him.”

The man squinted and stared hard at me before smiling in recognition.

“Oh yeah, Molloy. I’m Peter. You’re Pat’s boy, right? I remember you now. You’ve grown up quite a bit since I last saw you. Keeping well I hope.”

“Yeah, it’s been a while. I remember you too. I used to get candy here and once in a while I’d pick up a racing form for Dad. You haven’t aged a bit.”

It felt weird talking like this. I did not have much experience with idle chitchat, but this fellow seemed to expect it and I needed his help.

“Can’t complain, can’t complain.”

There was a pause in the conversation. I thought I had done my share, but he seemed to want something more. The place was empty of customers and kind of gloomy, but it looked reasonably tidy.

“The store looks good. It brings back memories.”

Peter nodded as if I had gotten the right answer in my quick search for appropriate bullshit.

“Yup, a lot of history here. I try to keeps things up to date without losing the old-time charm. Thanks for noticing.”

Oh brother.

“It would be hard not to notice. I’m in Ottawa now and you don’t get the same good feeling in the stores there.”

Pete nodded some more.

“Yup, I hear you, thanks again.”

I hoped that was enough.

“Does Dad still come by here ever?”

“Oh yeah, your pa’ still comes by now and then. Not as much as he used to and he’s calmed down a fair bit, but I see him.”

“Know where I might find him?”

“I’m not certain, but it seems to me he mentioned he lived in one of those apartments above New Beginnings, the second hand store on Apple Street. Do you remember it?”

“Yeah, I do. Thanks.”

"No problem. I hope you find him, and be sure to say hi to your old man for me if you do."

"I will."

I figured I should buy something. I was getting hungry anyway. I grabbed an Oh Henry and a bag of pretzels.

"I haven't eaten in a while. These should tide me over."

Pete snickered.

"Aw hell. For old time's sake they're on the house. Just be sure and say hi to Fit for me."

Fit was a nickname I heard people call me Dad once in awhile. I never knew why.

"I definitely will, but if anyone should be giving gifts it's me. Thanks again for the help."

I put five dollars on the counter and headed for the main street; King Street, I remembered.

"My pleasure," called Peter. "Good luck in your search."

I gave him a thumb up as I went back outside.

Although I did not specifically remember Apple Street, I did remember the second hand store New Beginnings and the general location it was in relation to Ritchie's and King Street. I knew Apple Street must be perpendicular to King Street and the two streets intersected. I just had to read the street signs. After only two blocks I came to Apple Street and I could see New Beginnings just half a block down. I had been mentally prepared for a longer journey, almost wanting a longer walk to get mentally prepared to see Dad. Walks between places were generally longer in Ottawa. Once again I paused in the street a few buildings from my destination to put my nerves and thoughts in order. My mind was a mixed up, complicated jumble of things that I did not have time to sort through at the moment. I pushed everything aside as best I could by examining the building I was set to approach.

It looked as if there were two apartments above the used items shop. The mailbox for apartment two had a magnet with the name O'Grady stuck to it. I pressed the button beside mailbox two and waited. Soon enough I heard some footsteps walking somewhere above the store and soon after they were coming down stairs.

222

When the door opened Dad looked significantly older and smaller than I remembered. His face looked thinner and his body looked softer. I briefly wondered if I would have recognized him in an unexpected passing. Probably. It seemed as if Dad did not recognize me at first, but only for a second or two. I watched recognition dawn upon his face with a strange mix of confusion and wary joy.

He did not say anything. To allow him to be sure it was me I held out my hand for him to shake. I spoke fairly quietly.

"Hi, Dad. Surprise."

It took him a couple seconds to speak.

"Molloy...you've grown."

He paused then as if he could not believe I could be standing there. He looked at me as if he expected me to waver and evaporate like a dream for a little while before he spoke.

"Would you like to come in?"

I smiled.

"I might as well now that I'm here? How've you been keeping? It's been a while. I tried to call ahead, but I couldn't find you until I came in person and even that was tricky."

Neither of us knew what to say for a little while so nothing was said. Dad moved back onto the stairs leading up to his apartment to let me into the small area between the base of the steps and the outside door. There was a plastic mat in the alcove for my boots and hooks on the wall for my coat. After I shed my outerwear I followed Dad upstairs.

Once I got up to the apartment Dad asked, "Ya' want anything? I don't have much, but I think I have some tea somewhere. I can put out some cheese and crackers if you're hungry."

"Tea sounds good if you've got it."

"I'll find it. I know it's here. I just don't use it much."

I sat on a blue and gray futon couch and looked around. Dad's apartment was pretty plain. It reminded me of my own in many ways, functional, but sparsely adorned with little in the way of extra amenities. My apartment seemed to have better lighting both from within and without and perhaps a little better airflow. Neither of us had a television, but I had a phone and a computer. I suspected Dad had none of the three modes of communication or entertainment.

Sitting on the small couch in the small living room while Dad prepared the tea I felt kind of sorry for him living alone like this. Then again what did that say about me since I lived similarly? I know there are differences in age and context, but these notions floated across my mind.

Dad carefully carried out the tea for each of us and handed a mug to me.

"Do you take anything in it? I should have asked before."

"No, this is good."

"I drink mine black too," he said.

I don't think either of us drank tea very often. Maybe Dad was trying to put something in common between us to help us get a good footing for our reunion.

Dad sat to the right of me on an odd sort of padded rocking-chair facing perpendicular to the direction I faced from the couch. I recognized Dad's chair from the house, but so far it was the only thing I recognized. At first the words between us were nervous and sparse, but we gradually felt our way through the haze. This is essentially how it went.

Dad said, "It's been a while, Molloy. I'm not even sure how long. How's it going?"

"Nothing too exciting. I have a job in a restaurant. I had a nice girlfriend for a while. I have an apartment kind of like yours. I'm doing okay."

"Good to hear. I think about you sometimes, all of you. I'm glad you're making out all right. Keeping out of trouble?"

"I try. I guess there's always trouble, but nothing super serious."

Dad chuckled, "I hear you."

"What about you, Dad? Okay?"

Dad nodded.

224

"Yeah, okay. Not bad, not bad."

Dad definitely seemed different. I had never seen him like this, without a trace of antagonism oozing from his character. Not without being a little tipsy anyway. It was as if he had put away every one of his weapons, surrendered to something.

It had to be said eventually.

I said, "I take you it sold the house."

Dad took a deep breath and nodded.

"Yep. We still owed a lot on it so I didn't come out with much, but I got something at least to start over with."

I could relate to nest eggs and new beginnings.

"When did you start...the new start, I mean?"

"Oh, not long after you left. A month later maybe, two or three at the most."

I started to feel a little emotional then. Not sad, joyful, or angry, just confused maybe, like I was not sure how I felt or how I was supposed to feel. I just felt something.

I said, "Sorry about leaving like that. I guess I should have probably said something."

There was an almost palpable silence between us for several seconds that almost seems to darken the room slightly. Dad alternated between looking at me and looking out a window that only looked out to the sky. His fist clenched once, but I did not sense anger. My guess would be he too was struggling with unclear emotions.

He said, "Don't apologize. I've never done you no favours. I know it."

"Let's not worry about anything like that. Things happen, things change, and not everything makes sense... especially when you look back on it after. I'm only here because I wanted to see how you were doing. Like you said, it's been a while."

Dad nodded.

"I actually understand where you're coming from. You always were smarter than me in some ways, but I get what you mean. I've thought it myself."

I almost felt sorry for Dad then, almost loved him, but I did not want things to turn all mushy and squishy. I was putting my life in order.

"Yeah, it's just another way of admitting things are too complicated for us to understand sometimes."

Dad laughed out loud.

"I'll go with that for sure."

I laughed a little as well. It was nice to see him laugh. It was a sign we had made it through to a clearing after a rough patch. I was curious about the house, but I did not want to put Dad on the defensive.

"Okay, so you sold the house. It's expensive and a lot of work for one person, so it makes sense."

He nodded a bit wearily.

"Yeah, it is. And it might sound kind of pathetic, but it's a pretty empty feeling being alone there too. It's hard to describe exactly. I'm not trying to make excuses or make anyone feel sorry for me. I know any bad feelings I got living there was mostly being reminded of all the stupid things I did there, the poor decisions. But still it was tough living there even if it was my own fault."

I was stunned to hear him say it. If his new demeanour had not partially prepared me for a more humble man, I may have been shocked into a longer silence instead of a short one.

"Let's not worry about it. Things got tough and messed up for all of us. We all had to find a way to start over, right? What happened is just the way it went. We got a new start and hopefully Mom and Kim did too."

Dad glanced hopefully at me.

"Ever hear from them?"

"No. I was hoping maybe you had."

Dad shook his head. Both of us seemed disappointed by the answers even though I doubt either of us was surprised.

I said, "All we can do is hope and wish them the best."

"Yeah, I wish it."

In some ways Dad seemed quite happy to see me, but he still gave the impression of being a little spooked by me showing up without warning. He still had not said a word about what he had been up to for the two years since I had seen him. All that had come out was that he had sold the house, and it had been me who had brought the matter up.

"I told you a bit about my new life. What about you? What have you been up to? Keeping well?"

"Well enough, I guess."

"You must have to do something to pay the bills."

"I got a regular part-time job and another piece work job that gives me stuff now and again."

"You're getting enough to keep on top of things?"

"Yup. No problem for now. I worry a little about getting old sometimes, but I guess everyone does."

"Yeah, even I do once in awhile and I'm sure it crosses your mind more and more as times goes by."

"That's for sure."

It took a lot of tries ending up at dead ends and uncomfortable lulls in the conversation, but neither of us moved to end our reunion and eventually we stumbled into some success in conversation.

"Can I get you another tea? I'd offer you a beer, but as a rule I don't keep it around anymore. Every Sunday, Andrew and me...Andrew's a friend in a similar situation... nurse two pints each at The Brock and watch the football games and shoot the shit. I'm pretty good at keeping that my limit for the week now."

"Tea's perfect. Then let's just sit, relax, and chat for a little while before I have to start heading back to catch the train."

"Okay."

I looked around while Dad was fixing up the tea. I sort of liked the place; nothing fancy, but rustic, tidy, and uncluttered, like a cottage that was only used once in a while to really get away from it all. It suited him, the new him anyway.

Dad brought the tea over. He had topped up his own as well.

"Here you go."

"Thanks, Dad."

When he had sat down in his chair Dad's face seemed more comfortable and conveyed a little more purpose.

"So what brought you around," he asked.

It was a reasonable question. Why now? Why not six months or a year ago or six months from now?

"I'm not sure. I think it's been in the back of my mind for a quite a while and it somehow made its way to the front. You are the only family I have a clue where to find."

Dad snorted an honest, sad sort laugh.

"I hear ya'. I didn't even have a clue where to look for you."

I started to apologize again, but Dad quickly noticed and put out his palm toward me to silence me. I only got out half a word. It put a brief halt to the conversation. Both of us looked back and forth between our tea and each other until Dad found something to say.

"I'm glad you came by. I'm glad you're alive and well."

"Likewise."

The words came hard for us, like chipping old paint off a sidewalk. Not that we did not mean the words, but there was so many events and so much empty space between them that it could not feel natural. But the words got said and now that they had been said it seemed important to make sure we did not let the moment get bogged down by their weight. I changed the topic.

I said, "How come you're so hard to get a hold of? You got an unlisted number or something?"

Dad's face looked a little ashamed and I immediately knew the answer and regretted asking.

"I don't have a phone," he said. "I'm trying to put away something every pay for the future so I cut out everything I thought I could do without."

Practicing a similar philosophy myself I could empathize with my old man, but a phone seemed like a pretty basic and inexpensive convenience to do without. I tried to keep my voice from revealing my sentiments.

"Do you miss having a phone?"

"Not anymore. I'm used to it. Besides, Brockville's not that big. I pay my bills in person or at the bank, and the few people I see now and again we just drop by, bump into each other, or arrange to meet somewhere. It's not a big deal."

"I actually try to keep my basic expenses down too so I know what you mean. Is your plan working out for you?"

"Not bad. It's coming along. I didn't get a ton from selling the house after paying debts, but what I did get I put most of it away. Plus a bit after every pay starts to add up. If I have a good run of extra piecework I can even put a decent chunk away. It comes in spurts."

I was relieved to hear this. Not only because it might mean Dad was fending reasonably well for himself, but it seemed a common thread we could build a normal conversation around.

"I have the same sort of method for saving back in Ottawa. If you stick with it, it adds up, eh? I do have a phone though."

Dad smiled.

"Well, Ottawa's bigger, I guess, harder to get around in person if you need something or want to meet up with someone. You're smart to start young...saving I mean. You always were the egghead in the family. I'm glad you're doing good."

As always, I have not repeated our conversation word for word. Many times our conversation stumbled into roadblocks with pools of silence blocking the way forward. If we had trouble getting going again Dad would reset the scene by offering more tea or a slice of cheese. Those two things seemed to be all he had to offer that were conveniently available. However, we both trudged ahead, determined, I suppose, to avoid wasting our overdue reunion now that it was suddenly upon us.

Dad tried chatting about football and other sports, but I was so hopelessly lost in that realm that I could not even fake it. I attempted to bring up something sports related regarding my running and general attempts at fitness, but Dad only looked at me blankly. Dad tried to talk a little politics, but that only made me realize it had never even crossed my mind to vote. I had no idea if there had even been an election of any kind during my stay in Ottawa.

In desperation, at one point I mentioned my dabbling in meditation. To my surprise, he seemed a little interested.

"I see a sign in one of the windows downtown about it and for some reason it always catches my eye and makes me wonder about it. How does it work?"

I did not want to bore him and extinguish his interest so I kept it very brief.

"I'm no expert, but it's mainly about focusing your mind and blocking out all the noise and clutter so you can get a sense of the things that really mean something to you."

Dad nodded.

"Doesn't sound that stupid actually."

I laughed.

"I like it. You should try it. It's something that's easy to do on your own and you can start with just a minute or two a day and see if it does anything for you. You might be surprised at how fast you get better at it if you do a little bit each day."

"I don't know. Maybe. Who knows?"

I dropped the subject. The rest was up to him.

Eventually, we found our way to three issues to which the majority of males can usually relate: work, money, and women. Here is the gist of these conversations.

Work

I emphasize Dad's role in the conversation since you know my situation well already.

I asked, "So tell me a bit about your work. What's your regular part time job?"

"I'm a night watchman at Phillip's usually three, sometimes two, sometimes four nights a week."

"The construction firm?"

"Yeah, but they're into more stuff these days. They do landscaping, property maintenance, deck building, tree removal, you name it. They're getting pretty big."

"What about your piecework?"

"Phillip's again most often. Mostly unskilled labour when they need it."

"Keeps you in shape a bit I suppose."

"Yeah, a little I guess. It comes in waves. It actually pays better than my regular job. No benefits though. I do get some with my regular part-time job, but they take a little of my pay each time to get them."

"It must be nice to have some benefits though."

"That's what they say. So far it's just cost me. I haven't got anything yet."

"Got a pension?"

Dad looked a little embarrassed again.

"I think so. I'll have to look through my stuff again. All that shit's on there."

I wanted to ask to see one of his pay stubs, see if I could tell what his benefits were from the deductions, but I figured I might be stepping over the privacy line by asking to look at his paycheck and then insulting him if I tried to explain his paycheck to him. Maybe another time when we were on firmer footing.

He asked, "You get benefits?"

"No."

"Ah well, you're young and healthy."

"For now," I said.

Dad laughed and nodded.

"Ain't it the truth."

Dad was quite interested to hear about my work. I did not tell him about *The People*, just Groovier's.

He said, "Sounds like you do just about everything there."

"I've been trying to make it so I can do everything. If anyone quits or calls in sick they have me to fall back on. I'm trying to make myself hard to replace."

"Smart. I actually tried my hand at the restaurant business. I could handle everything except waiting on tables. You wouldn't think it's so tough, but it's a real grind on your legs, back, and brain by the end of a shift. Plus half the customers act superior on you like you're their servant. I couldn't do the waitering well enough and I left the restaurant eventually 'cause waiting is where the possibility of real money is."

I agreed, a little guiltily.

"We share the tips among the staff at Groovier's, but I know what you mean. All the money goes through the wait staff."

We nodded knowingly at each other over this fact.

Home Finances

Dad asked, "So what percent do you set aside each pay for saving?"

"Percent?"

"Oh well, that's how I do it. I figured maybe you did the same."

"A percent of your pay?"

"Yeah, I put away ten percent of my regular part-time pay. It's all I can do if I really want to stick with it. It still adds up. Where it really kicks in is with the piecework. I put half of it away. It's easier to put that away 'cause even half the piecework money is a decent amount of extra spending money."

I had to hand it to him. I had a similar method subconsciously, but setting out percentages might be a better, more honest method. I took the opportunity to compliment him.

"Great idea for saving, Dad. I might give it a try from now on. I do something similar, but I like how your percentages idea lays down the rule so you can't fool yourself."

I think he could tell I meant it. He seemed to gain a bit of confidence.

Dad asked my advice.

"If you can afford only one at my age, what do you think is the best to go for, the tax-free savings account or the RRSP?"

Rather than me helping him it turned out he just gave me another good savings idea to think about. I only vaguely knew what he was talking about. I had heard of both, but I did not know the details about either.

"Umm, to be honest, don't know a lot about either of those things."

Dad looked honestly surprised.

"You should check them out. From what I've been told, if I understand it right, if you're saving the money anyway those are two of the best ways to go about it."

He told me what he knew about each of them and they certainly sounded like they were worth checking into. I especially liked the idea of a tax refund for the RRSP savings. Since he knew more about saving methods than I would given him credit for I asked him about something else.

"Do you know anything about stocks and investing?"

He shook his head.

"No, nothing. Do you?"

"Not much. I've been reading a bit lately about it and it sounds interesting. If I ever figure anything out I'll let you know. I'll definitely check into the RRSP and tax-free savings account. Thanks for the tips."

We talked about other home finance issues like rent, groceries, entertainment and other day-to-day costs, but I won't go into it except to say Dad did not seem to have a lot of entertainment costs. Lately, and for most of my life, neither did I.

Women

Dad asked, "Any pals in Ottawa? When you were here I know you liked to hang out by yourself quite a bit with your books and stuff like that."

"I guess I'm still a bit of a loner, but I go out sometimes."

"You're filling out like a man some now. Any ladies?"

He sounded hopeful. I had not specifically mentioned Aggie, only a generic girlfriend in passing. I sort of wanted to and sort of did not want to get into it.

"One actually."

"Serious?"

"Yeah, I guess."

"How long you been seeing her?"

"We actually broke up not too long ago. I think we were together around a year or so."

Dad might have noticed something about me when I talked about Aggie. He seemed to become more careful about what he said.

"The first break-up is the toughest. I know it doesn't help much to hear it, but nearly everyone's been through it. It's something to keep in mind when you're feeling low."

"You too?"

"Yup. It was so long ago I don't remember it too well, but I can always see her face and remember her name, Bonnie. It might not sound like a big deal, but nearly everything fades after you haven't been near it for thirty years or so but at least a little part of her has stayed sharp in my brain. When we split up it was like my whole life got sucked out of me and it seemed to take forever for it to grow back and start to cover up the hole."

He looked a little misty.

I had gotten somewhat used to Dad's new demeanour, but hearing him moon over his first girlfriend from a time when I had not even been born made me a little woozy and speechless. He must have thought I was silent for another reason because he felt he had to explain himself.

"I remember and miss your mother a lot too, of course, I was just trying to show I could relate to your situation."

"So what happened?"

"I honestly don't remember exactly."

Then with the first flash of anger I had seen during our visit, he snapped, "I expect I probably fucked it up like usual."

It startled and even scared me briefly, but he directed his anger only at himself. I tried to console him.

"I'm sure it's more complicated than that."

Dad nodded.

"Probably. What about your girl? What happened? You don't have to talk about it if you don't want to."

I tried to clear my head from the buzz of interference that arose whenever I got to thinking about Aggie. I had thought of her and us a lot, but I had not figured out much or come to any clear realizations about cause and effect between us. The hole had barely started to get grown over. I realized I had to stop secretly blaming *The People* for tearing us apart. I knew it was futile and largely false, but the idea loitered around inside me unless I made the effort to shoo it away. Even then it gradually crept back though it grew a little weaker each time. I figured this process was part of what would start covering up the hole.

I tried to lighten the mood by rolling my eyes and responding, "It's complicated."

Dad laughed with me, but I thought I owed him more than that since he had opened up to me. I tried to focus on saying the words, telling the basic truth, and keeping it simple.

"Her name was Aggie. It was great. I don't know what went wrong exactly. Our lines of work didn't fit too well together and that caused a bit of tension. It just seemed to end somehow, run out of steam."

I faltered here, not knowing what else to say, but feeling as if I could not have possibly said enough to sum up the relationship we shared. Dad seemed to agree. He waited patiently for me to continue.

"I don't really know," I said. "I think I just maybe got into it a little too much and too fast. I didn't let things unfold naturally maybe. I'm really not sure."

I suppose Dad could tell I was foundering. He spoke up.

"I'm not altogether certain what happened with my first gal neither, or the second one. Even the best one, maybe the last one, your mother, slipped away before I could come to my senses. Mind you, I'm not trying to play hard done by."

"I know Dad."

After a short uneasy quiet I tried to put our failed relationships behind us.

I asked, "Any new ladies in your life?"

"Not really. A little nibble here and there, but nothing to speak of. I'm still really getting my feet under me if you know what I mean."

"I hear you."

Not too long after, I sensed we were both pretty much finished talking and reconnecting for the time being at least. I did not see how it could have realistically gone much better and there was no benefit to pushing it farther. Dad put up very little resistance when I mentioned I should be getting back to the train station.

At the door we shook hands.

"I'm glad you came, Molloy. You're always welcome."

"Thanks, Dad. I'm glad too."

Before he let go my hand he gave it a short, harder squeeze.

"You've done real well. You were right to leave and go on your own."

49

Goodbye For Now

I am back in Brockville. My intention was to visit with Dad again, but during the train ride here my mind gradually turned toward the idea of taking a long walk around my old hometown instead. It suddenly seemed an excellent opportunity to assemble my closing thoughts for this diary. Of course, my story is not done, but then one's story is never done except perhaps when everyone dies and every last trace of influence one ever made upon another is gone. Anyway, I suppose if I am a real writer you will hear from me again sometime.

It seems to me the section of my life that gave birth to this book is coming to a close. It has been difficult to add chapters; my mind turns outward, moving on, even with a pen in my hand and my notebook open before me. I resisted for a while, but for whatever reason the peaceful journey on the train brought it to the forefront of my mind that it was time to say goodbye to my readers, be they real or imagined.

Things are going well at Groovier's. I am making myself as useful and indispensable as possible. I am working there full time, probably more. I have begun my online line courses to finish high school. So far the courses are going well, but they really just got started.

I walked nearly two hours after I left the train. I walked passed my old house and my old high school, retracing the route I always took between the two. I walked passed Ritchie's and even Dad's apartment though by this time I had decided I did not want to bump into him right then.

The longest part of my walk took me down the number two highway to the very edge of town where Angel gave me my tattoo. I stopped and looked down the long driveway at the house far back from the road. I could hear music. Maybe the same crowd still resided there. For a few moments I even wished I could drop in and have a brief visit with Angel so we could tell each other how things were going and reminisce, but that was not why I was here.

I was here to settle my past so that I could hopefully see my present and future more clearly. After I watched the house and listened to the music for a minute or two in the dusk, I turned and walked backed toward town along the shoulder of the highway. I walked to my left so I could see the cars that came toward me, but it was quiet with only occasional traffic.

Eventually, I got to the edge of Brockville where sidewalks were available again. Soon I came up to the St. Lawrence Park Campground. It was long past camping season and the idea of solitude within the abandoned oasis of organized nature appealed to me. I made my way to the town's only little beach, perhaps only thirty meters long.

Next to the beach was an elevated, reinforced, stone wall which protected that section of shore from the waves. It offered clear views across the St. Lawrence River to the lights of another country, the United States, only a mile away. I could also see down along my side of the coast, the line marking the southern edge of Brockville. It seemed as if Brockville had been my hometown almost forever before I left and it seemed like a lot longer than a couple of years since I ran away.

It was not yet completely dark outside and the moon was only a third full, but even so our satellite planet seemed unusually bright. Even in the dusk I could see a lot more stars in Brockville than I could see during the darkest night in Ottawa. It made me realize how these larger and larger congregations of human beings separated us all the more from nature, a self-inflicted isolation of the human race.

As I have implied, the diary is more or less finished. Personally, as I have said, God and fate willing, I am not nearly finished. I have more to live and learn, but for now what I can write about is done. My further evolution requires my full concentration. Maybe we can only reflect coherently upon our struggles in retrospect. Maybe that is why I had to condense and throw away large portions of my diary that muddled on laboriously in the present. Probably, like most things, it is different for every writer, every person.

I thought about having my tattoo removed or altered, but have decided against it. In some ways the tattoo seems like a misguided act to me now, but so do many other things I have done. For now it is just part of my body, part of my story. I regret that it is a permanent curse toward God, not necessarily because I suddenly believe in God, but because it is a permanent display of my ignorance, blaming something else for the situation I found myself in at the time. Perhaps I am keeping my somewhat embarrassing mark to atone for this error. If I think it is foolish to believe in God, it is even more foolish for me to curse that God.

Besides, I have more important and immediate concerns to figure out. Some things are as basic and childish as what I want to be when I grow up. Some are as simple, challenging, and universal as keeping at least one eye on the lookout for my true purpose or a soul-mate. Some are more personal, quietly aching questions such as how close a relationship do I want to maintain with my Father and what is a boy, a man, without his sibling, his mother?

I don't know the answer to any of these things, but I feel it is time to focus on finding the answers and to put this history aside.

It would be fair for the reader to ask what was the point of all this and since you have been kind enough to stick with me until the end I believe I must do my best to give you a reasonable answer.

I have written down a lot of things here, mostly about myself, nobody special. If you bumped into me on the street you would most certainly not differentiate me from any other straggler who ekes out a living working in a restaurant. Most likely, you would not notice me at all.

For whatever reason I decided to set to paper the mishmash of daily experiences, struggles, successes, failures, disappointments, and epiphanies that make up each one's existence. I edited and streamlined it into something as unique and comprehensible as I could. Since you lasted until the end it is fair to assume you found the odd worthwhile item here and there among the rubble to keep coming along with me.

The best point to it all I can come up with is this: if another person, you the reader for instance, put their whole story down on paper, arranged it in its proper order, and somehow made it known to the world around them, what a unique, insightful, and fine story it would be.

May our paths cross again.

May we roam in green pastures.

"...being a star might be a nice, happy, simple
life even though I know stars are not alive.
It could twinkle in the sky, a pinhole of
brightness in the black silence of outer space.
It might be lonely, but you could grant the wish
of the first person that saw you each night.
If they were a special person with a special wish,
you could even help make the world
a better place."